"*Being a woman is not a disease!*"

Ruth's tone was insistent. She *had* to convince both Dr. Mark Travers and the ruling Rajah of her medical skill.

"Miss Stafford," Mark said, "you must realize you've crossed the border dividing progressive West from time-anchored East. Educated women in India are the exception. The universities are turning out more, but Kanjihan doesn't boast a university. Here we live simply under our Rajah, and to him, all women have but one necessary function. Do I make myself clear?"

"Indeed you do," Ruth replied.

"The Rajah will come to accept you as a doctor," Mark reassured her.

If only you *would accept me as a woman*— Ruth wanted to say to the inaccessible but so compelling Mark.

Great love stories never grow old...

And we at Harlequin are proud to welcome you, our readers, to HARLEQUIN CLASSIC LIBRARY—a prime selection of time-tested, enduring favorites from the early lists of Harlequin's best-selling Romances.

Harlequin Romances have been read throughout the world for many years. Why? There are as many reasons as there are people. But longtime readers tell us that our books combine the enjoyment of travel, the intrigue of good plots, warm and interesting characters and the thrill of love. Each novel possesses an emotional appeal that sweeps you right into the wonderful world of romance!

As publishers of **Harlequin Romances**, we take a great deal of pride in our books. Since 1949 Harlequin has built its reputation on the solid base of quality and originality. And now our widely popular paperback romance novels have been translated into eighteen languages and are sold in more than eighty countries.

So...if you relish a classic love story, one whose appeal has lost nothing over the years, read the timeless Harlequin Romances in the HARLEQUIN CLASSIC LIBRARY. We hope you enjoy this story and all the others in our special selection of beautiful love stories from years past.

For a free catalogue of the books available, write to:
HARLEQUIN READER SERVICE
(In the U.S.) M.P.O. Box 707, Niagara Falls, N.Y. 14302
(In Canada) Stratford, Ontario, Canada   N5A 6W2

Doctor Memsahib

JULIET SHORE

Originally published as Harlequin Romance #531

HARLEQUIN
CLASSIC LIBRARY

TORONTO·LONDON·NEW YORK·AMSTERDAM
SYDNEY·HAMBURG·PARIS·STOCKHOLM

Original hardcover edition published by
Mills & Boon Limited 1958
ISBN 0-373-80004-5

Harlequin edition first published July 1960
Golden Harlequin Library edition, Volume XXV, published September 1972
Harlequin Classic Library edition published March 1980

Printed in Canada

CHAPTER ONE

RUTH FOUND CASSIE'S breakfast-time call particularly irritating that morning. It was all right for Cassie, draped in some ridiculous froth of a negligee in the middle of her great satin bed, no doubt disordered by at least a couple of snuggling poodles, ringing up simply because she happened to be awake before her breakfast tray or bath was ready, and pouring a stream of gossip into what she imagined to be a sympathetic ear.

"Look, Cassie, I'm busy," Ruth interrupted the other to say brusquely, "I've got *work* to do."

"I know, my sweet. Just hang on a minute though. I haven't got to the bit that will be sure to interest *you* of all people. As I was saying, you could have knocked me down with a feathah—but a feathah, my dear—when that awful Beth Ransome came in wearing the most ghastly shade of purple. Well, you know, my dear, there are those who simply shouldn't, and Beth's one. Oh, by the way, she calls herself Liz nowadays. Liz Ransome. Apparently it's smart to be Liz at present, whereas at one time nobody would touch a Liz with a barge pole . . . ."

Here a piercing "yip-yip" broke into the long soliloquy. "Shut up, darling!" Cassie said endearingly. "I'm talking to Aunty Ruth . . . ."

Ruth almost slammed the receiver down there and then. "Aunty" to a bundle of lamb's wool that took more to keep than two human children! That she would not stand for!

"Cassie, I'm off to work," she said firmly.

"But, darling, I'm going to tell you who she was with in just a teeny moment. You see, this purple sack caught my eye and held me absolutely fascinated with horror. It sort of shouted at Louise's decor and made everybody feel uncomfortable, the way a hiccup does in the middle of a suspenseful story. Oh! Did I tell you about Gussie running a four-minute mile? It wasn't official or anything like that, but I believe he's running everywhere now. It saves taxis."

"Cassie!" Ruth shouted angrily into the mouthpiece.

"Yes, well, I only wanted to tell you, darling, that Liz Ransome was with Bendy . . . ."

"Bendy?" Ruth echoed, trying to eat toast and drink coffee with her free hand.

"Darling, don't be tiresome!" Cassie scolded patiently. "She was with *your* Bendy. Benedict Sharn. You didn't even tell me—your own loving stepsister—that he was back in England!"

Ruth choked at last with the combined effort of eating, drinking, and listening to Cassie all at the same time, especially a Cassie imparting such news! Tears streaming from her eyes, she said, "Look, dear, I'll be seeing you."

"You bet!" Cassie said darkly.

"So goodbye for now!" Very firmly she replaced the telephone receiver and tried not to believe her tremblings denoted the fact that she was suffering from shock.

Benedict back in England after five years? He was doing so well in the States, too. She had read about him occasionally, referred to as "one of our younger, but no less brilliant orthopedists."

The Americans had a knack of coining words that fitted the subject and didn't appear so verbose as the true English equivalent. Here an orthopedic surgeon was still an orthopedic surgeon and would remain so forever and ever, amen.

Surely Benedict intended getting in touch with her? If he was going to cocktail parties he would at least have telephoned . . . !

More puzzled than hurt, she carried her crockery to the tiny sink and decided to leave everything for the woman who cleaned her small apartment daily along with the others in the building. She had let herself in for that early extra appointment, and getting through the traffic of central London for only a couple of miles took such ages, what with detours and one-way streets. All doctors should be equipped with wings, she pondered, so that they could literally travel "as the crow flies" about their business.

In the bedroom she gave a few quick flicks of the brush through her short, cap-cut ash-blond hair, moistened her surprisingly dark eyebrows with a fingertip, and outlined her lips with her favorite shade of orange tan. It was Glen who had introduced her to an orange-shaded lipstick.

"You're a golden type, Ruth," he decided one morning, "and that cherry isn't you at all. Try this."

Now she never used any other, and yet, when she had eloped six years ago with Benedict, she hadn't had a lipstick of any description to her name!

It was no use getting silly and sentimental, she told herself as she backed her Hillman out of the mews garage she rented close by. Six years was a long time and people changed. Benedict must have suffered jet lag, or he wouldn't have left her to discover from another source that he was back in England.

She followed a blue van almost all the way to Harley Street. The driver was the type who played "guess what I'm going to do next" by not signaling any of his intentions, apart from driving with both signal arms out—apparently stuck—the whole way. He stopped suddenly, overtook without warning, and finally— to Ruth's delight—collided with a barrow boy and brought the "law" upon himself. Ruth gave her name and address in case she was needed as a witness, and, half an hour late, presented herself at No. 9 Gifford Place, where a shiny brass plate announced to the world that here practiced:

Dr. Glen Meriton, M.S., F.R.C.S.,

the well-known plastic surgeon, and underneath was a smaller plate, yellower because it was newer, bearing the legend:

Dr. R. Stafford.

Ruth always had a desire to give the plate an extra rub with her cuff; it was a proprietorial gesture, and not too kind on her cuffs, so this morning she forbore and let herself into the building, feeling nervous and irritable because she knew she would now be running late all day, and that if Benedict should call on the telephone she couldn't really spare the time to speak with him.

"Miss Stafford," greeted the nurse-receptionist whose services the partners shared. "Your first patient was here before me this morning. Baby's awfully cross, too."

"I know, I'm sorry, Kath," Ruth said as she handed over her loose coat to the girl and slipped into the cloakroom to wash her hands. "It's been one of those days up to now. It may improve . . ." she philosophized as the wail of an unhappy infant smote her ears. "Can you come in?"

"Certainly."

The young and rather grubby mother who entered the consulting room with her child in her arms saw a tall, fair, immaculate, apparently cool young woman with every blond hair in place, her white coat loose over a forget-me-not blue dress, a pearl choker at her throat matched by small pearl studs in her ears. Ruth saw a dark-haired gypsyish girl with dirty bare feet in high-heeled open-toed shoes, obviously chewing gum, and the least affected by her wailing child of all three of them.

"You're Marlene Carter?" Ruth asked, consulting the card Kath handed her.

"Yes, doctor. You *are* a doctor, aren't you? Coo!" Marlene continued chewing. "I don't mind 'aving a woman doctor for baby, but me—I like 'em male!"

"Obviously," Ruth decided under her breath. She had noticed from the card that Marlene was not married, but that was no business of hers.

"You called yesterday," Ruth said kindly, "but you must understand, Miss Carter, that we work to appointments, which are often made weeks in advance. I tried to come early to fit you in, because you said baby needed help, but actually, I can't spare you much time as I was held up by an accident on my way here . . . ."

"Cor!" ejaculated Marlene. "Doctors are ruddy 'eroes. Can't stand the sight of blood meself."

"No blood," smiled Ruth, "only orange juice, fortunately. Now what's the matter with baby?"

The young mother laid the grubby bundle on the immaculate blue blanket covering the examination couch, and after removing several pins exposed a wizened little creature soaked at both ends and smelling sour. Its gaping mouth was twisted in a way Ruth had learned to recognize only too well. The baby had a harelip.

"Mmmm!" Ruth murmured and dismissed Kath as they both heard Glen Meriton arrive. "Baby's very pale, Marlene. How's that?"

"'Cause she don't go out much, I expect," decided the mother. "But she's all right, doctor. Got good lungs."

"They won't remain so forever without fresh air," Ruth chided gently. "Why have you brought baby to me instead of taking her to a hospital?"

"Because I want 'er done proper, that's why," Marlene as-

serted succinctly. "National 'Ealth's all right fer most things—
I 'ad 'er under National 'Ealth—but this is my kid's face an' I'm
not muckin' about with that!"

Ruth, who had received the impression that "baby" was little
more than an inconvenience to the girl-mother, now felt a
dawning of warmth toward the other.

"I can assure you that most hospitals have consultant
surgeons who could adequately deal with baby. Our Mr.
Meriton is a consultant at Welch's; that's the big hospital off
Mayfair. You haven't got a husband behind you, Marlene, and
you could never afford . . . ."

"I got twenty-five quid," the girl said proudly and delved
down into her bosom to produce a somewhat bulky envelope,
which she threw onto the desk, "and I want baby doin' proper,
by *you*, doctor, because I've taken a fancy to you, see? I'll come
clean with you—" Marlene obviously was no stranger to
American films "—though I want you to know I would 'ave 'ad
baby done in any case. I gotta chance to get married to the
father. He's a seaman an' been on the South American run, so
baby was a bit of a shock to 'im, see?" Ruth nodded, trying to
keep abreast of Marlene and of Glen's movements next door at
the same time. "I written an' told 'im about Gloria—" this was
apparently the mite on the couch "—only I told 'im she was a
beauty, see? Well now 'e writes an' says 'ow about 'im an' me
doing it proper an' givin' Gloria a pa? So I . . . ." Marlene was
only nineteen and her eyes suddenly filled with tears.

"And baby needs some surgery before daddy sees her, eh?"
Ruth added gently. She went to the nearby cupboard and fished
out a small towel. "I think her immediate need is a clean diaper.
Here, use this, and pop the soiled one into this plastic bag until
you get home. Well, Marlene, you've posed me a problem. I
should send you off to the Children's Hospital . . . ."

"They got a waiting list a year long," Marlene grimaced.

"So you found out that much?" Ruth smiled.

"Yes." The other flushed scarlet. "Caught me out, there,
didn't you, doctor? It isn't that I have anything against National
'Ealth, only there isn't time to spare in waiting."

"When are you expecting the, er, child's father?" Ruth
asked.

"In six weeks."

"She ought to be done right away," Ruth decided, busily
probing and examining the baby's mouth. "Fortunately there's

no cleavage in the palate. What am I going to be able to do for you, Marlene? We haven't a bed in our private clinic for weeks . . . ."

"Oh, lor'."

Just then the phone on the desk rang shrilly. This Ruth had been expecting. Glen had been in for five minutes and they always had a conference of sorts before the real business of the day started.

"Good morning, dearest you!" Glen greeted with his usual extravagance of words. "What kind of client *have* you got in there?"

"Sorry about that, sir," Ruth smiled. "Not of the usual variety. Do you think I could have some emergency operating time tomorrow and a cot in the clinic?"

"Have you gone mad?" Glen demanded.

"I must have done. I need humoring."

"You need certifying, girl, if you're taking on what Kath has just described to me. This is Harley Street, my love, not the Old Kent Road."

"Thank you, sir, I knew I could count on you," Ruth said sweetly and replaced the receiver. She glanced up at Marlene. "Have baby at this address at eight o'clock tomorrow morning. You can leave her with the nurse and phone up about two o'clock to inquire. There's no need to worry; it's the sort of operation we take in our stride."

"And . . . and will she look like . . . other babies afterward, doctor?" Marlene asked wistfully.

"Prettier than most, I suspect," Ruth smiled. "Isn't she like her mummy?"

"Oh, go on!" Marlene caught up her baby and made for the door. "I'll be seeing you then, doctor."

"Good morning!"

Marlene was replaced, as Ruth had expected, by Glen Meriton, dark, urbane, and—at this moment—thoroughly outraged.

"Ruth, in case you haven't heard, this is a welfare state, but we do not practice public welfare from this address. You're building up quite a clientele among the lame dogs. I won't have it!"

"I thought we once took an oath on behalf of lame dogs," Ruth said quietly.

"Possibly," Glen frowned, "but there are plenty of hospitals where they can receive attention without fouling up *my* clinic."

"I'm sorry," Ruth said, tight-lipped. This wasn't the first time she had displeased her senior and patron by what he described as her "social" behavior. "It won't happen again, sir."

"I hope not." Glen Meriton couldn't be angry for long. He was clever, he was rich, and he was a snob; all these things Ruth acknowledged along with her liking of him. His women patients doted on his dark good looks, inherited from his Portuguese mother, and had proven his discretion by having kept secret from their contemporaries the fact that he had renewed their sagging faces and made their beauty good for another ten years at least.

Ruth's job as the junior partner was to perform the plastic surgery she had learned from Glen, on children or young people who needed it. There was the case of the small boy who had broken his nose in a fight; the beautiful doll-like girl who had a large brown mole right on the bow of her lip; the baby who had been badly cut about the face when an electric light bulb exploded; and the young man who had lost the whole of one eyebrow, thanks to a refractory Bunsen burner. These, and more, had her to thank for their restored appearance, and she was glad she had been able to help. Occasionally, however, a few people got past Nurse Greyburn and into her consulting room without any idea of what it cost to be treated by the partners. Once Ruth discovered their need was genuine she was sunk; she could no more have turned Marlene and her baby away than fly, even though the girl's twenty-five quid would only just clear the operation costs. She would have to foot the nursing fees out of her own pocket. As Glen often said, she was a fool about such things.

"I don't know why I don't shake some sense into you," Glen observed, his dark eyes lazily smiling forgiveness. He put his hands on her shoulders and—before she realized what was happening—planted a kiss firmly on her lips.

Kath coughed significantly from the open doorway.

"Your ten o'clock appointment, sir."

"Right-o!"

Ruth stood looking after him a little helplessly. It was the first time he had ever done that, and she felt somewhat shaken. Glen had always been Glen, her teacher and senior. She had never before thought of him as a man who perhaps occasionally beheld her as a woman beneath the platonic starch of her white coat.

Kath, too, was obviously shocked by what had occurred, for she didn't meet Ruth's eyes when she showed the next patient into her consulting room.

CHAPTER TWO

RUTH WENT HOME at the day's end feeling unsettled and peculiarly disgruntled. It seemed to her that some crisis was about to come to a head, and yet she was not aware that any crisis had been imminent. It was not only that Benedict had made no attempt to contact her all day, though this was beginning to be a rub with her by now and threatening to turn septic; it was also the situation generally at No. 9 Gifford Place ever since Glen had kissed her. There had been no more than the usual significance in his invitation to take her to lunch at his particular haunt, the Waverley Grill, but there had been disapproval exuding from the usually gay and friendly Kath as she handed Glen his black Homburg and light coat and answered some casual request from Ruth with strangely accusing brown eyes and an obedient, though cool, "Very well, Miss Stafford."

"I wanted to talk to you about Kath," Glen said as they occupied his usual table in the window alcove and ordered T-bone steaks on the head waiter's recommendation. "She tried to give me her notice this morning. I was flabbergasted and refused to accept it. Told her I'd be sunk without her. Have *you* said anything to upset the girl, Ruth?"

"Me?" Ruth flushed indignantly and then blushed even more hotly as she suddenly saw the light. Kath, who didn't have any boyfriends and admitted she was happiest during working hours, was nursing a secret passion for Glen, her employer. It was not so improbable when one looked at Glen in a considered way. He was not only blessed by nature in the way of good looks and a firm, black, sleek thatch, but he was pleasant, well-spoken, and considerate to his employees. Last year he had paid all expenses and sent Kath's widowed mother on a health cruise after an attack of pneumonia. He had a whimsical way of silencing words of gratitude, but could even he shrug away the declarations of the human heart?

"If I were you I'd let Kath go if she wants to," Ruth opined.

Glen paused with his fork halfway to his mouth, his lips inelegantly apart with shock.

"For heaven's sake, why?" he demanded.

"Because she's twenty-eight and would make somebody a good wife if she was allowed to."

"Am *I* stopping her?" Glen wanted to know. "I asked her if she was thinking of getting married and she denied it. In fact she didn't seem to be able to say why she wanted to leave. She appeared to be upset."

"Because she's in love with you, and this morning she caught you kissing *me*."

"Good Lord!" Glen ejaculated. "That was just a casual salute, old thing. You must be mistaken."

"I may be, of course. But Kath has hated me ever since. We were one happy unit first thing this morning, but now she thinks you and I are 'carrying on.'"

"Good Lord!" Glen said again, turning things over in his mind. "Women are the deuce," he decided. "After all, Kath knows I'm married."

"Which fact makes me less than the dust in her sight," Ruth concluded. "You shouldn't go around saluting your junior partners like that, Glen. Supposing *I* get ideas?"

"And have you?" Glen asked provocatively. "My dear Ruth, you'd better know that my wife is jealous of you. If I'm late home, I've been with *you;* if I don't kiss her with fire and passion, it's because I have been kissing *you*. I made this morning's assault on you quite deliberately. I wanted to be just a little guilty for once."

Ruth was toying with her food.

"You shouldn't play with fire, Glen," she advised quietly.

"I know," he murmured somberly. "At times I'd give anything to be going home with you. You're quiet and restful and soothing. But I know that if once I did find myself alone with you, those three qualities would probably be discounted in favor of . . . ."

She met his eyes sharply.

"Don't go on, Glen, please! I feel lonely today somehow, and only too ready to listen to someone whose flattery makes me think I'm needed. You already have your niche in my scheme of things, and it's not as my lover!"

"Touché!" He smiled at her. "That's what I call restoring

the situation. I can't see you behaving furtively, either, Ruth. It was just a seed Madge planted in my mind. A pity about Kath. She'll have to go, I suppose. A nuisance! She was supposed to keep my women patients off me, not to join their ranks herself.''

"I could be horribly mistaken," Ruth interjected.

"No," he said thoughtfully, "you're right—as usual. She was always ridiculously eager to do anything for me at any hour, and the verses on birthday and Christmas cards she sent . . . . They could be termed sentimental, I suppose. I wouldn't like Madge to get her claws into Kath. It's just as well for her to move on out of harm's way.''

"You don't seem to mind Madge having her claws in me," Ruth complained suddenly.

"Because you can take care of yourself, my dear. If ever you can't, I shall take care for you. In this niche, pet, you have a friend in need.''

"Well, thank you!"

They were laughing again now as the waiter brought dessert and, somewhat offended, removed the liberal remains of cold steak. "I think I prefer you as a friend in need to the other thing. Thanks for letting me have the emergency time tomorrow, Glen. I'll try not to impose on your good nature in future.''

"If you do I'll exile you to Kanjihan.''

"And where on earth is that?''

"Kanjihan is an island in the Indian Ocean, somewhere off Bengal. I was at Oxford with the raja, who still keeps in touch with me and sends me the occasional invitation to visit him. As a matter of fact, I heard from Ajil yesterday. He has been in an argument with a tiger, had his cheek ripped, and is positively raging about the scar the mainland hospital has given him. He wants me to go out and undo the damage.''

"And will you?''

"What an idea! I couldn't spare the time. Would *you* like to go? Expense no object, you understand?''

"Do you think the raja would accept my services in lieu of yours?''

"He would if I told him the pupil is abler than the master. . . .''

"Glen!" Ruth's eyes shone moistly as she regarded him across the table. "That's not true, but . . . thank you for saying it!''

"I'm not so sure it isn't true," he told her frankly. "In this game one has to recognize one's limits. I know mine and I keep well within them. There's no reason why I should confine you, however. Whenever you're ready to move on, I'll understand."

They had both temporarily forgotten all about Prince Ajil Rahmat, Raja of Kanjihan.

MISS NOBLE, WHO OCCUPIED the basement apartment and took all Ruth's calls while she was out, stated there had been no telephone messages at all, but that Miss Cassandra Belampton had been in person.

"What did Cassie want?" Ruth inquired. "She knows I'm away all day."

"Yes, she knew that, Miss Stafford. She wouldn't write anything down—you know how she is?—and we were talking about her little dogs most of the time. They *are* dear little things. I think she said you had to be ready at seven-thirty."

"Whatever for, Miss Noble?"

"I don't know, Miss Stafford. Miss Belampton is so difficult to follow. Anyway, it *was* seven-thirty. I got the time quite clearly."

"I have no intention of going out this evening," Ruth stated flatly. "If I can reach Cassie I'll tell her so. I'm tired and it's an operating day tomorrow. Thank you very much, Miss Noble. I'll go up now."

"Oh, God, let him have written!" she silently prayed as she let herself into the apartment and looked around at its bright shining neatness. The cleaner, Mrs. Dodd, had placed three letters on the table, addresses downward. Ruth deliberately removed her hat and gloves, shook her hair free, and then casually approached them. The first was her telephone bill; she might have realized it was something of that nature by the buff color of the envelope; the second was a lengthy autobiography from Jean McWade, a friend of medical school days who was dedicating herself to Hippocrates somewhere in the Canadian backwoods. This could wait until later. The third envelope was addressed in a long illegible hand that made her heart contract with both unbearable relief and pain. It was from Benedict Sharn, the only man she had ever really loved, and whose wife she had been for six short hours before Sir Esmond Sharn had caught up with the runaways and pleaded the case for a little patience and a family conference before proceeding with the business of marriage and living together and perhaps raising children of the union.

He had made it all sound very grave and serious. But being desperately in love and needing each other was all that seemed important. Ruth was only eighteen, Benedict just twenty-one, and they were both studying medicine in Edinburgh at the time. It had seemed so simple to go on studying *and* be married; after all, they were in Scotland where Ruth's age was no obstacle to marriage. But someone—Ruth had always suspected her stepsister, Cassandra—had told Sir Esmond, and he had to raise such topics as a family and sources of income.

To his son, Sir Esmond had privately mentioned quite casually that although he couldn't dismiss Benedict's right of succession to the baronetcy, he could certainly disinherit him and would do so forthwith unless the young fool allowed the marriage to be annulled. This was a powerful argument indeed, but had to be interpreted later for the young bride's benefit.

"Darling," Benedict had said, "perhaps we were a little impulsive. We thought things would carry on much the same only that we'd have each other—" here he paused to embrace and hug her to him desperately "—but now I see there would be complications. You might have a baby and then you'd never qualify to be a doctor, and anyway, it won't seem long to wait if we both put our backs into it."

"I'm your wife, no matter what they say," Ruth had stubbornly asserted, "and I'm all for telling your father to go away and leave us alone."

"Dearest!" Benedict had gasped over her. "You're so sweet and so . . . so naive. I do love you. What would we do for money, sweetheart?"

Her eyes, large and pansy-blue, had suddenly questioned his.

"Why didn't you think about that before, Benedict?"

"Because I was in love with you and dotty, I suppose."

"And you're not in love with me now?"

He kissed her tears away before they fell.

"Angel! Of course I am. Only not quite as dotty since dad arrived."

"I'm sorry he found us, Bendy."

"You won't be five years from now when we have the wedding of the year with all the trimmings and things. A girl has a right to bedeck herself fittingly on such a day."

"I shall always think of today as my wedding day, no matter what you or anyone else says."

However, since only one of them was apparently prepared to contemplate love in a garret, mammon had won for the time being. The marriage was quietly annulled on the grounds of nonconsummation, grounds Ruth would have been deliriously happy to have frustrated if only to show Sir Esmond you can't dispose of human beings with red blood in their veins as you dispose of garbage. But having found his son, the baronet hung onto him watchfully, and at the earliest possible moment, Henry Belampton had arrived to escort his erring stepdaughter back to her outraged mama. There had been a dreadful terrifying scene during which it was threatened she would be removed from medical school, along with "all that nonsense about dedicating herself to mankind."

"The first man who looks at you and snap!" Mrs. Belampton had said accusingly. "I made that same ridiculous blunder in my youth. There's no need that you, Ruth, should suffer as I did."

"But, mommy, you were in love with daddy, you always said so, and you only married Henry to get some money for us. You said that, too."

CHAPTER THREE

RUTH TOOK HER PRECIOUS LETTER to the window seat, where the evening sun cast the golden light of a benediction over her fair head, and tremblingly slit open the envelope.

It was not a long letter, but for once Benedict had written very much to the point. She had at times wondered (faithless one) if he never intended coming to the point. He began:

> My dear Ruth,
>
> You must excuse my long silence (*three months' duration on this occasion*), I have been doing a coast-to-coast lecture tour involving eight states. I'm home for at least three months—maybe forever. (*What did he mean by that?*) My future is distinctly hazy at the moment. I've got to see you, dear girl, at the first possible opportunity (*. . . but that was last evening, surely, when Cassie saw him escorting Beth Ransome at a cocktail party . . .*) as you have always loomed large on my future's horizon. (*Poetical,* Ruth frowned, *but I don't like to describe myself as "looming" anywhere.*) Will you phone my club to say if you can have dinner with me this evening? Leave the selection of a place to me; nowadays the thought of roast beef, yorkshire, and two veg. plays my ulcer up. (*Bendy with an ulcer at twenty-seven? Impossible!*) Anticipating our meeting,
>
> > I am,
> > As ever . . . .

Ruth folded the letter thoughtfully, then excitement overcame her and she glanced at the clock. It was almost seven already.

In two skips she had reached the telephone and dialed the number of Benedict's club. A steward replied. Mr. Sharn was in the bath. No, there was no extension in the bathroom. Madam would have to leave a message.

"Please tell Mr. Sharn to join Miss Stafford for dinner at her apartment," she stated somewhat bleakly, thinking how dreary these third-person invitations always sounded.

The steward gave a well-bred little cough and asked her if that would be all. A little deflated, Ruth replaced the receiver and tried to recapture some of her former excitement. Bendy was coming at last, and she would have him all to herself for the first time in six long years. They would enjoy an intimate little dinner here by the fire. If Benedict had a gastric ulcer he would probably be glad of one of her light-as-air mushroom omelets and a froth of trifle to follow. Everything would be daintily served and she would wear. . . .

"I'm not even bathed yet!" she exclaimed happily and turned on the hot tap as she passed the bathroom on her way to undress.

Ready at last, she surveyed herself critically in the long cheval mirror. Shining fair hair—which she wore short for convenience' sake—waving at the temples and taking a natural dip behind her ears, fearless blue eyes with a sweep of dark eyelashes framing them, a small, rather tip-tilted nose, and a well-curved emotional mouth above a dimpled chin. Cassie called herself a "gamine" type and referred to her stepsister within her hearing as "statuesque," but behind her back as a "monster." Actually, Cassandra Belampton resented Ruth's extra inches along with her determination, ability, independence, and other attributes of strength of character. Cassie was really one of the pampered and spoiled little lapdogs of life.

When their parents had died together in a car crash two years previously, Henry Belampton's daughter had come into a great deal of money. Fortunately, Ruth's five hundred pounds had served to help her complete her training and take a working partnership with Glen Meriton. She had wanted no more of the Belampton estate than the right to break away and lead her own life apart from Cassie and her cloying friends. Cassie, however, was not so easily shaken off.

Donning an apron, Ruth sang happily in the tiny kitchen as she soaked sponge cake with sherry, added segments of banana and glacé cherries, and then made a custard to pour over the whole. Until the steam disappeared she couldn't put the trifle into the fridge. She then opened a tin of tomato soup and put it into a pan to heat slowly. The omelet would have to be made fresh, of course.

The shrilling of a bell made her jump suddenly, nervously,

and she had lifted the telephone receiver before she realized it must have been the doorbell, and that Benedict had probably arrived.

Her heart raced as she whisked off her apron and smoothed her hair. Six years, and she was as much in a dither as she had been when she eloped with her twenty-one-year-old sweetheart. She was twenty-four, a qualified surgeon and a responsible citizen, yet her emotions were still those of an errant undergraduate.

A pulse beat visibly in her throat as she opened the door.

"Darling!" Cassie greeted affectedly, rising to her elegant tiptoes as though kissing her stepsister was akin to saluting the Statue of Liberty. "I see you're dressed and ready. We're going to Frascati's. Come in, Jimpy, old thing! Ruth'll find you a whiskey and soda or something. Give Jimpy some whiskey, dear. He's an absolute *sponge* for spirits."

Ruth collected herself as a somewhat negative individual in dinner clothes edged into the hall and looked around him curiously as though expecting to find chickens in such a small place.

"Remarkable!" he decided, and seeing no whiskey in evidence, poured himself a large port from the decanter on the side table.

"Sorry, you can't stay, Cassie!" Ruth said firmly, having met some of her stepsister's hangers-on previously. "I meant to put you off but I forgot. I never go out Tuesday evenings. I'm operating tomorrow."

"But you're *dressed,* dahling . . ." Cassie accused and nosed her way into the kitchen. "You're cooking? . . . Silver out for two . . . Jimpy! I do believe Ruthie has a *follower.* What a scream! Is it—" she flashed wicked amber eyes at the other "—that divine Meriton you work for?"

"I work *with* Glen Meriton," Ruth corrected, "and no, it isn't. Goodbye, you two. Have a lovely evening."

"Oh, pooh!" Cassie grimaced. "We haven't gone yet. Jimpy hasn't had his whiskey. He's moribund without it."

"Morbid, weet," corrected her escort.

"She was probably right the first time," Ruth decided. "I have no whiskey in the apartment, Cassie, and my brandy is purely for medicinal purposes."

"Jimpy's awfully medicinal," the other girl confided.

"He needs to grow his beard before he becomes an alcoholic,'' Ruth said unkindly, but Cassie's boyfriends were almost insult-proof, and Jimpy woefully helped himself to another port. "Off you go, poppet, and take your litter with you,'' she insisted, "otherwise I shall have to throw you out.''

"She's big enough to do it, too,'' Cassie told her swain, immediately succeeding in making the other feel as big as the side of a house. "When she was sixteen she weighed nine stone and was always bullying poor 'ickle me.''

"Poor 'ickle you used to fight with tooth and claw,'' Ruth smiled forbearingly. "At least my elephantine tendencies were my only defence against you.''

"Oh, come, Miss Ruth,'' Jimpy gallantly interposed, "you're only lavish in the nice feminine places . . . .''

"Well, thank you!'' The surgeon thawed in the young man's direction.

"Cassie's a bit retarded in every way,'' he opined.

"Absolute oaf!'' that young lady flashed at him. "I told you to be nice to Ruth, not necessarily recite eulogies at her. Anyhow, we're not wanted here, so let's go.''

"Splendid idea!'' Ruth agreed, opening the door with a flourish.

"You'll be sorry for treating me like this one of these days,'' Cassie observed maliciously. "We were going to take you out to dinner and then the theater. We had a nice man all lined up for you, too. You should relax more, elder sister. Everybody knows how frustrated professional women really are. Especially when they've been let down once already . . . .''

"Please go, Cassie,'' Ruth advised calmly. "I'll look after my frustrations in my own way.''

"With meetings in your apartment, I suppose?'' Cassie inquired. "You only *look* innocent, Ruth. *I* know more than you think . . . .''

They both saw Benedict Sharn at the same moment. Cassie's voice faded into a somewhat nervous giggle. She said, "Oh, so it's *you* Ruth's expecting?''

Ruth held out her hand, not wishing to display affection in front of an audience.

"Benedict!'' she said in a small choked voice. "Goodbye, Cassie!''

"Certainly. Jimpy!'' that young lady commanded imperiously.

"I wouldn't like to think I was breaking anything up," Benedict Sharn smilingly observed.

Cassie turned in the doorway and looked up at the whole handsome six-feet-two of the new arrival, her amber eyes catlike.

"You already have broken things up, Benedict," she said ambiguously, then she flashed an angry glance at her stepsister. "Some people just won't see it."

It was Benedict who looked the more embarrassed as the door closed on the intruders, and Ruth, who had been wanting to hurl herself into his arms in an abandonment of longing, checked herself and decided he should make the first move.

"I . . . I thought we'd have dinner here, just the two of us," she announced breathlessly as he didn't attempt to embrace her. "You said you wanted to talk."

"Yes, that's right," he agreed, licking his lips. "You're looking very pretty, Ruth."

The compliment fell over her like dry ice, leaving her unmoved. As she reentered the tiny kitchen she put a hand to her eyes as though shielding them from a blinding light. The truth was like a light, she supposed, as she had just recognized the truth in Cassie's intentionally hurtful words.

Benedict *had* broken the existing contract between them, not once, but over and over again. Though he had been of age at the time of their runaway marriage, he had allowed himself to be frightened into an annulment by the threat of disinheritance. The vow "for richer, for poorer" had meant nothing to him. He had allowed himself to be persuaded that they should not see each other for a year, and at the year's end he had gone to the States where he had remained for five years, apart from one unsatisfactory, almost grudged, working visit. If he still loved her, she would have been the first to hear of his return to England, but such was not the case. Goodness knew how many people were aware of his homecoming, how many parties he had attended since his arrival.

I'm just one of the welcoming throng. Ruth decided with a feeling of shock after all her excitement. *I'm glad I've realized it in time to save face at least!*

She didn't dare investigate her heart at this stage. Pride, when divorced from mere arrogance, was essential to self-respect, and Ruth determined to retain her pride at least.

Benedict Sharn could not read her countenance as she entered with the soup and they began to eat. She was smiling and almost impersonal at this stage. They talked shop and he discovered that she was not only a very attractive woman but a knowledgeable doctor also. She did not once delve into the remembrance of their early association, and he realized that sooner or later he was going to have to remind her that once—for such a little while—she had borne his name and willingly joined herself to him, trustingly offering her fair young body for his tenderness and pleasure. At that point the cup had slipped and everyone had urged on him the belief that he had enjoyed a providential escape.

Now, regarding Ruth's poised intelligent beauty across a table graced by candlelight, he wasn't so sure they had been right in their advising, or that this pleasant young woman was the scheming, conspiring title-hunter they had made her out to be.

CHAPTER FOUR

THE MERITON CLINIC, or Nursing Home as it was sometimes called, was small, ostentatious and painfully select, Ruth had long ago concluded. It stood in its own green belt of lawns and flowering shrubs. The building was of no particular era, or even of one national style. Its portico was decidedly Spanish, but the overhanging roof of moss-green tiles was somewhat reminiscent of Bavaria, and the non-functional green shutters of Switzerland. The whole had been built to suit the requirements of a claustrophobic actor in 1928, and to either side, leaning on each other and seemingly gossiping about the intruder, were the familiar gray Georgian houses that make up the greater part of residential London.

The clinic was within walking distance of Gifford Place, but no one was ever seen afoot in that neighborhood apart from the mailman or an occasional itinerant foreigner who had probably mistaken his *gauche* from his *droit* at Marble Arch.

It was really much quicker to walk, Ruth decided, as she guided her Hillman into a stream of more opulent Rolls-Royces, Daimlers and Jaguars, and pulled up outside the clinic twenty frustrating minutes later.

The nurse-in-charge met her in the staff cloakroom.

"I have your baby all ready, Miss Stafford," she announced, and her eyes twinkled merrily. The young surgeon's "waifs and strays" were beginning to be well-known and an accepted fact by now.

"I hope she wasn't too grim, nurse," Ruth said apologetically.

"Oh, no," nurse Kilkenny smiled. "You forget I was trained in a Dublin slum hospital, Miss Stafford. Young Gloria was a bit fussy when she came in, but she's well nourished and contented now that she's fed, clean and dry."

Ruth was only half listening. She had had a bad night and looked heavy-eyed from lack of sleep. She concentrated all her mind on the forthcoming operation and by the time she was changed into her operating clothes and sliding her hands into gloves, she began to feel alert and somewhat jerkily aware of all that was going on around her.

Glen said admiringly, "The most classical proboscis I ever achieved, I do believe. Pure Grecian. What do *you* think, my dear?"

Ruth said, "If that's Mrs. Farland, I wouldn't have known her. What did she want a new nose for?"

"Pure novelty," Glen shrugged. "When one already has mink and diamonds, why not a new nose if one is tired of the old one?"

The unconscious subject of their discussion was removed from the table and the operating room nurse spread a fresh sterile sheet.

"I'm ready," Ruth nodded as Glen went over to the sink, and Marlene's baby was brought in looking like any other pink and white sleeping infant apart from the drawn-up curl of the lip.

Glen, rescrubbed and gowned, wandered over to watch the woman who had once been his pupil, at work.

"Hm!" he announced as the last stitch was inserted. "I don't think anything else will be needed to ensure that young lady's fair share of masculine admiration later on. I wonder if she'll remember to thank you?"

"I don't want her ever to know," Ruth stated. "If my work's good enough there's no reason why she should."

"How much is this costing *you*?" Glen asked quietly.

"Oh, the mother paid twenty-five quid down," Ruth told him frankly. "As the father's coming home to marry her, I don't want to dun the girl for more. Weddings bring their own expenses."

"Put it down to experience, nurse," Glen told the nurse-in-charge who had come to escort the baby back to her cot. "Don't prepare a bill." To Ruth he said, "Give the mother her twenty-five quid back and tell her *not* to recommend all her friends to us!"

"Oh, Glen! You *are* a darling!" Ruth exclaimed, and then she did something she had never previously done in his presence. She wept openly and had to turn away quickly to finish her cry in private.

She was in a scarcely controlled emotional state for the remainder of operating time. Glen watched her keenly. Her work was faultless, but she was too ready to laugh and then quickly to sink back again into some dark abyss beyond his ken. His assistant was not normally an emotional type, and he realized that there had been a gigantic upheaval within her during the past twenty-four hours. When they arrived back at Gifford Place he summoned her into his consulting room and asked Kath to prepare a pot of tea.

"I'm going over to Welch's before I knock off, Ruth," he said apparently casually, "so I just want to get one or two things off my mind. Firstly, I know you're not very happy working with me. I don't want you to think you have to stay on out of loyalty. Well?" he smiled quizzically as Kath entered and set a tray down on the table between them. She still avoided Ruth's eyes, and looked somewhat reproachfully at Glen as he ignored her completely.

"I'm sorry you think I so obviously don't enjoy working with you, Glen," Ruth sighed. "That savors of disloyalty in my opinion. Actually, I enjoy working with you enormously, but I do wish your practice was more general. That's my only complaint."

"You mean you would like your services to be available to Brixton as well as to Mayfair?"

"Yes."

"But, my dear, that's physically impossible, and you know it. We're two specialized people and we do very well out of it. You're not going to be silly enough to suggest I should work for nothing, are you?"

"Of course not. Why are we talking like this, Glen?"

"Because I've been watching you all day, and you're obviously under a strain. I'm too fond of you, Ruth, to want you tied to me against your will."

"Oh, Glen!" Once more her eyes brimmed over and she found herself gathered expertly against his broad chest. "It isn't you or my work that's upsetting me today. I . . . I didn't sleep well last night." She glanced up at him and decided to confide. "You see, Benedict's back."

"Oh!" There was a wealth of meaning in that one monosyllable from Glen Meriton's lips. He knew all about the role Benedict Sharn had played in his assistant's life. Ruth had told him of the elopement, describing it self-consciously as one describes an indiscretion. He had been wondering for some time when the romance was going to flare up in a more permanent phase.

"There are as good fish, Ruth . . ." he comforted.

"What?" She brushed her eyes uncomprehendingly, then she smiled uncertainly. "Oh! It wasn't like that, Glen. Bendy *did* propose to me again."

"Then why are you in such a tizzy today, girl? Wedding nerves?"

"No." She eased herself away from him. " . . . I turned him down."

"You . . . *what*?"

Glen almost scalded his elegant chin in his surprise. "You tie yourself to a man for six whole years and then calmly turn him down when he comes up to scratch? Care to tell me about it?" Glen asked.

"Well, there isn't much to tell, really," Ruth murmured as she sipped her tea. "For years I've been a woman in love and waiting. I don't think I could have waited without the consolation of my work, and knowing it was his work, too, always helped. I wanted Bendy to be proud of me. I was tremendously proud of him and all he was doing. He used to pose me his exam questions and then tell me his answers; pages on pages of detail . . . ."

"Didn't you skip it to see if he said he loved you at the end?"

"Yes," Ruth smiled wistfully. "You seem to know exactly how it was, Glen."

"The man's an egotist, obviously. They are only capable of loving themselves. You have faithfully reflected his perfections all these years, and he has suspected he wasn't all that marvelous close-up. Hence he has kept his distance as long as possible and held you hog-tied and adoring him. Something has happened to bring things to a head all at once. What was it?"

Ruth looked at the other admiringly.

"Old Moore couldn't have known more," she decided. "Yes, Benedict did have a spur to decide his future suddenly. He has been working at the Velades center in New York. Regis Velades was the founder and an orthopedic surgeon himself. He has told Benedict that he will make him director of the center in his place providing he marries Olga Velades, his granddaughter. This would be an amicable arrangement all around because Benedict's family is titled but has no money, and Velades is rolling in money and thinks it would be 'cute' for Olga to have a title . . . ."

"You didn't just act nobly and back out?" Glen interrupted.

"No, I'm not in the least noble. I simply wanted to be loved and desired by the man in my life. Not unnatural, surely?" Glen raised his eyebrows and waited. "Finally Benedict got around to saying he was still in love with *me*, but he made it seem a nuisance and inconvenient with so much at stake. He would have to get a job here, he grumbled, and from what he had heard, most specialists became bankrupt or shot themselves in our welfare state. When he finally asked when it would be convenient for us to get married, I told him never. He was surprised. But he . . . he hadn't tried to make love to me all evening. I wasn't prepared to be a business arrangement."

Glen was smiling secretly.

"I would rather like to have been there," he decided. "Did he take your refusal well on the whole?"

"No. He told me I was out of my mind. 'You were my wife once,' he reminded me, 'and I refuse to be tossed away like an old glove.' Then there was an attempt at a love scene, such an obvious pathetic attempt, I felt rather sorry for Bendy thinking I could be swayed by masculine physical superiority. It was that that made it all so finally over for me, Glen. I've grown up and away from Benedict Sharn. There it is. Let's face it."

"But you feel shocked and unsettled, eh, my girl?"

"Yes," she frankly admitted. "You'll have to be very patient with me. I suppose I'll get over it in time, but just now life seems horribly empty."

"You'll probably try to fill your need urgently and unsuitably," Glen pondered. "That's the deuce about women. They need love as a man needs a shave. I think for a while you'd better turn to me, old girl. Not in *that* way," he assured her kindly as her eyes questioned his, "but when you feel desperate or lonely ring me up and we'll have dinner and a quiet natter somewhere. How about this evening?" he asked her. "Are you doing anything?"

Beyond his broad back Ruth saw a figure framed in the anteroom doorway, an elegant figure trimly gowned and wearing a mink stole caressingly around her shoulders. Following the direction of Ruth's gaze, Glen looked around and then sprang sharply to his feet.

"Madge!" he exclaimed. "What on earth are you doing here?"

"Eavesdropping," the woman announced shamelessly. "I thought I would come and see what you were up to, darling.

We spend so little time together lately. How are you, Miss Stafford?''

"Very well, thank you, Mrs. Meriton." Ruth had risen to her feet also.

"I didn't expect to find *you* in my husband's consulting room," the other woman stated, "but I suppose you're often in here talking shop?"

"That's right," Glen said rather too hastily. "Do you want a cup of tea, Madge?"

"No, thanks. Not your stewed remains," his wife refused and again turned to Ruth with a malicious smile and pale eyes that looked up from under heavy lids. "Did I hear my husband making a date with you for this evening, Miss Stafford?" As the other flushed but didn't answer, she went on with a teasing laugh, "The dreadful creature had already left word he wouldn't be home to dinner. Never marry a handsome man, my dear. Such creatures spend very little time with their wives."

Glen, who had been regarding his wife in the light of a tiresome interruption, now flushed dully and warned, "Don't start clawing Ruth, Madge. She looks on me as a somewhat elderly brother."

"But she's going to find out one day that you're *not* her brother, isn't she, darling?" Madge Meriton asked. "You know, Miss Stafford, when my husband accepted you as his partner all my friends warned me it was a mistake. 'Even professional men and women are only human,' they told me, 'and he'll be spending twice as much time in her company as in yours.' 'Ah,' I said, 'but it's *which* time that's important, isn't it?' Shortly after that, Miss Stafford—" the other woman looked piercingly at Ruth now—"my husband began to sleep in his dressing room!"

Ruth felt humiliated for Glen's sake, having his private life thus exposed to view.

"All this is none of my business, Mrs. Meriton," she said coldly, "and your friends should be aware of men and women working amicably *and* platonically together in every field these days."

"Oh, *I* believed in the platonic nature of your relationship until today," Madge Meriton continued excitedly, "then Nurse Greyburn told me my husband *kisses* you, Miss Stafford, and I hear him asking you to meet him for dinner this evening with my

own ears. Really! What kind of a fool do you *both* take me for?''
She glared furiously from one to the other.

"Go to your own room, Ruth," Glen said in a strange tight
little voice, "unless you want to witness an assault!"

"No," Ruth said calmly, "I can see all this through your
wife's eyes, Glen, and it *does* merit an explanation." She
proceeded to tell Mrs. Meriton briefly what she had told Glen
and added, "I was naturally upset, and your husband was
lending a sympathetic ear. That's absolutely all there is to tell.
Nurse Greyburn did perhaps witness one perfunctory peck
between us, but the fact that she was there to see it eliminates
any savor of intrigue, I think?"

Now Madge Meriton looked somewhat uncertainly in her
husband's direction.

"Well, if I've misjudged you, Miss Stafford . . . ." she began
uncertainly.

"You have, *and* your husband," Ruth said firmly. "He's the
most loyal person I know. In fact, you've planted one or two
rather interesting ideas in my mind, but too late for me to pursue
them. You see, I'm leaving Gifford Place *and* your husband's
practice . . . ."

"This is news to me!" exclaimed Madge Meriton, while
Glen looked out of the window.

"Yes," Ruth sighed. "We had just agreed that I'm not cut
out for an exclusive practice. As a matter of fact, he asked me
yesterday to do one last job for him. What was the name of that
island in the Bay of Bengal, Glen?"

"Kanjihan." He looked at her admiringly. "You'll go to
patch up old Ajil, Ruth?"

"Yes." She looked obliquely at the somewhat discomfited
Mrs. Meriton. "Obviously I ought to remove myself from the
scene until I at least lose my reputation as a husband-seducer.
You can book my air passage to India as soon as you like, *sir*."

That "sir" was a final defiance as she swept out of the room
with her head held high.

Informality had always been the rule between the partners,
and look what it had entailed! She had almost been named in a
divorce case!

Kanjihan would provide a respite, give her time to think about
a future without Benedict and about her work now that she was
casting herself off from her patron.

When she got home that evening she took out her atlas and looked at the map of India and Pakistan. Kanjihan wasn't even named, but she saw that the coastline of the province of Bengal was serrated into a thousand jagged little islands and inlets.

Weren't there reputed to be tigers in Bengal?

"I'd rather face a tiger any day than a jealous woman," Ruth decided. "In any case, Kanjihan will just be an incident in my life."

So she innocently contemplated what was to prove to be the most shattering episode of her young life.

CHAPTER FIVE

BENEDICT SHARN WAS not at home when his father died suddenly of a coronary thrombosis while in the middle of tending his beloved prize roses. The news reached him at his club two days after that dinner at Ruth's apartment. As he had not been on very affectionate terms with his parents, he refused to make a hypocritical display of grief over Sir Edmond's sudden demise. He was shocked, certainly—the old man had appeared to be good for years—but having overcome his shock in the bar of his club, he realized he had everything to gain, as was an elder son's natural right. He was the new baronet; Velades would be tickled to know that. Also, his father's estate, when turned into hard cash, would at least keep the wolf from the door for the rest of his lifetime, if it had not been hacked into too many small pieces. He would have to go home, of course, and see that the old man was decently put away in the family vault, before raising the more earthy subject of the dependents' future existence. One thing he was determined upon this early in his bereavement: his brother Aubyn, who had recently distinguished himself by placing a red flag on the dome of the Bodleian in Oxford, could jolly well come down and think seriously about doing a job of work.

In the train rhythmically beating out the miles to the country seat in Herefordshire, he felt suddenly English and steeped in the traditions all around him. In the States it had all slipped from him like a cloak, his birthright and his background, as he struggled to make his mark among men who respected only physical or mental superiority and who had familiarly addressed him as B.S. or even Bud. Over there the general freedom, which had allowed him, an Englishman, to seek and win honors in his profession, had affected him strangely, becoming almost an ideology that made everything old and hidebound—like his native country—appear pathetic and futile. The historic became synonymous in his mind with the inept and defunct. The old tree had deep roots but had ceased to bear fruit. He almost succumbed to surrendering his nationality and allowing the new young growth to absorb and nurture him. Only his acquaintance with old Velades stayed his final capitulation. Regis Velades was a Spanish royalist who had fled his country and found sanctuary in the days when the United States really meant those words emblazoned on the Statue of Liberty: "Send me your homeless . . . ."

Regis had given his brains and his manipulative fingers to those same United States. His heart he had left somewhere in Valencia, where an old white house had nestled among its orange groves, somnolent in summer to the cooing of the indigenous doves, and friendly in the winter because one could shut the windows against the sharp attack of the *barbash* blowing from the Pyrenees.

"Tradition," he told Benedict, "is a country's character. This America—" he blew what can only be described as a raspberry "—no character. What character do you find in a dollar bill, my boy? America—she is dollar."

He paused to utter a conspiratorial cackle as he rubbed his hands together gleefully. "Sometimes I send American dollar to help restore His Imperial Majesty! You see. One day only tradition will be left in the world. These upstarts will blow one another to kingdom come. Hold on, boy. Hold onto your past."

Olga, the granddaughter, was, at twenty-three, pure unadulterated United States female. She was pretty, she dressed well, her legs were good, she ate like a horse, and she retained vital statistics of enviable proportions. She was already overindulged by her tradition-minded grandparent and likely to be more so as time went by. And she firmly believed that her physical attractions, backed up by the platinum of her million-dollar setting, were the open sesame to anything she desired in the world. So far she had not desired Benedict Sharn, but Regis had made his offer in unmistakable terms to his lieutenant.

"If you are free to love little Olga and can make her love you, this clinic is yours, my son, from the day of your marriage, and all that goes with it. You want that in writing? You bring Olga here to me wearing an engagement ring and I write . . . ."

Benedict was not exactly noted for his modesty. He had spent five years in a place that did not encourage hiding one's light under a bushel. He was a good orthopedic surgeon and he enjoyed being told so. If a patient ungratefully omitted to remind him, he would say, somewhat offended, "You've had the best treatment under me, I hope you realize . . . ." and then the patient would assure him that was so obvious a fact it hadn't seemed worthy of mention.

Tantalized by Regis Velades' offer, Benedict had decided to come home to England for a vacation and think about it. He didn't want to hurt Ruth, of all people. God knew she hadn't ragged him about their separation. She had been patience itself. Even his father had got around to saying, "I suppose you'll be claiming your bride soon? I admit I was wrong about Miss S. Occasionally when I'm in town I look her up, and she's a nice intelligent girl who should fill the bill at Larne Hill one day as Lady Sharn . . . ."

So Benedict had made up his mind to do the right thing by Ruth; that being to ask her to share his life, fully understanding the sacrifices he would be making if she agreed to do so. If her devotion was real and true and unselfish, she would appreciate the gesture and—battling against her natural inclinations—hand him back to the Velades Clinic and the waiting arms of the directorship and Olga.

If all this could have been arranged over the telephone it would have worked beautifully, he felt sure. But in all decency he had to arrange a meeting, and that was, as always, his undoing. He had said all he intended to say, but the proud golden head opposite him was still poised after his peroration. The grave large eyes affected him strangely. He wanted to kiss the pout of the trembling moist lips. He became with each passing moment so physically conscious of the woman opposite that Olga and the Velades center had faded in the immediate urgings of his masculinity.

"Darn it, Ruth," he had suddenly exploded, "I never stopped being in love with you! If it was to be the biggest mistake of my life, I would still have to marry you and find out what lies behind that Mona Lisa promise of yours. So, darling, when?"

Ruth had looked at him very squarely and said promptly, "Never, Bendy. You've made it very clear how everything has changed between us. I wouldn't stand between you and your ambitions for anything. After all—" and she smiled that little Mona Lisa smile of hers "—we're told love is only a very small part of a man's existence."

In that first moment he felt almost relieved by her decision;

there had been no tears or repinings, no scene. In the next his
relief gave way to a growing resentment. How dare she
withdraw the devotion of six long years when he had been
driven—by a fever of desire—into asking her to become his
wife? He began to urge and argue, but Ruth's mind was
apparently quite made up against him. At last he had seized her
in his arms and tried to kiss her into a realization of the bliss their
union promised. She merely submitted, however, which made
him feel at a loss as he finally released her. The kiss had meant a
great deal to him—absolutely nothing to her. He began to fear
that coming here to deprive, he was instead going to be deprived
himself. Within his breast he felt the stirrings of a mild panic; he
had gulled himself into thinking of his tie with Ruth as a
millstone weighing against his future, but now that he had spent
a short two hours in her company the idea of a future without her
was not so lightly to be contemplated. He failed to move her on
this occasion, however, and now he was stung. He resorted to
begging a woman to marry him, and again he was refused.

"I thought you loved me, Ruth," he accused her on that
second evening.

"I did—maybe I still do—but my loving you isn't enough for
marriage. Marriage is two people who are all the world to each
other. You told me how much of the world you would be losing
if you married me. It happened once before; I couldn't bear not
to be sufficient a second time, Bendy."

"And if I assure you you're all I want?"

"No, Bendy. It was never real enough. We must go our
separate ways and find our own reality."

"Ruth, I refuse to let you go! Once you bore my name."

"Once, yes," she had sharply agreed. "Everyone assured
me I had no right to it soon after. You included."

"You're bitter, Ruth. This is spite, isn't it?"

At that she had confronted him, looking very lovely with her
flushed cheeks and flashing eyes.

"And you profess to love me?" she had asked. "Please go,
Bendy. I have to make my preparations for my trip to Kanjihan."

"Where on earth is Kanjihan?"

"It's in the Bay of Bengal, and for me it's a working trip. I'm
flying out on Friday."

"But, Ruth . . . . " Benedict looked at a loss. "I do think now

that I'm home you should at least stay and argue this business
out to our mutual satisfaction.''

"I was home for six whole years, Bendy. You must have had
some leave in all that time.''

"You never complained . . . !''

"No. I must have been mad. Good night, Bendy!'' Again her
eyes flashed warning.

His answer was to seize her again and kiss her fiercely. This
time she was not submissive. She wriggled and fought like a
mad thing in his grasp.

"If you attempt that again,'' she told him, looking angry and
disheveled, ''I'll . . . I'll hit you.''

So he had returned once more to his club wondering if he
could continue his pursuit of a lady who used his own words in
urging his abandonment of her. Did Ruth seriously no longer
care about him or was she merely playing him like a fish who
was doomed to be caught in the end?

Two days after that he heard his father was dead, and when he
returned to London a week later as Sir Benedict Sharn, the
seventh baronet, plus the pittance of six thousand English
pounds (his father having made all four surviving members of
the family equal) to his utter consternation Ruth had literally
flown away from him—to Kanjihan.

CHAPTER SIX

THE SMALL LAUNCH tut-tutted its way fussily up to the wooden pier and disgorged a brown-skinned individual with a chestnut thatch of hair badly in need of trimming. Several Bengali gentlemen at the pier-head were wearing either turbans or topees. Only an Englishman would thus expose his head to the heat of the midday sun in this latitude, his limbs below army-type khaki shorts and bush shirt also exposed. The Englishman's eyes were a clear pale gray, screwed up against the sudden strong glare of the sun. He strode along biting on the stem of an inverted pipe, and he was very, very angry.

"Dandy-wallah!" he called sharply, and two individuals sleeping under the shade of a cotton tree came to life as a few coins were shaken like dice against their ears.

"Sahib?"

One of the fellows pulled his loose *dhoti* through his legs and knotted it around his middle.

"Where to, sahib?"

"The hospital."

The Englishman climbed into a contraption that somewhat resembled a sedan chair, known locally as a dandy, and the two dandy-wallahs started off at a loping run along the dusty winding road leading inland.

Mark Travers continued to grind his teeth on the stem of his pipe as they jogged through a small *jhil*—or swamp—steaming and mosquito-infested, as he knew it to be. One small monoplane, which he was prepared to pilot himself, and a reinforced D.D.T. spray mechanism, and that particular threat to the health of the island's population would be at least minimized, if not wiped out altogether. Getting blood out of a stone would present less of a problem than obtaining money for Kanjihan's health service from the Rajah.

"Elephants, tiger shoots, even the bloody army!" raged Mark. "And now this . . . this latest craze of his! He'll drive me

straight up the wall one of these days, and then what'll happen to
those thousand poor devils over on Katra?''

The dandy-wallahs edged fastidiously over to the side of the
road as a leper approached ringing a small bell and announc-
ing—as in biblical times—that he was unclean. Mark observed
the fellow to see what progress the disease had made on him.
One hand, he saw, was minus fingers, the nose had collapsed
and the eyes were beginning to stare in the sunken sockets.

"Too far gone for Katra," he decided with professional
regret, for a leper was too common a sight to his eyes for him to
feel personally for the sufferer. Doubtless the fellow was
returning from the hospital where—in an isolated but nearby
cypress grove—Dr. Jarwhat Singh would have given him an
injection if only as a gesture of goodwill.

As the dandy approached the hospital a blaze of red
rhododendrons appeared by the roadside, and in front of the
three-winged wooden building a lawn of savannah grass had
been contrived and tended. At intervals were beds of heady-
scented white bauhinias, with petals resembling settling but-
terflies, and ramrod straight among the virgins the yellow-
tipped scarlet or red-hot pokers, apparently reaching to capture
their heat from the blazing sun.

Mark paid off the dandy-wallahs and ran up the steps into the
hospital, briefly saluting the patients who were well enough to
occupy the verandas. Most of the patients slept in the heat of the
day, but as the superintendent marched down the corridor
dividing the female from the male wards, a woman moaned
gently and with infinite patience. She was probably in the throes
of death. These people just wouldn't cry out until one could do
no more for them, he had long ago discovered.

Breezing into the private office at the rear of the main
building he malevolently regarded the figure asleep on a cane
chair tipped back on two legs. The young man's feet, in
"chaps," were sprawled on the desk and he was snoring gently.

Mark kicked the chair and the young man slid to the floor,
muttered an oath, and observed, "So you're back!"

"I'm back all right," Mark said savagely. "You know what
the blighter wanted with me? I'm to give full cooperation to
some damn fool surgical sculptor who's flying out to pretty up
the beautiful face. Whatever this fellow wants he must have, no
matter what the expense. I tried asking for a few things *we*
happen to need, seeing that the rupees were being flung around.

Not a hope! Not even a blooming thermometer! I could have punched H.H.'s beautiful nose! And why not, seeing this plastic bloke is coming out to fix him?''

"Cool off, brother,'' advised Matt Travers soothingly. "You'll have a coronary if you carry on like that in this heat. Take up yoga and learn to fix an unseeing eye on all that is unpleasant and intransmutable. Do as Ajil does and look after number one sahib, *and* number one sahib's younger brother of course. We're up against a brick wall, Mark. We do what we can.''

"Sorry!'' Mark Travers smiled apologetically. "I do let fly at you, old son, don't I? It's just that I wanted better doctoring for you when you qualified.''

"What better doctoring is there? Grant that we get just about everything here at Kanjihan?''

"But everything,'' Mark nodded. "You haven't seen cholera yet, laddie, and pray heaven you never do. What's this? A letter for me?''

"It's addressed to the superintendent. I nearly opened it but didn't. Well, I'll go and set up an infusion for Ramjat Lal.''

Mark Travers slit the blue airmail letter open without real interest, then as he read he looked for a signature on the letter. There wasn't one. Now he frowned as he began reading the anonymous letter once more, deciding only a woman could have written so, with a woman's perception, malice, and smallness of mind.

Dear Sir,
I write to inform you that you will shortly be entertaining a
member of your profession who is supposedly an expert in
plastic surgery. I would advise you to treat this person with
extreme reserve. Handsome is as handsome does, but Miss
Stafford (as she calls herself, though why a woman who
has been through a marriage ceremony should have the
nerve to call herself 'Miss' I do not know) has not behaved
very handsomely to me. Thanks to her I am at present
estranged from my husband, and she is only coming to
Kanjihan with the idea of lying low for a while, I feel sure.
I believe Miss Stafford is reasonably efficient, but socially
she has proved a menace.
    Don't say you have not been warned.
                                                    A Friend

Mark Travers shuddered with distaste.

"What bitches women are!" he decided contemptuously, then he swallowed and looked again at the letter in his hand. The raja hadn't told him the newcomer was to be a woman. Possibly even Ajil himself didn't know. The plastic surgeon was the partner of an old college friend of His Highness, a sleek Sam called Meriton, who wrote amusing anecdotes that were duly related at the palace dinners to which the hospital superintendent was invited occasionally. Meriton was probably married to the creature who had written this letter.

"Anonymous my foot!" Mark exclaimed, crumpling the missive into a ball and throwing it into the wastepaper basket. "But if it isn't adding insult to injury to ask me to cooperate with a plastic surgeon who's a woman into the bargain! I'll give the lady social menace when I get hold of her! Azar!" he roared suddenly, and as a salaaming servant appeared in the doorway, "Bring char! Quick!"

"*Tekai, sahib! Tekai!*"

Now Mark leaned back on two legs of the chair, thinking up suitable tortures for members of the fair sex who dared invade the island of Kanjihan and have the audacity to expect cooperation from him in such medical frivolities as plastic surgery.

CHAPTER SEVEN

RUTH, WHO HAD cooled her heels unavailingly in Karachi for almost a week because the monsoon season was particularly violent this year and precluded all flying across northern India for days at a time, now found herself cooling her heels in New Delhi, unable to do anything about either the weather or the delays in her journey. Fortunately, nobody else seemed to worry about her; the raja had replied to her explanatory telegram with:

Enjoy yourself in Delhi my good fellow stop. As soon as is felicitous will send personal plane to same stop. Time is still on our side stop.

Kanjihan

This missive was addressed to Mister Roth Stafford, and Ruth smiled as she realized Glen had obviously not made her sex clear to his chum, the Indian prince. She thought at first she had better telegraph again and correct this misapprehension, for obviously a man traveling alone in the east was no novelty, but a woman might well be subjected to rigors and unhealthy curiosity not conducive to either her well-being or her peace of mind. She thought again, however. She was safely ensconced in a hotel in Delhi and had merely to wait here until His Highness' private plane called for her and deposited her in Kanjihan. It was not unpleasant, this place, the seat of Indian government; there were wide modern streets where sleek cars hooted all day long, and handsome buildings and churches. Perhaps tomorrow she would hire a tricycle and go and see Old Delhi, where the past—so she was told—had not budged for five centuries. But it was difficult for her to relax and be carried along in a stream of life moving at so leisurely a pace it might be said to ooze, after the strict timetable existence of these past disciplined years.

Though she was herself delayed by the rains, the mail planes were obviously still getting through, for while she was in Delhi she had quite a crop of letters sent c/o the air line by which she had traveled. There was a somewhat telling missive from Glen.

My Dear Ruth,

I forgot to say don't hurry back. Make it your annual leave, old thing. Unless Ajil has changed he never does today what he can possibly leave until tomorrow, so travel at his speed and relax.

Protocol decrees that he tell you what to do. Therefore your suggestions are slid forward diplomatically, preferably through a third party, and always phrased 'if Your Highness pleases!' I can see all this getting out that old red flag of yours, but when in Rome—you know?

My dear wife decided she was due for a stay with her mama after the almighty row we had following your exit. I also told Kath what her tale-bearing had almost precipitated, and she collapsed into tears and told me—as you had feared—that she had been in love with me for some time and couldn't see straight for her jealousy when she thought that you and I . . . but enough said! She has decided to take a job in the district, so the driving lessons I gave her last year should come in handy.

I am taking on a promising lad from Malaya (British parentage) who is interested in plastic surgery with a view to practicing in Singapore on postleprous patients. By the way, you should keep your eyes open on your trip and you'll probably see some interesting leprous specimens. . . .

Though she had been qualified for almost three years and had seen many unpalatable sights in her time, Ruth still could not suppress a shudder whenever she thought about leprosy. There was that about the disease that gave it the aura of the ultimate evil in the sight of medical science. In a way it was akin to malignancy, though it was symptomatically divergent: cancer bred cellular tissues the body did not need; leprosy destroyed those that it did need. Each made the sufferer secretive, anxious not to divulge that, which, if confirmed, could so acutely alter the course of a life, and, if neglected, a lifetime.

Shaking such thoughts from her fair head, Ruth opened a long rambling letter from Cassie urging her to have a good time and mentioning ambiguously that she, herself, was having a wonderful time with a certain good-looking baronet.

I don't believe in exporting our aristocracy, and I shall do my best to keep him in the family. No names, no pack drill!

Ruth smiled as she opened the third letter, which was from Benedict. He didn't mention having taken Cassie out. In fact it was—after six long years—a love letter as of olden time. He told her she was his one, his only love; and if he had to follow her to the ends of the earth, he was prepared to follow.

Only don't tell me to abandon all hope, my own, my sweet, my patient Ruth. Such love as was ours cannot die. I admit fault, that I neglected my love, but it was to pursue the career I realized I would need to support us if my father ever again threatened me with disinheritance. I want only to see you ensconced at Larne Hill; perhaps, in time, blessing me with a child . . . our child . . . ? Ah, my dearest Ruth . . . !

She read this missive twice before she decided she liked it. It was extremely pleasant to be told one was a necessity to someone's very existence. Benedict's whirlwind wooing of her had been all she had known of emotional love between man and woman; thereafter she had considered herself engaged and had warned off all trespassers from her lonely, often aching, heart. She was emotionally shy, almost undeveloped. If Bendy wanted to start all over again, that was up to him. She wouldn't discourage him, but would prove twice as hard to convince.

During dinner at the hotel, Ruth was conscious of another European occupying the table on her left. The fellow would have passed for an Indian, he was so brown-skinned, but she had already noticed his light gray eyes investigating her, and he had an English way of wearing his clothes, white jacket and black bow tie. Most Indian gentlemen wore the pyjamalike trousers and knee-length cotton jackets with the forage-type cap prevalent among members of the Indian congress party. An occasional Sikh was to be seen in full turban with jewels, under which would be pinned his long hair by which—he believed—he would one day be plucked up into heaven.

Ruth liked the Sikhs. They were what she had imagined of India, their fierce black darting eyes, curling beards, and impenetrable hauteur.

Ruth looked around as she tackled an excellent curry, and in doing so she caught the full gray-eyed glance of the European and flushed against her will. He looked the no-nonsense, outpost-of-empire type, now so much depleted as a species. His glance was direct and investigative and assessed her at one and the same time. During coffee, which was served on the veranda overlooking Government Square, he came up to her and introduced himself.

"My name is Travers, and I believe your name is Stafford. I think you know of me?"

"I'm afraid I don't," Ruth said, withdrawing her fingers quickly from the firm handclasp. "Should I know you?"

"You presumably received a telegram informing you of my coming. I am flying off back to Kanjihan at daybreak tomorrow. You are supposed to accompany me."

"Oh!" Ruth didn't like the fellow's manner much. He might have suggested collecting a bale of bedding with as little enthusiasm. "The telegram I received mentioned a private plane but not the name of my escort. I think that was remiss of somebody." He stared at her.

"Well, obviously I can't be expected to fly off into the blue with—with any Tom, Dick, or Harry."

"Why?" he asked calmly. "Have you an obsession about white slave trafficking, Miss Stafford? I presume you *are* Miss?" His eyes were gimlets now.

"I am, yes," she replied, and for some inexplicable reason her own gaze dropped momentarily. "As to your reference to white slave traffic, Mr. Travers, that actually hadn't occurred to me, but I am civilized enough not to agree to being picked up casually by the first strange man I meet."

"Then how long does one have to wait before one qualifies as an acquaintance?"

"Are you trying to be insulting, Mr. Travers?" she asked, rising to her feet and discovering he was the tallest man with whom she had ever been angry. It was almost physically impossible to feel so angry and keep looking up.

"Look, Miss Stafford," he shrugged, "sleep on it. I am taking off for Kanjihan from the air terminal about eight-thirty a.m. tomorrow. If you overcome your ridiculous feminine scruples—or whatever they are—be there on the dot. I can't get a flag out once the big stuff starts coming in. If you prefer to continue your journey by the usual air lines, they'll put you down in Calcutta. After that you'll travel by rail the hard way, at a hard time in horrible climatic conditions. My advice to you, young lady, is to go back where you belong while the going's good!"

"And who asked you for advice?" she demanded. "I'm expected in Kanjihan, am I not?"

"No, you are not expected, Miss Stafford," he said incisively. "A Mr. Roth Stafford is expected by the Rajah. He won't enjoy the joke of your arrival one little bit, and I can't see him letting you touch him. If you go back and I explain, it'll be far the better thing. Westernized as His Highness imagines he is, it isn't to the extent of putting his facial beauty into a woman's hands."

"I gain the impression that not only are women contemptible in your sight, Mr. Travers, but women plastic surgeons doubly so."

"Do you, Miss Stafford?" he said calmly. "Believe me, you flatter both subjects. I never think about either. Good evening!" And with a slightly mocking bow he left her seething.

To go back to England now seemed the desirable thing to do after that little contretemps, but having come so far and at such expense it seemed foolish to take a stranger's word for it that she would not be welcome. Maybe the Travers man had some axe of his own to grind with the Rajah and was discouraging her to gain his own ends. She looked him up in the visitors' book where he had signed himself: Mark Travers, F.S.M.S., M.D.

So he, too, was a doctor! Maybe he was the one who had bungled the Rajah's wound in the first place and didn't relish the idea of being shown up by such a contemptible creature as a woman! Well, she'd show Dr. Travers she wouldn't creep away like a cur with its tail between its legs. She'd be at the air terminal in good time tomorrow so that he wouldn't have any excuse for leaving her behind.

CHAPTER EIGHT

RUTH DECIDED SHE had no reason to change her initial impression that Dr. Mark Travers was an unpleasant and ill-mannered person by the events of the following day. For one thing, he was obviously furious to find her waiting for him at the air terminal, her baggage checked and cleared and neatly piled up close to the small Auster aircraft bearing the insignia of the Rajah of Kanjihan.

"Oh!" was his dismayed greeting. "So you've decided to brazen it out, have you?"

"Much to your obvious disappointment, sir, yes, I have, if there's anything to brazen out. I don't feel guilty of anything and I refuse to apologize for my sex. I like being a woman."

"There's no need to be blatant about it," he said curtly. "It's as well to remember you are now in a country where most women are kept veiled. That's one of the best things about India."

She didn't answer, so he turned his attention to her baggage.

"You can take one of those and a hold-all," he told her.

"But . . . but . . . I need everything," she said quickly. "It's not all clothes. I have instruments and equipment I'm going to need."

"They'll follow," he said languidly and signaled a porter to approach with his cart. "Which is it to be?" he asked adamantly, and, as she looked ready to argue, "Look, I'm not flying a bus. She's a twin-seater—" he patted the little plane "—not a freighter. I want to get off now, so make up your mind, Miss Stafford, and let's go."

Once they were airborne she realized that flying in an Auster was going to be something of an ordeal for her. She was not the best of travelers, and as pockets of air rolled the craft first this way and then that she began to look greener and greener in the tiny cabin behind the apparently blithe singing figure at the control panel. The cabin was upholstered in royal purple and beige. H.H.'s monogram was everywhere, but though Ruth searched she could find nowhere to be sick.

The singer's ballad stopped in midair as he was tapped on the shoulder and the situation made clear to him. Then he began to laugh heartlessly. Reaching down between his knees, he pulled up a leather bag, took out a packet of sandwiches and said, "Here. Go and enjoy yourself with that."

Ruth staggered back to her seat positively hating the creature, and now he was singing again, "Pale hands I loved, beside the Shalimar . . ." occasionally looking over his shoulder to ensure that the leather bag was coming in handy.

Feeling a little easier she eventually dozed, only to be aroused by Dr. Travers shouting, "If you look down, Miss Stafford, you'll see the Taj Mahal. We're flying over Agra."

She craned against the small window and saw a golden dome flashing in the sun. The ornamental gardens of the great tomb looked lush and green, the fountains like so many diamonds exploding over pools of royal blue silk.

"The best view is from the air," he called. "One gets the depth of the colors."

"Thank you," she said coolly. "It is impressive. How green it all is down there. I didn't know India could be so lush."

"Lush, did you say? At this time of the year the Valley of the Ganges is a quagmire. Last year two thousand souls lost their lives in the floods."

Agra was left behind, and he didn't speak again until he announced "Cawnpore!" then "Allahabad!" at which point she was ill again and lay down on the two seats provided.

"Fasten yourself in!" Mark Travers called a little later. "We're going to land."

"Thank goodness!" Ruth decided and could have wept when she discovered they were merely refueling, having arrived at Benares.

Leaving her to refresh herself in the airport rest room, Dr. Travers disappeared into the city while mechanics tuned up the plane. When he returned he was carrying an article resembling a fire extinguisher, that was fastened underneath the aircraft with a lead and a button passed through into the cabin. He seemed highly satisfied with this operation and suddenly thawed toward his passenger as she climbed rather rockily aboard.

"Now look here, Miss Stafford, we don't like each other very much. Check?"

"Check!" she agreed faintly.

"But we're both in the medical profession. Check?"

"Check!"

"So I may need your cooperation in a certain venture later on before I put you down on the palace airstrip. In the cause of Hippocrates, of course. Now fasten yourself in."

"Could you . . . please, Dr. Travers, could you make it not bump so much this time?"

"I can't control the flow of air, Miss Stafford, much as I fancy myself as a superior being at times. However—" rather self-consciously he dug deeply into the pocket of his flying-suit "—I did get you these . . . ."

He handed her a small bottle labeled in Hindustani.

"It's all right," he assured her as she questioned him. "It only says take two for vomiting. Even here a poison is quite distinctly labeled with skull and crossbones."

The day was now well advanced and the sun had blazed throughout. It was difficult to see the earth for steam. Only occasionally the silver thread of the Ganges broke through in an unmistakable dazzle of light, and once when the white gyration of steam changed into a brown pall Mark Travers observed, "The only good thing to be said for Calcutta is from this altitude, and that is that it's far enough away."

"I take it you don't like Calcutta?" Ruth asked conversationally.

"I do not. I trained in Calcutta. I saw enough of it, and it never improved in my sight. Most of all I have a boyhood memory of the riots there after Gandhi's arrest. I never saw murder in cold blood before, but Hindu and Muslim, who had hitherto worked and played together as friends, suddenly couldn't bear to breathe the same putrid air and struck one another down like ninepins in the streets. But all this is past—" he shrugged "—the Muslims have partition and Pakistan, the Hindus have India and long bitter memories."

"Where do the remaining Indian princes fit into all this?"

"Very few are still completely independent. Our own Rajah is subject to the government in that he pays taxes and must observe federal law. He is, however, his own chief magistrate and prime minister. He also maintains a private army, which provides background color for the occasional durbar he throws for the benefit of tourists, and has no other useful function as far as I can see—'' here Mark Travers expelled a long painful sigh as though the subject of His Highness' private army was merely an irritant to him and he was glad to have done with its ''—and he maintains his own medical service.'' Here came a distinctly hollow laugh. ''I am the director of said medical service, but the title, I assure you, is purely honorary. I do not direct. I do as I am told and at as little expense as possible. Do you see?''

Ruth did, suddenly, all too well.

''You mean he economizes on health, of all things?''

''He does to my way of thinking, but India has a lot of catching up to do, and we in Kanjihan are no worse than most. Ajil—I mean His Highness—can't see any good reason why we should forge ahead of others in this particular field, making Kanjihan a shining example to all public health facilities. He makes me so mad. He thinks nothing of putting on a shoot for a few visitors at a cost of twenty thousand rupees (that's about fifteen hundred pounds sterling) yet last year our old autoclave at the hospital blew up and he hasn't replaced it yet.''

''Now I know why you resent my coming,'' Ruth said, feeling rather guilty at her blind acceptance of the expense-no-object offer. ''I thought it was personal.''

''How could it be personal when I didn't know you, Miss Stafford?'' he asked.

With a woman's perception she replied, ''You gave me the impression that you knew all about me, Dr. Travers, and liked none of it. But I *do* see your viewpoint in all this. You think of me as a medical luxury. I did my general training, you know, and when I specialized it was with a view to working among children, particularly accident cases threatened with scars or disfigurement.''

''But Monsieur Meriton is hardly in that line, is he?'' Mark Travers sneered.

''No. But, like you, I was in no position to dictate my future when I left hospital. I had no money. I needed a patron.''

''Meriton?''

''Exactly.''

This time he looked around at her squarely, so that the aircraft appeared to be flying itself.

''Is he your patron still?''

"While I'm on this trip, yes. Actually, we have agreed to dissolve. I don't know what I'll do in future."

Mark Travers clutched the control column fiercely as he realized that the anonymous letter was so far proven right. This woman was using Kanjihan as a pause between events in her life. Fair-faced as she was, it was as well to remember the devil used many disguises, and surely the devil might descend upon Kanjihan looking innocent and rather ill, as Ruth Stafford did at this moment.

"We're going down now," he snapped, realizing he had almost been taken in and weakened toward her himself when she had confessed her poverty. "Fasten your belt, but take that thing like a hose pipe in your hands and press the button when I say."

The plane dived suddenly toward green forest and sea, making Ruth gasp fearfully.

"Now!" yelled Mark Travers. "Press!"

Ruth pressed, overcoming her nausea, and from the contraption under the plane a jet of pest eradicator fanned out like silver smoke.

"Good! Another run in. Press!"

They swooped, turned, and swooped again and again; six runs in all over the mosquito-infested swamp on the island of Kanjihan.

When it was over Ruth felt like death itself and asked, "Please, when can I get out?"

"I'm landing now. The palace is on the mainland. I live on the island and we have two lesser isles, Katra and Inj. If His Highness has witnessed the use to which I put his plane there'll be hell to pay, but as there'll be hell to pay when he hears he's paid for a woman surgeon to be flown out, we may as well get the lot over."

The Auster alighted on a lawn-smooth landing strip behind a fabulous, Arabian nights, sugar confection of a palace, shining in the evening sunlight like a mirage. Ruth could absorb but little of it as she crept on tottery legs out of the plane and was helped into a waiting jeep by a salaaming character in a blue turban. Her stomach felt unable to cope with food, but she wanted to drink as never before in her life. Even two magnificent tuskers stomping from foot to foot in the palace yard, with a jangle of their tethering chains, failed to impress her. She might have seen elephants every day of her life for all the notice she

took. She allowed herself to be salaamed into a cool little
anteroom where she begged for tea, her tongue feeling strange
and swollen. The servant who had thus far monopolized her
said, *"Tekai, memsahib,"* and disappeared.

She heard Mark Travers march past on his way into the
Presence; this was shortly signified by an outburst of such
human fury that words were unnecessary. The tidal wave of
invective rolled on and on until it merged into the general silence
and somnolence of the surroundings. Finally Mark Travers
could be heard retraversing the marbled corridors. He stopped in
the doorless archway of the anteroom where Ruth was now
drinking iced tea to her heart's content.

"That was H.H.," he told her wryly and smiled. "At the
moment he loves me not."

"Does he want to see *me* now?" Ruth asked.

"No, he doesn't, dear lady. He's hopping mad at Meriton
also for not making things clear."

"But I can do anything Glen can do!"

"I don't doubt it. I'm to billet you at the hospital. Come on!"

"Now look here, Dr. Travers," Ruth said dangerously. "I'm
not an Indian woman in veils and I demand to see the raja. Just
let him try shouting at me!"

"I would advise you to leave quietly. . . ."

"I'm not asking your advice," Ruth snapped and marched
off down the corridor, looking back over her shoulder and
hating that smiling cynical face more than anything in the world
at that moment.

"May I see His Highness, if His Highness pleases?" she
added quickly as a soldier on guard duty questioned her
approach to the royal apartments. The soldier was unbending,
however, and simply put his rifle in her path when she tried to
pass. There was nothing for it but to retrace her steps and try not
to look at Mark Travers when she reached him.

"Put in a request for an audience tomorrow," he advised.
"I'll personally recommend you to Ajil."

"Ajil can go to hell!" she said violently, near to tears. "Who
does he think he is anyway? I have come a long way from home
to do him a service, not the other way around. I think someone
needs a few lessons in courtesy and hospitality. After all, being
a woman isn't a disease, you know!"

"You've had a bad day, Miss Stafford," he sympathized,

"and you haven't yet realized you've crossed the borderline dividing the progressive west from the time-anchored east. Educated women in India are the exception rather than the rule, and even those few are regarded indulgently rather than seriously. Of course the universities are turning out more and more, but Kanjihan does not boast a university. Here we live simply under our raja, and we never—but *never*—tell him to go to hell, rattle us as he may. To Prince Ajil women have but one necessary function, Miss Stafford. I make myself clear?"

"Vulgarly so," she snapped as they climbed into the jeep once more.

"He will have to be broken in to the idea of you in your professional sense, but why should you worry? It's not costing you anything."

"Which is obviously a rub with you," Ruth snapped.

The darkness had fallen suddenly like a cloak, and she felt no better that now this hateful Travers man had to guide her by the elbow into a waiting motorboat, and that because she was decidedly nervous she huddled up against him during the brief crossing to the island. Even then the ordeal wasn't over, for she was helped into an unseen conveyance and jogged along in a darkness from which gleamed many seemingly evil eyes. Only the padding feet with the conveyance in front, bearing Mark Travers, were a comfort to her, but when at last they pulled up in the familiarity of a hospital compound, the relief was almost too much for her and she whimpered hysterically.

On the lighted veranda of the hospital a young man lounged and looked curiously at her as she descended from the dandy.

Mark introduced his brother and then looked somewhat at a loss as the newcomer crumpled into a heap at his feet.

Matt Travers picked her up and looked uncertainly at Mark.

"Poor traveler," Mark explained, "and hasn't had a bite to eat all day. Where can we put her?"

"My room?" Matt volunteered. "I'll sleep on the veranda. But . . . this is a woman, Mark!"

"Clever boy! That's what arrived, old son, and H.H. has declined with thanks. By the way, did you see my spraying of the *jhil* with the Auster? I knew I'd never get another chance like that with the regular pilot sick. I . . . ." He stopped speaking, for obviously the younger brother wasn't attending. His eyes looked strangely dark as he regarded the helpless woman in his arms, and Mark realized this was probably the first time Matt had held a woman so and guessed at the effect it must be having on him.

"Put her into bed and we'll send an *ayah*," he snapped suddenly, "and take that silly expression off your face. She's not made of glass, boy! She's probably hard as nails and tough as old shoe leather, normally. Get rid of her and report to me."

"Yes, sir," Matt said obediently and turned away, self-consciously carrying his burden.

CHAPTER NINE

ON THE THIRD day after Ruth Stafford's arrival in Kanjihan, Mark Travers was a very worried man. Though he was but thirty-three years of age, he felt old and ill with worry and responsibility. His brother Matt was seven years his junior, and since their father had died in the late raja's service he had tried to be everything to the younger boy; father, mother, friend, counselor and mentor. Obviously Matt had turned to him on every account until now; and—just as obviously—Matt considered himself capable of conducting his first love affair quite unaided. He didn't ask his brother if he might be allowed to fall in love with Miss Stafford, he just did so; his rapturous eyes and frequent withdrawing into his own private thought world were evidence enough of the impact the presence of this female was having on him.

So far, Mark realized, Ruth Stafford seemed unaware that she had a rapt admirer in the younger Dr. Travers; she was perfectly at ease in their company, as one member of the medical profession is with others of her kind. But Mark suspected that all women regarded masculine declarations as tributes to their ego, and that Matt had only to stumble out those first incoherent phrases of devotion to start her on a pursuit of scalp hunting that would be merely amusement on her part, as an experienced woman of the world, but probably the whole world—or its end—for the young lover.

He couldn't claim Matt away from her. They had always been friends, and very close, and he wouldn't want to damage his own relationship with his brother for a woman's sake. The newcomer's sex was as much of an inconvenience at Kanjihan's General Hospital as it had been at the palace, and after he had watched Matt taking Ruth off on some expedition, this being his day off, Mark decided to do something about it. He left his Indian assistant in charge and once more made his way across the narrow sound to the mainland, bound for the palace.

Though he owned a car—a vintage Rolls that had once known the distinction of carrying the king of Nepal on his many tours, and was therefore somewhat of a graybeard among cars—it was not much use to him on the island, especially during the rains. So he had garaged it for the duration in the nearby town, and used either ricksha or dandy when he was in a greater hurry than his legs would carry him. Today, however, he decided to walk to the palace, and stepped thankfully out of the burning sun into the welcome shade of the giant eucalyptus trees that flourished in this area. Colorful bulbuls darted among the branches overhead, and occasionally a mother dangur chided her baby and chattered raucously for a moment or two before succumbing to the sleep-inducing heat once more.

As Mark Travers climbed the gradual rise leading to the palace he paused occasionally and looked back at the expanse of sea, blue and glittering under the sun. There were many craft darting around: native dugouts with homemade sails, well-patched and colorful; and even a clipper, probably one of the few surviving in the Andamans or the Maldives and cruising through the Sundarbans to Dacca. Nearer home was a scattering of yachts, for to own and race a yacht was the ambition of young men of substance in the district, and though Matt Travers was not yet exactly a young man of substance, he had saved and—with Mark's help—had bought a yacht, which had been his single passion until Ruth Stafford's arrival.

Now they were probably combined in his day's entertainment, Mark thought wryly, woman and yacht; both graceful, beautiful, capricious and—in foul weather—undependable.

"I suppose he'll learn," Mark growled aloud, "but it's natural I would have preferred him to learn with another beginner. According to my anonymous correspondent, Miss Stafford has just about been through the book!"

The sentry at the palace gate did not even question his entry, and now Mark strode on down an avenue of blossoming azure jacarandas, past a gardener who dropped his secateurs readily to make a deep obeisance to the doctor sahib, and through a fountain court where an *ayah* was playing ball with Ajil's heir, the small Prince Narhad. The child ran to him, calling out in English, "Uncle Mark! He wants sweetie!"

"He" being the princeling himself.

Mark, however, had to show his pockets empty and promised

not to be so remiss the next time. He then passed on into the cool
precincts of the palace and formally requested an audience.

He was not really surprised when this was promptly refused,
for he had been prepared for Ajil's sulks, so, whistling softly, he
retired without argument and walked openly along in full view
of the royal apartments.

As he had intended, Ajil's curiosity was aroused by his visit,
and having administered the rebuff the raja now walked out
onto the wide veranda and called, "One moment, my friend.
Perhaps we had better speak together after all?"

"If Your Highness pleases," bowed Mark and advanced at a
run up the veranda steps.

In a moment the two were shaking hands and laughing as
though nothing had ever been amiss.

"Come in! Come in!" invited Ajil, who was wearing the
loose robe he lounged around in during the heat of the day. "I
don't know why you come at this time, but welcome! One day
you will walk in the sun once too often and I will have a madman
for my medical director. But what difference? I think this man is
mad already. Do you agree, my dear?"

In the long cool lounge within the rani was wrestling with a
sewing machine and obviously not getting very far with it.

"Oh, Dr. Mark!" she greeted. "No, I do not think he is mad,
Ajil, but *I* am! This damn contraption!"

"Let me see," Mark offered, after saluting the princess.
"What is this, Your Highness? A sew-your-own-sari session?"

"I have to learn to work the thing before I can teach my
women. It is not like the old machine, which is worked by the
feet. When we go to Europe next year I will need many new
clothes. Oh, what is wrong with it?" And Her Serene Highness
kicked the machine sharply.

Mark explained that the new toy was an electric model and
needed to be plugged into the wall socket, and leaving the rani
quite happily in the midst of her admiring women, the two men
wandered off to Ajil's private study and sat regarding each other
steadily for a few moments.

"I was very angry with you the other day," Ajil remembered.
"I wanted very much to dismiss you—never see you again.
Now you know."

"I'm sorry," Mark said sincerely. "I was rather rattled
myself, I suppose, and took advantage of our long association to

use your plane for my own ends. If I may put forward a point of view, Highness, I thought I could show some profitable return for what would have otherwise been a completely empty venture. I knew you wouldn't approve of a woman surgeon.''

"Oh, that," Ajil nodded. "I cabled my friend Meriton regarding this . . . this deception."

"Has he replied?" Mark asked.

"Yes. At great length. Charged to me, of course." Mark raised his eyebrows but said nothing. "And he insists there has been no deception. Miss Stafford is fully trained and able to take care of any specialized surgery I may require. Perhaps we should investigate this lady. Yes?"

"I never thought I'd hear you submitting to petticoat experiments," Mark said sharply. "I really came to see if Your Highness pleased to speed Miss Stafford's return home."

"She is not pretty?" the raja inquired.

"But she is—I suppose," Mark answered and added, "fair, Anglo-Saxon, if you like the type."

"I am Bengali," Ajil smiled. "Do *you* like the type, my friend?"

"My brother does, unfortunately," Mark said sharply.

"Ho! ho!" The raja now fancied he understood the beginnings of a situation. "So the lady has made her choice and it is not you, eh, Mark? Shame for the jealous chip on your shoulder!"

"I couldn't care less," Mark said promptly. "Matt hasn't known many European women, and he's naturally impressed by the first pretty face he sees. Unfortunately, I have been led to believe that the lady in question is somewhat of a *femme fatale* back home. Such a one would not take my brother seriously. I don't want him hurt."

"You come to ask my advice?" Ajil inquired, now intrigued.

"I came to ask when you were thinking of sending her packing."

"But I'm not at the moment, my friend."

"Then can she stay at the palace?"

Ajil half smiled.

"A *femme fatale* here?" he shrugged. "Her Serene Highness wouldn't appreciate that, I don't think! No, Mark, you must not shoulder your troubles off onto me. After all, Matthew is not a child and you cannot protect him from his own emotions forever. If you think this . . . this woman is bad for him, take her on yourself." At Mark's stare of utter incredulity Prince Ajil laughed again. "I mean that," he insisted. "You are a very good-looking fellow when you forget to either sneer or scowl, and I would fancy your chances against Matt any day. Charm the lady away. Then perhaps your brother will hate you, but either way he's got to grow up."

Mark new that although his friend was joking he was also talking a good deal of sense. Matt could not dwell in the cocoon forever. If he, Mark, was not prepared to stand by and watch him emerge only to singe his wings, he must do something about the situation himself: assert his masculinity, efface his brother in competition for the lady's interest.

Somewhat bitterly he indicated the small drawn scar on the raja's left cheek.

"And all for that dimple!" he said scornfully.

The prince was immediately dignified again.

"I do not care for your tone, Mark. I do not like it when you despise me."

"Well, you must admit. . . ."

"I admit nothing and you know nothing. Always nowadays we quarrel, you and I. Once we were boys together and we scoffed when they said east was east and west was west, and that never the twain would meet. They met ideally, we vowed, in our friendship. We were sufficient in ourselves to bridge all gaps between east and west. Poor young fools we were! Now many years have passed and we are east and west again, and I *do not* give in!"

"Well, I'm sorry," Mark said stiffly. "I did not mean to offend Your Highness."

"Said with a curl of the lip your apology offends me the more," Ajil murmured broodingly. "You are so aggressively British, my friend, and imply such pity for anyone in disagreement with you. I know how your mind thinks," he went on, whipping up his passion as he proceeded, "and you have decided this raja is a fool who has grown beyond your British kenning, with too much money and too little sense to spend it wisely; who takes his friends to shoot the tiger and puts new howdahs for his elephants before an autoclave for your hospital. Remember, Dr. Travers, it is *my* hospital and that you are my medical director. I give you this post when you are a young untried man because you are my friend. I take great risk, but I am no fool, and I have no regrets except when you grow too big for your shoes at times . . . ."

White-faced, Mark asked suddenly, "May it please Your Highness to excuse me now?"

"No, it does not please me, my friend. I must come to a conclusion with you. Only your insufferable arrogance is troubled at the moment. You wish to be excused to stalk back to your quarters and write your resignation. I know this. Correct?"

"Dead right!" Mark said through his teeth.

"So before you go I unburden my heart to you. It is not my dimple, as you call it, which has necessitated my bringing a surgeon at great expense from London; this is merely my excuse. In realty I am thinking of the little one, my daughter."

"The Princess Kiran?" Mark asked.

"That one. If I am guilty of vanity, call is compassion, a father's pity for the young saddled with a curse of ugliness. I love my daughter, Mark, and I cannot bear that she should grow up as she is. To my people the princess is a mystery, a legend almost. If they knew the truth, their superstitious minds would associate the child with evil spirits, curses, and the like."

"She should have been hospitalized when she was three months old," Mark said curtly.

"Again I plead the feelings of others. Her Highness was ill, as you know, with the tragedy of having borne a disfigured child. I wanted to reassure her, and my gods, that I could accept this tribulation and bear it . . . for myself. Now I find I can no longer bear it for . . . Kiran."

"So Miss Stafford is to be consulted?" asked Mark.

"Yes, in great confidence. *I* will be her obvious patient, but in reality my small injury will be a cover for the princess. I want you to assess this lady, find out if she is as competent as Meriton states, and give me her character. If she is less than efficient in all matters, back she goes to the U.K. But be fair, Mark, and do not allow your feelings for your brother to turn you from a person who may prove to be Kiran's savior. Do this for me, please, before you resign."

A smile quivered on Ajil's full lips.

"Would this operation be performed at the hospital?" Mark asked, his face expressionless.

"Naturally."

"Then we'll want a darn sight more than a new autoclave."

"You are excused, my friend," said the raja in his high clipped tones.

CHAPTER TEN

RUTH LEANED BACK over the shining blue water and asked, "Am I a good crew, Matt?"

"Learning fast," the young doctor smilingly assured her, his brown body shining with sweat and spray above his white naval shorts. "Can you bring her about now and remember to duck?"

Ruth untied the ropes of the mainsheet and swung herself lightly under the boom as it lurched across, then she tied off and lent her weight to the port side.

"Are there many Europeans hereabout?" she asked.

"Quite a few. Chiefly in advisory capacities these days, and quickly replaced, as soon as they have served their purpose by their Indian pupils."

"And European women?"

"Practically nil. But the climate in Bengal is scarcely suited to members of the fair sex. We get an occasional bigwig's wife or daughter who's handy with a rifle and who has an ambition to bag a tiger, but when the shoot's over the lady departs with her prize and that's that."

"Then ideally it's a bachelor's life, eh?"

Matt Travers regarded his compassion through his long veiling lashes. His eyes were as brown as chestnuts, warm and soft, unlike his brother's steel bores.

"I wouldn't say ideally, Ruth. I'm no bachelor at heart. In fact—" he thought a moment before he spoke, wondering if she would rebuff him "—seeing you has made me realize it's time I got married. I'm no woman hater as Mark is . . . ."

"*Is* he a woman hater then?" she asked quickly.

"He hasn't much faith in womankind, I'm afraid. You see, he was once engaged to be married. Her name was Marcia. I was just commencing my studies at the time and I thought she was a smasher. I don't know what went wrong—Mark would never talk about it—but she eventually married an Australian and is living in Colombo. But must we talk about two people who *aren't* here, Ruth?''

Something in his tone made her glance at him obliquely, and she said coolly, "The answer to the shortage of marriageable females in the district is a trip to London, Matt. There are still plenty of surplus women around there. Doctors are quite a high priority, too.''

"Don't tell me you're considered surplus, Ruth?''

"I don't think I'll be here long enough to confide my life history, Matt. After today I shall inform His Highness that if he doesn't require my services there are plenty who do back where I belong, with people who can appreciate a woman both as a doctor and as a colleague. I think there's much more satisfaction in having a man for a friend than as a lover. Like you and me, Matt. I feel I can really relax with you without sex rearing its ugly head.''

"You do?" Matt asked a little faintly, suddenly finding the tiller rather still. "That's good.''

Ruth smiled into the wind, considering she had steered that particular course rather well.

"I don't really understand the geography, Matt. I thought Kanjihan was just an island.''

"Actually, there's quite a slice of mainland and three islands to Kanjihan, but in prepartition days the royal residence was on the largest island—ours—which gave the island of Kanjihan importance. Unfortunately, an outbreak of cholera wiped out the island's population and the raja wisely burned down his palace and cleared off to the mainland, where the royal family has lived ever since. Inj is a pleasant little island, known as the raja's garden, for all the fruits and vegetables for the royal table are grown there. Katra is our leper asylum. A thousand souls live there, and Mark is trying to make the community self-supporting. He gets enormous satisfaction out of his job.'' Matt sighed hard.

"Don't you?" Ruth wanted to know.

"On the whole, yes, but I'd like to practice decent surgery. Old Ajil's tight on the rupees.''

"So I gathered from your brother,'' Ruth said dryly. "You'll have to go elsewhere for your surgery, Matt.''

"I would hate to leave old Mark. We've always stuck together.''

"If he'd married his Marcia you'd have broken away, wouldn't you?"

"I suppose I would, but he didn't. Look, Ruth, while we're discussing the might-have-been there's a squall bearing down on us. Take your sheet in quickly, or else come and hang on here, will you?"

A black cloud had blotted out the sun, and as the wind struck suddenly Ruth crawled along to the stern while Matt stepped over her and hauled in the mainsheet with difficulty.

"Mind getting wet?" he roared above the wind.

"No. Not if that's all."

"We'll hope that's all." He laughed with the enjoyment of being in the teeth of danger. "We'll be driven ashore somewhere. I can't decide where. With luck we may find an uninhabited island and then you'll be compromised, young lady."

"Even in India?"

"Even here."

"I refuse to be compromised when I'm hungry. I'm ravenous."

"We've been out longer than I intended. I'm sorry, Ruth."

"Rough with the smooth," she acknowledged, her hair plastered to her head with rain and seawater. "It was lovely when we started."

MARK TRAVERS GAZED from one to another of the soaked figures as they appeared in the lighted compound and suddenly saw him.

"Capsize?" he asked conversationally, trying to ascertain from Matt's expression whether or not he was emotionally disturbed after the hours he had spent in Ruth Stafford's company.

"Not quite," replied the younger brother. "Ruth keeps her head in an emergency . . . ."

"Well, thank you!" she smiled and bowed slightly " . . . and we were tossed up on Inj. When the squall had blown out we came back by ferry."

"Had a nice time, Miss Stafford?" Mark then asked pointedly.

"Yes, indeed. Actually, I've been testing Matt's loyalty. I've done my best to persuade him to leave Kanjihan."

"Oh?"

"I don't think it's the ideal school for a surgeon."

"No. We don't profess to be Guy hospital."

Sensing a reproof in his curt tone she turned away with, "Well, I must bath and change these clothes. Please excuse me."

Matt watched her go and Mark decided, *the affair's static, thank goodness. It's about as you were with him.*

"You'd better change, too," he said aloud, "and then have a look at your patients, or had you forgotten them?"

"I had rather," the other replied easily. "Thanks for reminding me."

RUTH HAD BEEN ASKED for her opinion regarding a special case and Mark was showing her through the hospital.

Kanjihan hospital proved to be a pleasant medical surprise. Though the building itself was somewhat lacking in architectural enterprise, and was even repaired at intervals with mud and adobe filled in the gaps in worn timbers, the wards were pleasantly antiseptic, the beds startling white, and the patients obviously well cared for and happy.

The nurses, who walked outside in the familiar tunic and sari, here looked like any European staff in plain blue dresses and snowy aprons. Some of these girls wore caste marks and were incredibly beautiful. The head nurse was a Portuguese nun, as was the operating room nurse.

"Our operating theater is our Achilles' heel," Mark Travers explained as he flung open a door and revealed an ancient hide-covered operating table which reminded Ruth of any G.P.'s examination couch. "A Hindu likes to keep his guts inside him, as you will gather."

"Is this where Matt works?" Ruth asked thoughtfully.

"It's where he develops his frustrations. However, I'm hoping you might change all that."

"Me? How!"

"Nurse—" he addressed the bright-eyed nun in the doorway "—please bring the child in here, will you?"

Through the door weaved a strange little procession headed by a turbaned individual with darting black eyes as sharp in their suspicious glances as the *kukri* he wore at his waist. Behind him came a woman, heavily veiled, holding by the hand a small girl, also veiled to the point of suffocation.

Mark Travers pointedly closed the door on the party and bent down to bring his face close to the child. Her bright confident eyes were full of the laughter her draperies successfully disguised, and it was obvious they were not strangers to each other.

"Did you come to see me, Kiran, or to catch another monkey?"

The child shook with mirth and looked for approval of the joke into the accompanying adults' faces.

"Will you stay and have tea with me?" Mark persisted, and as the child nodded, Ruth thought, *he loves children and they love him, yet he has this bitterness against women as a sex and may never have any of his own*.

The little girl was now perched on the travesty of an operating table, and turning his head a little Mark said, "Are you any good with kids? She may be shy of letting a stranger see her."

Ruth said, "Kiran's a pretty name. My name's Ruth."

The child's eyes were grave, assessing, but not hostile.

"Have you any children?" came from under the veils in a distorted tone Ruth knew only too well.

"No, but I'm going to have one some day." Mark looked interested at this swift calculated reply. "When I do I shall call my little girl Kiran perhaps."

There was only a halfhearted movement of protest from the child as Ruth lifted the face veil away and exposed the fissured upper lip she had expected to see. Now the child's gaze was proud and rather defiant, though the lower lip trembled with a promise of tears.

"It's such a pretty little face," Ruth decided, apparently to herself, an investigating spatula already inside the child's mouth. "There's just a very small job needs doing to put everything right, Kiran, my dear."

"Memsahib is the doctor I am to see?" the child asked of Mark, who was obviously gospel around these parts.

"Yes, Kiran. This is Miss Stafford. Dr. Memsahib."

Now it was Ruth's turn to feel startled.

When the procession had gone out of the theater and they were alone once more, Ruth turned to the medical director.

"She's a rather special child, isn't she?"

"How do you make that out?"

"For one thing she speaks English. Not all Indian peasants do that nowadays. Also, those people with her were not her parents, as I thought at first, but servants."

"I salute you, Dr. Memsahib!" Again that title gave Ruth an

unaccountable thrill. "As a matter of fact, that was Her Highness the Princess Kiran, daughter of our raja. She is the true reason for your presence here."

"But . . . ."

He held his hand up in a silencing gesture.

"If you feel yourself capable of undertaking the task of performing surgery that will allow the princess to lead the normal life of the educated Indian, I will give you my absolute cooperation in all things. But don't do it out of vanity or if you only *think* you can help. Be very sure and keep silent about your charge. The raja has never allowed it to be known that his daughter is . . . disfigured. Perhaps it's possible you can help. Perhaps not. Take time to decide. Now I'm going to give the princess some tea."

Ruth continued strolling through the hospital, considering her course of action very carefully. It was one thing to promise to help any harelipped child, quite another to undertake to help a princess whose life would revolve around her personal beauty more than anything else. It was a bad fissure, not the simple disfigurement from which Marlene's baby had suffered. It might take weeks, months, several operations, and the child was only seven years old.

"I'll do it if she can stand it," Ruth resolved to Mark Travers late that evening.

"She'll stand it," he promised, his eyes very keen even at the end of a busy day. "Kiran is royal right through."

"Well, then," she said uneasily, "that's that."

She went to bed wondering what she was letting herself in for, and Mark Travers was not the least of her worries.

CHAPTER ELEVEN

"TIME IS STANDING STILL," Ruth pondered dreamily, sitting on the bungalow veranda in the hot humidity of morning after a night's torrential rain. "Absolutely still. It's uncanny."

A clump of teak trees made a dark retreat for the island's wild life beyond the compound wall. The gray monkeys were gossiping che-che-che-che-che, angrily or laughingly as the case might be, and occasionally a gibbon whooped, traveling on his spidery arms with a careless abandon that made even the winged creatures look clumsy by comparison. Into the compound itself wandered a Muslim girl driving her goats. The leader wore a bell; he was a fine Billy with a beard even Socrates might have envied. He rallied his wives and offspring to him with a commanding na-ha-ha-ha-ha and led the party, without the girl's aid, around the back to the milking shed.

The girl squatted in the shade under a wall and drew figures with her stick in the sandy dust. She was only a poor peasant girl. In fact, her family's sole income was derived from the goat's milk supplied daily to the hospital. Ruth had once tried to talk to the girl, but she was painfully shy and suspicious of everyone. Mark Travers had observed that as a Muslim she had received ill treatment during the riots and had never forgotten it.

"I noticed she was scarred," Ruth had said.

"More than scarred, poor kid," Mark had said bluntly. "She won't let a man near her."

Ruth rose and stretched, realizing how quickly one succumbed to the ennui induced by great heat. Ten steps across the compound demanded the gathering of physical energy one would normally expend in a hundred-yard sprint back home. Such heat—when accompanied by ninety-eight percent humidity—was draining. One should be content to lie down in the shade of some giant tree and tranquilize oneself in the hypnotic regarding of velvet-green verdure.

"Where are you going without your hat, may I ask?" Mark Travers suddenly demanded from behind her.

"I'm not going anywhere. Anyway, *you* never wear a hat!"

"That's different. I was born out here. You get your hat on immediately and take those salt tablets I put out for you."

He moved past her and then turned as though her grimace was a thing he could feel.

"I'm quite capable of ramming them down your throat myself, Miss Stafford," he smiled, looking hatefully cool and efficient and energetic in this enervating atmosphere.

"Oh, I'm sure you are," she readily agreed. "Such an action measures up to the rest of your courtesies, Dr. Travers."

"If I thought there was any future for me in social graces, Miss Stafford, I would practice them. You must excuse the elephant its skin, you know."

She felt strangely rattled by this encounter, as by others. They never met, she pondered, unless it was head on. Every word that passed between them was charged with either challenge or ambiguity; even their "good mornings" were either flat statements or inquiries, never innocent and spontaneous greetings as intended.

"Hello!" came Matt's cheerful voice, pleasant enough for two, Ruth decided. "The Doctors Travers are coffeebound. Didn't Mark tell you?"

"He might have mentioned it," Ruth lied, wondering why. "I've just had coffee. I do nothing but drink coffee and blank my mind. There's a busy surgeon's life for you!"

"It'll get livelier," Matt promised. "Then you'll be glad of this period of lotus-eating. In fact, it looks like it's shaping up already. We got our new autoclave by this morning's ferry. I'm going to collect it this afternoon. Care to come?"

"No. Please excuse me, Matt," Ruth said quickly.

"You have something better to do?"

"No. Something else. Letters . . . ." Once more she had lied and her conscience smote her. Matt had never again made advances toward her, so it wasn't that. It was simply that with him out of the way for an hour she could promise herself the dubious pleasure of his brother's companionship. No man had ever alternately ignored and provoked her so before; she found the situation difficult to accept or believe in. One day he had taken her on an expedition to the center of the island, which was craggy and volcanic in origin. The climb had been steep, the fossilized lava treacherous and sharp as flint where it pierced her ankle on occasion. For miles, it seemed, they trudged over this unhappy terrain and she had bitten her lip until it bled rather than complain to that upright surefooted figure always maddeningly ahead.

His "You all right?" on one occasion had been an imperious command that she had better be all right, not a question requiring any answer.

Her "Of course" had been torn from her pride, for she could feel her own blood slippery inside the lamb's-wool socks he had made her wear, and her head thudded with blood deprived of natural salt. Sweat had soaked her clothes which were uncomfortably attached to her like an outer skin.

At long last, when she had become quite callous to physical suffering, she saw him unfastening a rucksack on some flat ground beneath a peculiar inverted red tree. She counted the steps it took to reach him: eight-seven-six-five-four—she made a little skip out of four because she stumbled—three-two-one-collapse under the tree. Her gasping breaths were audibly painful, yet she couldn't seem to fill her lungs and wondered dispassionately if she was about to die of suffocation.

"Do you suffer from asthma, Miss Stafford?" Mark Travers had asked conversationally, and as she didn't answer, "The fresh air may have been too much for you. We're three thousand feet up here, but of course you have quickly become accustomed, breathing the steam of the delta. I'll show you a splendid view a mile on. Have a curry puff."

He had placed one of the cakelike globes on a napkin beside her before he heard her speak.

"I . . . can't . . . go . . . on . . . ." was dragged out of her.

"What do you mean you can't go on?" he asked sharply. "You'll have to either go on or back, you realize?" Then the incredible happened. She allowed a small whimper to escape her lips, and this became a full-blooded howl as he pulled her roughly to her feet and shook her.

"Stop it!" he commanded. "Stop it at once! Do you hear?" She not only heard but obeyed immediately.

"What hurts?" he demanded and spoiled it by adding, "I can't stand a woman bawling. You can't get any sense out of 'em once they start that."

"My feet, mostly," she said. "I don't think my shoes were very suitable."

He allowed her to flop down again and unlaced her offending shoes. They had scarcely any soles left. The white lamb's-wool socks were now the blackened purple of congealed blood.

"My God!" was wrung from him, and she opened her eyes, stupid with pain, to see his face as though he had just unmasked himself. Concern, gentleness, horror, and guilt sped across his countenance as he peeled off what remained of the socks, apologizing for the bits of skin that came away with them.

"Why didn't you say?..." he murmured over and over again. "Oh, lord, what a mess!"

"I'm sorry," was torn from her. "I seem to be a nuisance to you whatever I do, Dr. Travers."

"A nuisance?" he echoed strangely. Then he gave a rather hollow laugh. "Being a nuisance is something one can't help, Miss Stafford, but what you've done to yourself this day is sheer idiocy. What were you trying to prove?"

"I don't know," she said as he bound her feet in linen and covered them with fresh socks from the rucksack. "I suppose if you thought I could tackle an expedition of this sort I wasn't going to argue. Now we both know I'm a softie." She turned her head away quickly.

"No," he said, very thoughtfully, "you've proved you're no softie. I don't know how you did it when your poor feet must have been raw for the past hour. I wandered into the bazaars when I was a child and watched the fakirs settling for the day on their beds of nails under the blistering sun . . . but they learn to do it by discipline and long practice. I suppose it's my fault. Frankly I . . . I don't know much about women. It's a shock to discover their physical fraility allied with a fantastic capacity for suffering, and I feel very guilty about all this. I often spend my time wandering about up here; it's wild and lonely and . . . and ageless somehow. Matt likes the sea, yachting and swimming, waterskiing, and all that. You've shared his days without turning a hair. Obviously you're not up to sharing mine."

With that last pronouncement the mask of arrogance and masculine superiority had been donned again. The moments of intimacy created between pain and healer were past. She was a burden again, a poor wretched feeble woman whose very presence 3,000 feet up a mountain was purely a physical embarrassment.

"How am I going to get down?" she had asked weakly as he threw her shoes, with a grimace of distaste, over the lip of a precipice.

"I shall carry you."

"Oh, no!" her cheeks flooded crimson, though she tried to control her blushes. "You can't do that!"

"I not only can, Miss Stafford, but will insist on doing so. There aren't many alternatives. I could leave you, of course, and send a bearer up for you, but you would be frightened, possibly, by lammergeiers and eagles, and you obviously have to be rescued before sundown. No, loathsome as the prospect appears to you, dear lady, these arms will have to hold you, but I can promise you not a single sullied thought shall despoil the contact thus forced upon us."

She had turned her head away proudly, angrily.

"Can't you discuss anything without sneering?" she asked.

"That's asking a lot. What is a scorpion without his tail?"

"Less poisonous," she answered quickly, and he was actually laughing as he dumped the rucksack and lifted her—as though she had been a child—up into his arms and set out, surefootedly as a mountain sheep, upon the homeward trail.

Four days later Ruth didn't care to remember that expedition in detail. She was embarrassed to recall his physical tenacity that had never wavered until he deposited her on her bed and sent Nurse Angelina to her with her gentle ministrations. He hadn't bothered to see her again himself. Dr. Singh had examined the feet, once they were bathed, and prescribed for them.

Seeing her on the second day hobbling around in open-toed sandals in the compound, Mark Travers had approached with a face like thunder.

"Miss Stafford! Get inside and put on those boots I sent to you!"

"Oh, stop bullying me!" she had quickly protested. "Boots are so hot and I'm quite comfortable in these."

"No doubt," he smiled acidly. "But in this compound is the dust of many feet. Some of them leprous. Do I make myself clear?"

He made himself so horribly clear, as always, Ruth pondered on this day as Matt went off to have his coffee. *Now he's yapping about a hat. If I don't wear one I'm quite likely to fall down with sunstroke just to prove to him right, as usual. Oh, damn the man!*

She was wearing her own shoes today, and stockings, upon which Mark Travers insisted. Her feet were just about back to their normal size and practically healed, but she had begun to think her personal energy had been sapped for all time by the enormity of that physical ordeal.

"Come along, Miss Stafford, your salt tablets," the hated voice ordered briskly as she reached the veranda, now in the cool shade of overhanging boughs of Persian lilac, with blossoms whose perfume was reminiscent more of lily of the valley than its English counterpart. "You haven't been the same girl since I nearly walked you to death, so at least allow me to medicate you as I think fitting."

She swallowed the salt tablets with iced water and felt Matt watching her, saying with his eyes what she had forbidden to his lips.

"I want you to rest this afternoon, Miss Stafford," Mark announced conversationally. "This evening I'm to present you at the palace."

"Oh," she said somewhat bleakly. "Am I finally to be accepted then?"

"Wear something pleasant, but quite informal," he proceeded, ignoring her sarcasm. "I'll be wearing a sports jacket, and the womenfolk hereabout don't overload themselves with jewelry on these occasions."

"Thanks for warning me," she couldn't resist saying. "But for your timely advice I might have worn my pompadour brocade gown and a tiara!"

Matt laughed suddenly and then stopped short as his brother regarded him askance.

"I . . . I'll be pushing off back to that infusion I'm setting up," the younger man said quickly and bounded off down the veranda steps with a brief salute in Ruth's direction.

"Your spirits are somewhat restored, I'm gratified to note," Mark Travers observed as he poured more coffee both for her and himself. "You're obviously feeling kittenish today, Miss Stafford."

"If I was," she said, "I am now in the right company to restore me to my usual deep depression."

"You really don't like me, do you?" he asked on a note of

true inquiry. "I mean, it's not just a feminine pose or something on your part?"

"You were utterly impossible from the moment of our meeting!" she snapped at him.

"I know. But supposing we had started from scratch, without any previous knowledge of each other, what then?"

"But I *had* no previous knowledge of you, Dr. Travers. Did you have any of me?"

"No, no, of course not!" he said hastily, and she knew he was lying and hating himself for it. "How could I possibly know anything about you here in Kanjihan?"

He felt as though the anonymous letter was written all over his countenance, with its phrases like "social menace" and "woman who has been through the marriage service" trebly underlined. Somehow she hadn't seemed such a social menace up there on the mountain with her feet covered in blood, and she hadn't the sexual assurance expressed by most married women, confident in their power over men and uplifted from curiosity by their natural fulfillment. This woman was as physically reticent and yet as curious as he was himself, as though she had only peeped through all the forbidden doors leading to ecstasy. She angered and antagonized him, but he had not attempted to persuade her to be otherwise.

Now, suddenly, he wondered if the writer of the anonymous letter knew any more about the real Ruth Stafford than he knew himself.

CHAPTER TWELVE

RUTH STILL HAD THAT ODD feeling of being suspended in time as she dressed for the evening. It was actually a mere two weeks since she had boarded the transcontinental airliner which had carried her as far as Karachi, yet she seemed to have entered another dimension in which her past life had no part. She found it even difficult at times, to believe that she was a qualified surgeon, wondering if that part of her had been left behind along with the shining green tiles, plate glass and chromium of the Meriton clinic. A new elemental Ruth appeared to wake each morning with the sensation of a person emerging from an anesthetic, from a place where sounds were sharp with the significance of something that had already happened, a thing of such tremendous importance it was already deeply accepted in the subconscious mind, yet over which the act of awakening had drawn a teasing veil.

Ruth would lie and marvel in this state of primeval delight, loth to open her eyes and assure herself that there had been nothing truly delightful about her trip to Kanjihan so far. In fact, once true wakefulness had been achieved—with the aid of "char" served in a fragrant brown jug—the whole business of her visit was rapidly cut down to size. She was on the whole mistrusted, despised, and climatically unsuited for the project. She had quickly succumbed to prickly heat and had lost her natural color. With a pale buff complexion and hair decidedly in need of the beauticians who specialized in catering to the fine gold floss with which she had been blessed all her life, she hardly felt her feminine charms were exactly impressive. And while she wished to keep in full control of the situation where Matt Travers was concerned, by not emphasizing her good points with the most encouraging of adornments, she still wanted to look her very best whenever the elder brother was around, if only to hope for a lifting in that expression of utter impassivity with which he appeared to be permanently endowed.

Mark Travers' coldness, his keep-off-the-grass mentality, which he fancied protected him from all comers and for all time, was a constant challenge to all womankind, Ruth decided. She didn't like to think of him in his little medical kingdom, after she had gone, as unaware of her existence as the permanence of the shore is unaware of the separate individualities of waves breaking upon it. One wave—she determined—ought to break right over him one of these days and drown him in a realization of hunger and loneliness and frustration and amazement. It would dwarf him from a giant of arrogance and self-importance to a mere pigmy of emotional need. Though she might never see it, she liked to think such a thing could happen, that the man really was a creature of flesh and blood, with appetites, dreams, and desires like the rest of them.

Though he had advised "wear something informal," she had a desire to disobey him and present herself at the palace in something arresting and rather shocking like a backless gown with prominent "falsies" wired into it and ablaze with sequins.

She didn't possess such a dress, however, though Cassie wore those outrageous models as casually as she kissed.

I'm going to the palace primarily as the surgeon who is to operate on the princess, Ruth told herself sternly, *and if I annoy Dr. Travers I may also annoy the Rajah without meaning to.*

Therefore she selected a dress of pale blue spun silk with a matching jacket, and merely adorned herself with plain pearl studs in her ears. Neither a ring nor bracelet did she possess, and even her watch was too workmanlike for evening wear, so she looked more casually dressed than any woman paying an afternoon call to take tea with her aunt. The scissors, which had been intended merely to trim, had finally hacked her hair into a veritable urchin cut; the more she panicked, the worse she made it, until finally it wouldn't lie down at all.

After repeated urgings from the bearer, who was the superintendent's personal servant, Mark Travers himself appeared outside her window, which opened onto the veranda.

"Are you ready?" was all he said, apparently not noticing the originality of her coiffure. "H.H. won't like the idea of his barge being kept waiting."

"Will I do?" she demanded, determined not to be ignored, and turning around with a slight swaying of the hips, like a model on a dais.

"As if my opinion counted with you one way or the other!" he said impatiently. "Come on!"

He disappeared along the veranda, and with a last desperate attempt to smooth her unruly locks she seized her evening bag and a loose white coat and dashed after him.

"You look smashing, Ruth," Matt told her as he leaned against the bougainvillia-entwined veranda rail outside the hospital. "I wish I could swap takes with Mark."

"So do I," Ruth agreed as she was bundled unceremoniously into a double-seated ricksha known locally as a "bukoo." "See you later, Matt!"

Mark urged the two runners to get a move on, apparently not at all offended by his companion's stated preference for another's escort.

. . . and it's not strictly true, either, Ruth admitted to herself. *This brute at least stimulates me by the very fact that I fail to interest him. But if Matt had been here beside me so close in the darkness, he would at least have held my hand and breathed a little warmly against my neck.*

Only the pad-pad of the rhythmic running feet was to be heard until they reached the swamp, then a frog chorus—like so many out-of-tune euphoniums in concert—made the air hideous with raucous croaking.

"India," said Mark Travers, as though to himself. "The frogs at night destroying the nonpareil of beauty as expressed by the water lily breathing ere she dies. So, always, hand in hand go beauty and ugliness, creating in this context the commonplace we accept as our heritage."

"Are you quoting or expressing an opinion?" asked Ruth.

"Thank you for even wondering, Miss Stafford." She could hear the smile in his voice. "My opinions are rarely poetical, worse luck. I was roughly translating from Hamar, circa fourteenth century. 'There is nothing perfect in the world, for perfection is only in our ending.' "

"I'll settle for the best possible," Ruth decided.

"But then you are both practical and prosaic," he told her.

Somehow the observation stung and stayed with her like an insult. Was she as practical as all that? In her work—yes—one

had to be, but outside of work there was plenty of scope for
dreaming, and she had done her share of it. Prosaic? . . . There
she couldn't defend herself. It was other people who were
observers of the person who walked around bearing one's name.
One might think of oneself as charming, mysterious, and utterly
feminine, and be categorized by the Mark Travers of the world
under the heading "prosaic." Bitter the pill indeed, and it took
her a long time to swallow it.

The crossing to the mainland was made in Prince Ajil's
private barge, which appeared to Ruth to resemble the craft
plying up and down the Grand Union Canal, even down to the
small inconvenient cabin upholstered in leopard skin. It was
obviously stout in its timbers, however, for the arrival at the
jetty was signified by a head-on collision which sent everybody
flying and fused the lights.

"All right?" Mark Travers asked, picking her up from a
debris of periodicals in a corner of the cabin by the light of a
flashlight.

"I . . . I think so. What happened?"

"Nothing happened. We arrived, that's all. Some clot had
berthed at the jetty without leaving his parking lights on, and we
hit him. That's typical Kanjihan and breaks the monotony."

A very big opulent American manufactured car was waiting
at the jetty, and Mark indicated it casually.

"It appears we're in favor at the moment. Ajil has sent the
Buick for us."

"If we hadn't been in favor what might we have expected?"
she asked, sliding into the immensity of the air conditioned
interior.

"Depending upon the depth of our fall from grace, the
Mercedes Benz, or the old V-8, even the Hillman estatewagon
or the Morris eight."

"All those cars . . ." Ruth marveled, " . . . and no decent
roads!"

"You're catching on quicker than I anticipated, Miss Stafford," he said with a mocking little bow. "You are now in the
land of Topsy Turvy and nothing is really as it seems!"

"I'd like to believe that, Dr. Travers," she bowed back,
"then I might have hopes for even you!"

She could have sworn the air in the car grew as thick as smoke
for a few moments after her teasing pronouncement, as though

charged with the electricity of scarcely controlled human intent. But as the sleek car drew up outside the palace that gleamed like a jeweled crown reflected in its ornamental waters, Mark Travers stepped out and offered her his hand, looking cool, urbane, and quite unruffled by her gibe.

"I think you can safely look after yourself once we're inside," he suggested. "You're not a child at its first social function and neither am I a nursemaid. I'll be seeing you back when it's over."

Which is a very nice way of saying get out from under my feet for an hour or two, Ruth pondered, conscious that the hand under her elbow was as aware of her as a woman as a bedpost might be.

THE RANI, HER SERENE HIGHNESS the Princess Rosala, was still rather like a child in her reactions to a "party," and her husband—who was devoted to her, although it had originally been an arranged marriage—indulged her more than most husbands even in this new India. Today he had sent for the jewels he had inherited under his father's will and had discovered an emerald bracelet that he had sent to his wife "with compliments," a phrase he had adopted ever since, as a young man at Oxford, he had received a note in his rooms inviting him to the dean's study the following morning. It had been signed "With Compliments."

Rosala had gasped with delight upon receiving the bracelet. Not that she hadn't plenty of jewels already, but each new item usually meant that Ajil was pleased with her and had demonstrated his pleasure in this so pleasurable a way.

She already had emerald pendants falling from large golden earrings, and to match the jewels she wore a white tunic edged with brocaded silver, and a green sari that somehow brought out the hazel tints in her merry brown eyes.

Finally, accompanied by three of her women, she went along to the children's apartments so that they could see her in all her glory.

"A levee, mama?" queried Princess Kiran, taking in the beauty of her mother slowly as though there was too much to absorb all at once.

"No, darling, just a little dinner. Half a dozen guests."

"He wants Uncle Mark," said Prince Narhad from his cot.

"I'm sure Dr. Mark will come and see you, darlings. Now I must go."

The door behind them breezed open and Mark Travers stood revealed, Ruth Stafford behind him.

"Your Highness," he said suddenly. "I'm sorry!"

"You are expected, Dr. Mark," Rosala assured him. "As if such an old friend needs to ask if he may enter! Come in!"

Kiran, in her nightclothes, now did a most pecular thing. She rushed past Mark and wrapped herself around Ruth's knees so that she couldn't move.

"Look at my mama, Miss Stafford, how beautiful she is! You are going to make me look just like her, aren't you?"

Ruth had not yet been presented to Her Highness, but she didn't think this was a moment for the formalities. She looked at the rani, resplendent in her sari, with her black hair smoothly drawn back from her face. She wore a caste mark in the center of her forehead and her high cheekbones supported a face as lovely as anything to be seen in all Asia. Her eyes had ceased laughing and held an intensity of such pain as could hardly be borne during the interval of waiting for someone to speak.

"Miss Stafford?" urged Kiran, tugging again at Ruth's skirts.

"Just like your mother, darling, I promise," Ruth said confidently and wonder from what source she had drawn her confidence. "You promise to be brave and I'll do the rest."

"Oh, I can be very brave . . ."

The rani was serenity itself again by now.

"Miss Stafford, you don't know how welcome you are in Kanjihan. Perhaps my husband and I have appeared to be neglectful, but we are slow in our appraisals and anxious not to be mistaken in our judgments."

Ruth gave a slight inclination of her head and briefly touched the slim proffered hand with her own.

"I hope I don't disappoint anyone, Your Highness—" her glance flickered over Mark Travers in the background "—and most especially Kiran."

She held the child to her for an instant, then allowed her to obey her mother's gesture of dismissal into the charge of her attendant ayah. When they had gone into the bedroom beyond, Rosala asked, almost desperately, "There is really hope that surgery can . . . can? . . ."

"Surgery can do wonders these days, Your Highness. I am

prepared to be judged on the final results. Unfortunately, it will take some time.''

''Don't worry, Miss Stafford,'' Rosala said almost blithely. ''Dr. Mark, you must make Miss Stafford's stay pleasant as well as profitable. Build her a house. Get her anything she wants.''

''*Anything*, madam?''

''Absolutely anything, Dr. Mark. Please excuse me. We have other guests.''

''You heard what she said,'' Ruth mused as they left the nursery apartments together a few minutes later. ''I'm to have *anything* I want, Dr. Travers.''

''Oh, yes, I heard,'' he shrugged. ''Do you fancy the moon for a start, Miss Stafford?''

''No, thank you,'' she said cuttingly, ''not in present company. Actually, I was thinking that my needs could very well be yours—in a professional sense. You had better stop your elegant sneering long enough to decide what you want for your hospital, hadn't you?''

CHAPTER THIRTEEN

DINNER WAS PERHAPS hardly the word to describe the meal to which about half a dozen guests were entertained by the royal pair of Kanjihan province. Ruth thought it better resembled an indoor picnic, for everyone lolled around in attitudes of absolute repose on piles of many-hued cushions, and was served from various dishes of assorted precooked meats and patties and sandwiches, the contents of each item clearly labeled in both Hindustani and English.

Afterward Ruth learned that in India it is difficult to sit at one table and share the same menu with guests of so many different religions and beliefs. The Muslim will not touch pig, so for him ham sandwiches are out, also the slice of pork with its many and varied garnishings; the Sikh will not eat beef, the cow being a sacred animal. There is also another sect that will refuse both chickenmeat and eggs. Truly a hostess hasn't the easiest of times providing for such a mixed bag.

Ruth, who was hungry and enjoyed a little of everything presented to her, little knew what pleasure she was bringing to both the rani and her domestic staff by her display of appetite.

As Mark Travers had elected to sit cross-legged beside a Muslim merchant for the meal, Ruth had time to look around her and study the other guests. She had been introduced as memsahib, a visiting doctor from London, and Rosala had indicated she would sit beside her, as they were the only two women present.

The room was magnificent, a dream of pearly gray and pink-marbled walls with water running under an iron grill in the center of the floor sending up waves of coolness and displaying occasionally the darting flash of a goldfish in its depths. The window apertures were unglazed, yet each possessed a casement of gold filigree, as these were all open to the warm scented air of evening, and also, incidentally, to swarms of mosquitoes, moths, and hornbacks. The splendid figure of a sentry could occasionally be seen parading outside on the marble terrace, giving the scene the appearance of a gigantic film set dressed for showing in glorious technicolor.

A intervals on the walls were images of the god Krishna. He was never one person as is Buddha, or Mahomet; he either had a woman's face, a man's body and many arms; or a bird's head and tiger's claws; or he was man and animal both. Also, he had many different names. Sometimes he was Shiva and sometimes Vishnu.

One guest intrigued Ruth in that he placed a small dish in front of one of these images and proceeded to pile it with various items of food and succulent fruits. Ruth would not have been terribly surprised to see the birdhead animal descend and eat its fill. The food remained there, however, growing staler as time went by, and the Hindu, who was wearing a white forage cap and pajamas, went back to his neighbor and continued his chat with obvious contentment of mind.

All this was to stir in Ruth a curiosity about India, its peoples, and its religions, which she found fascinating and utterly absorbing. Before the evening was over she knew Krishna in seven of his accepted guises, and that God, to the Hindu, is in all things and all mankind. The gift of food was a tribute because the giver's wife had been sick and was now restored. That it was his host's food made no difference apparently. It was the gesture that counted.

Rosala Rani began to chatter energetically once the food remains had been removed and the servants brought in a choice of tea, coffee, and various spirits.

"How do you like our part of the world, Miss Stafford?"

"I'm afraid I haven't seen enough of it yet to express an opinion, Your Highness. At the moment I am still coping with your climate—not very happily."

"It will come in time," Rosala smiled. "I remember thinking I could never in a thousand years cope with yours."

"Your Highness has been to England?"

"But of course. I went to school near Brighton for five very happy years. I even took my Higher School Certificate and asked my father if I might be allowed to go on to Oxford. That was asking too much of him, however; my marriage was all arranged by that time. I was very sorry to leave Brighton."

Ruth looked at the princess and tried to imagine her as a schoolgirl in gym suit and socks, her dark hair in two plaits tied with regulation navy blue ribbons.

"Would Your Highness object to a rather personal question?"

"I know it!" Rosala said delightedly. "All our European visitors ask if I knew Ajil before I married him! That is your question, Miss Stafford?"

"Yes," Ruth said apologetically. "I suppose you think our curiosity impertinent."

"Not at all, my dear. I think there is a great deal to be said, still, for arranged marriages, and as I saw Ajil long before he saw me, I could have refused him if he hadn't been to my liking."

She turned a somewhat impertinent assessing gaze on her husband who was deep in conversation with the other menfolk.

"I think now, as I thought then, that I am very fortunate in my father's choosing. My sister's husband was forty and she was sixteen when she married him, but—" Rosala shrugged "—they are very happy and have five sons." Her lovely face brooded for a moment. "Miss Stafford, I dreaded having a second baby after . . . after Kiran. If that should ever happen again! . . ."

"Most unlikely, Your Highness," Ruth assured her. "In fact, I would say it couldn't happen again to you. The incidence is about one in two thousand births. You mustn't let it worry you for the future, and Kiran will be . . . all right in time."

"You hesitated, didn't you, Miss Stafford? You're not absolutely sure?"

"I'll do my utmost, Your Highness. Will you accept that?"

Rosala looked deep into the sincere blue eyes, the color of which reminded her of cornflowers rioting in the meadows behind the school she had attended as a girl.

"I have every confidence in you, Miss Stafford, and so has Kiran. You impressed the child very much from the moment you met. It was as though you were the first person to make her feel . . . beautiful, if you know what I mean?"

"But so she is!" Ruth exclaimed. "I could see the child as she was intended to be—as I mean her to be—God willing! I hope you will impress upon His Highness the urgency of securing whatever I may need. Quite frankly, I wouldn't perform an autopsy in the operating theater as it is at the moment.''

''You can leave the raja to me,'' Rosala Rani said confidently. ''Order from Calcutta—or even London—anything you may require. After all, it is for our precious daughter, the Princess Kiran.''

With that last remark the invisible curtain fell between the eastern and western mentality, Ruth decided. It wasn't important that other parents had children who could benefit from up-to-date surgery; the benefit was as incidental as crumbs falling from the rich man's table in this land of the survival of the privileged. Looking across the room, she met the challenge of Mark Travers's glance, and he was so evidently approving of Rosala's friendly overtures, seeing in them a means to an end for himself.

I am the open sesame to all he wants for himself and Matt and has failed to wangle, she thought wryly, *and with that his interest in me ends. But need he make it all so obvious?*

There was a sudden commotion outside the palace, and a servant brought news that was of apparent interest.

''Come along!'' It was Mark Travers grabbing her arm. ''There's a cobra out on the terrace. The *chuprassie* says he's a ten-footer, at least!''

Ruth found herself clinging to him as for dear life as she watched the deadly creature uncoil to the prodding of pointed sticks. Its skin shone as though wet in the reflected light, a thousand-faceted emerald green paling to yellow on the underside.

''He's throwing his hood,'' Mark said excitedly as the cobra's neck swelled out on either side of its wicked black eyes. ''There he goes! He's annoyed now!''

With the speed of the flick of a whip the creature struck here and there at his tormentors, and Ruth began to feel sick.

''Isn't it . . . dangerous?'' she asked.

''Of course. But who's afraid of a little danger?''

Rosala was shouting as loudly as anyone, even encouraging the raja to join in the fun.

''I'm going to faint, I think,'' Ruth said calmly and swayed as she stood.

She never quite lost consciousness, though the shouting

became distant in her ears and all sensation merged into a between world of uncomplicated peace and fragrance. When she eventually stirred and opened her eyes she mutely accepted the tinkle of running water and a breeze of cool air wafting across her face, and as though continuing a conversation she said calmly, "I am."

"Oh, so you're back with us," Mark Travers stated in relief. "I was wondering how long I was going to have to sit here playing punkah-wallah." He laid down the palm leaf he had been using as a fan. "Do you often pass out like that?"

"I wasn't aware that I had passed out, and no, I don't," she answered him shortly. "I remember now! The snake! It was awful!"

"That was no snake, ma'am," he jeered, using a broad American accent. "That was the real McCoy. A King cobra. You needn't have worried. Nobody gets hurt—often; not even the villain of the piece. He's been put in Ajil's private reptile house where he'll live right royally on chickens and Bengal hares."

"Have I been out here long?" she asked, looking around her at the moonlit-washed gardens.

"About fifteen minutes," he told her, "but I didn't mind a breather myself. Anyway, the party's breaking up now. We can go home whenever you're ready."

"Home?" she asked, startled.

"Sorry! The hospital is the only home I know. Obviously it can mean nothing more to you than an inconvenient lodging."

"No, I wasn't sneering, honestly," she said sincerely. "You and your brother have a very attractive home on the island. I always feel I'm putting you out though . . . ."

"You're to have your own house. Official orders," he stated.

"No, there's no need for that. An extra room built onto the bungalow is all that's required, then Matt can move back into his own quarters."

"He'd like to be nearer to you, especially at certain times of the moon," Mark Travers said slowly, gazing up at the partly broken plate floating in the indigo sea above them. "When one is young enough at heart to feel the stirrings of romantic excitement, even the movement of a pretty woman in the next room can arouse the feverish craving we call love."

Feeling her own heart working at full power now, Ruth said

quietly, "I hope Matt never becomes as cynical as you are, Dr. Travers."

"He will if he finds the wrong woman first."

"As *you* did, I suppose?"

He glanced at her sharply.

"Maybe, Miss Stafford, but we will not resort to personalities if you don't mind."

"That's what you say," she accused him, "but you're getting at me all the time. You think Matt is a little in love with me already, and you probably wonder what he sees in me . . . ." She indicated herself briefly. "I know I'm not much of a catch in your eyes!"

"Oh, I don't know," he half smiled, surveying her anew. "You have a lovely figure and that dress becomes you. I *do* notice such things, but I don't go around with my tongue lolling out over every pretty woman I see. I'm far too hardened for that sort of thing. But I have the vague primeval stirrings of desire on occasions, like any other normal male. At such times I either work harder or write a sonnet."

"Rather than do the natural thing and succumb, I suppose," she said nastily.

"Miss Stafford, are you ever so backhandedly challenging me to prove my normality?"

"I would never insult you by calling you normal, Dr. Travers. I concluded long ago that formaldehyde must run in your veins."

"You did it again!" he said admiringly. "For a woman who swoons at the sight of a cobra you certainly don't realize the danger in the creature you're arousing now!"

With a battering of white wings and a haunting hoot an owl flew out of the tree above their heads and swooped on some creature creeping along on the grass. Ruth was startled by the incident and acted instinctively, and the arms into whose protective embrace she flung herself closed around her so fiercely she felt her ribs creak in protest. Before she could frame a question her lips were otherwise engaged. Surely he was not only kissing her but drawing the very breath from her body, subjugating her will and her reason in a masculine demand that brought all physical sensation into one measure of elemental truth. She had never been kissed like this in her life before and somehow knew that with the passing of the entranced moment she might well never know such a kiss again. It was fever, it was fire, it was yearning and fulfillment all in one. The heady-scented water lilies, the carnations, the falling blossoms of the jacaranda, all made a sensory background to an ultra sharpness of the senses thereby fulminated in two human beings.

It was Ruth who disengaged herself at last.

"Mark!" she gasped, using his name for the first time as though there was no end to discovery.

"Let's go," he said, drawing her back toward the palace.

"I . . . I can't," she decided, wanting to hide her face in his lapel.

"Ruth," he spoke gently and yet commandingly, so that she raised her eyes to his, marveling at her own desire to be obedient, "we must say good-night to our hosts, mustn't we? Now be a good girl and come along."

Of course she must resume normality, she told herself sternly. Mark Travers hadn't declared eternal love simply because he had kissed her once on the mouth. He probably expected her to forget the incident as quickly as possible.

There was no reading his countenance on the journey back to the hospital. He didn't even attempt to hold her hand, though she wouldn't have rebuffed him, she knew. The whole of a somewhat fantastic evening had suddenly boiled down into that brief physical encounter in a palace garden. Somehow Ruth felt sure it would from now on color the whole of life for her, and glancing up at her companion as they climbed into the bukoo for the last lap of the journey, she wondered if he had been stirred as she had been, as his mouth had pressed muscularly on her own.

"Good night," he said calmly at the veranda steps outside her room. "Watch out for snakes, won't you?"

"I don't think I'm afraid of mere snakes now!" she assured him, her voice still uncertain.

"Sleep well, Ruth!" He went off, whistling, to the other side of the house.

She stood listening until there was no sound but the stirrings of the creatures of night; then, with a sigh, she undressed and crept under the mosquito netting and into bed.

"I mustn't fall in love with *him*," she decided. "Tomorrow everything will fall back into place with Dr. Travers senior as unbearable as ever."

But he had kissed her.

Always now she would remember that, when he chided or

sneered or haughtily withdrew. That moment of intimacy would always lie between them like a pool whose depths they had only ruffled before discovering that here they could drown together if they so chose. He wouldn't want to drown in delight, she pondered bitterly; it would mean too much giving for a person as self-loving as he was. It was more than likely he would put up a danger sign instead and expect her to keep herself clear of it.

Morning seemed to arrive on the coattails of her still troubled thoughts, and she fancied she hadn't slept a wink until something struck her cheek and caused her to open startled eyes and look around her. The mosquito net had been tied back and the *ayah* was singing softly in the kitchen. Somebody smoking a pipe had obviously just passed by on the veranda. Ruth put her hand up to her face and recovered the crushed blue trumpet of a jacaranda blossom.

But there were no jacarandas on the island!

With this knowledge she smiled suddenly and put the blossom between the leaves of her bedside book. It had told her what she wanted to know more expressively than words could do. Mark Travers associated her in his mind with a flower . . . not—as she had feared—with a snake!

CHAPTER FOURTEEN

"THERE!" RUTH ANNOUNCED, her eyes shining. "What do you think of your theater now, Matt?"

"I think it's a honey, Ruth, and all thanks to you."

The younger Dr. Travers lovingly ran his fingers over the steel and chromium of the new operating table and the lever that, when manipulated, could raise the head or foot or even turn it to face a different way altogether. There was a powerful new arc light over the table, and other more mobile lamps mounted on flat chromium bases with adjustable arching uprights. The walls had been tiled in pale green and this color was continued into the thick sound-deadening rubberized floor covering. The autoclave hummed pleasantly in the background and row upon row of immaculate instruments shone in the glass-fronted cupboards occupying the whole of one wall. Washing arrangements were also much improved. The one cracked basin previously in use had been removed, and now there was a row of three in an ancillary building that had been added to the theater and also served as the surgeon's changing room.

"Makes one feel like work," Matt smiled. "But who's going to use it after you and I are both gone, Ruth?"

"You and I ...?" She looked a little uncertainly. "Now don't make me feel guilty at this stage, Matt. What do you mean, you and I both gone? Only I'm going away eventually, surely?"

"Oh, no," he said firmly. "I've thought a lot about my career and future since you arrived, Ruth, and I've decided I can't allow Mark to nurse me through my whole life. When our father died Mark was a true guardian to me. He took this job as Ajil's medical director because it provided the means to see me through my studies and put a good job into my hands. I only just scraped through my first surgical, and I'll never be happy until I've bettered my degree, but I can't expect old Mark to keep forking out the fees. I think I need a couple of years as surgical registrar in a really good hospital. I've made up my mind to apply in London, or maybe Edinburgh, or Manchester.''

''Does Mark know about this?''

''No. But he does know I'm not little brother any more.'' He glanced sharply at Ruth in a way that brought the color flooding to her cheeks. ''You can't help not feeling about me as I feel about you, but living in close proximity to an attractive woman has naturally stirred my physical curiosity. I'll never settle my curiosity here, will I?'' He smiled again, and she realized it was the teasing of a man who knows his own powers and is saving them for the right moment. Matt Travers had indeed grown up; later than most perhaps, but not discreditably.

''I didn't know you wouldn't be using this theater, Matt,'' she said in a stunned little voice. ''I thought it was a dream come true for you.''

''Oh, Mark's not such a bad old surgeon himself on the quiet,'' he said dismissively, ''and Singh's working for his degree. I don't think he'll ever desert Kanjihan, outside of taking his exams. Well, I'm going out for a sail. Coming?''

''Er, no, thanks.''

''You never do these days, do you, Ruth? You're not afraid of me stepping out of line, are you?''

''Of course not, stupid! I just don't feel like it today with Kiran's first operation facing me tomorrow. Ask me next time.''

''Okay.''

Ruth was thoughtful as she walked down the corridor, her hands in the pockets of her loose white coat. She had grown to love this little hospital in the middle of an island, had made her contribution to its running for some weeks now, acting as either physician or surgeon—even pathologist when required. All the white workmen had been busy around the place bringing the theater up to date and building her a house. Though she had protested that the latter was an unnecessary extravagance, a two-storied timber and asbestos building was rapidly being erected in a nearby clearing. It had seven rooms and two baths.

''What do I want with two bathrooms?'' Ruth had asked blankly of Mark Travers.

''You're so shortsighted, Ruth,'' he had said patiently. ''After you're gone I'll have a real house where I can entertain a guest sometimes. Don't you think the medical director deserves a decent residence?''

At this she had flushed. That "after you're gone" had been too glib, as though the idea didn't trouble him one bit.

He'll mind about Matt though, she told herself on this day, *and probably assume the worst, that I'm behind this decision. When I first arrived I did tell Matt he ought to break away.*

She sighed, for though she had often thought about that first visit to the palace, and particularly those enchanted moments in the moonlit gardens, there had been no further sign from Mark Travers that he even remembered, though they had easily adopted the habit of using Christian names with each other.

He seems to prefer the formaldehyde, she decided gloomily as she reached the veranda door and beheld the bush-shirted figure busily engaged with the foreman who was in charge of building the house. It was as though he left his brother and his guest to take their pleasure in the new theater; his interest so obviously lay here.

She strolled across the hot dusty compound very slowly, knowing that she wasn't wearing a hat and not caring. Her hair was bleached almost white by now and looked carelessly attractive, curling around her ears.

"Hi!" she greeted in a comradely voice, and as he turned to raise his hand in greeting she pressed on, "Are you the medical director of Kanjihan or the minister of works?"

"You mean I'm neglecting my hospital?" he asked calmly.

"No," she decided. "Mark Travers wouldn't neglect one love for another. He's much more likely to be a Jack-of-all-trades and master of the lot!"

"Not quite," he denied, watching the joists being fitted into the roof. "What I can't reasonably accomplish I leave alone. Every man should acknowledge his limitations."

"Do you ever start something without finishing it?" she asked and realized she had felt a perverse compulsion to challenge him all day, as though she was inwardly spoiling for a fight.

"Frequently," he answered her, meeting her gaze quite frankly. "If one didn't start, one wouldn't realize one's inability to reach completion, would one?"

And he knows darned well what I was talking about, too! Ruth pondered, swallowing her chagrin.

"I think women are a little more adventurous," she pressed on. "I, personally, would go at least halfway with anything before I admitted inadequacy." Now she commanded his full attention for the first time and could feel his eyes on her as she gazed up into the jungle of roofing timbers.

"They're doing a good job up there," she decided, her lips quivering despite herself.

"Yes, Ruth, they are," he said thoughtfully, "because I'm personally seeing to it. Where's Matt?"

"He's taking out the *Nancy Lee*, as usual. He asked me to go along. I think I will. I'm bored." She turned away.

"No! Please don't go with Matt, Ruth!" he said quickly, and she realized he was genuinely upset by the thought of her accompanying his brother.

"Why?" she asked sharply. "Why shouldn't I go? What else is there to do at this moment?"

"I would like you to help me with the accounts," he said lamely. "Please!" he insisted.

"Oh, all right." She shrugged. "I'll be one degree less bored doing that, I suppose."

She was surprised to find that he had turned away with her and was accompanying her back to the existing bungalow, which was little more than a lean-to at the end of the hospital proper.

"I know you think I've neglected you," he said in a strangely uneven voice. "I do. I have to."

"Whatever brought on this confession, Mark?" she asked sharply as Matt left the bungalow wearing dazzlingly white shorts and a silk shirt that rippled to the muscular movement of its wearer. "Why should you think I consider it behoves you to keep me entertained?"

"Now he's gone I propose to tell you why," Mark said darkly, "so settle down on the veranda for a powwow. Ill humor often precedes sunstroke," he added pithily as he clapped his hands and gave instructions to the old bearer to bring iced lemonade for himself and the memsahib. "You'll go down with a blinder as sure as the dhobi-wallah's the blackest man hereabout."

"Well," she observed, stretching her legs and listening to the ice tinkling in the glasses, "as you were saying?"

"I was saying I would like to have an affair with you, Ruth, but I can't. I'm sorry."

It seemed to her that every word he spoke was written in black on a gray curtain of suspense. He spoke quite normally, but words of such impact were each separately stunning. They fell on her ears like stones into a millpond, sending ever widening ripples confusing her power of comprehension.

"What did you say?" Her voice sounded as though from afar off, thin and high in tone.

"You *did* hear," he leaned across the table to assure her. "I have presumed my attentions were not unwelcome to you that evening up at the palace, and neither was the thought of a romantic interlude reprehensible to me. But Matt is more than a little in love with you, and I'm thinking of him."

"Do let's think of Matt!" she said faintly, reaching for the lemonade as though it was whiskey.

"Naturally I consider him," Mark proceeded. "As I have said, I could have enjoyed . . . well—" meeting her eyes he saw her flush readily and knew she understood him perfectly. "—you're a very lovely and attractive person, Ruth, and a woman of the world." Here she choked and took refuge in her handkerchief. "I sounded Matt out about his feelings, ragged him a little. He said you weren't interested in him and he had accepted the fact. 'I'll get over it in time,' he told me. 'It isn't as though I have to stand by and watch *you* making love to her. I think it must be hellish to be in love with someone and find her in somebody else's arms.' " There was a short uncomfortable silence. "Well, there it is," Mark said shortly. "He's my brother and . . . and you're just passing through, so to speak. A year from now and you'll have forgotten all about Kanjihan and its repressed medical inhabitants." He drained his glass.

"I . . . I don't know what to say," Ruth managed to blurt out at last, wondering where all the words in her vocabulary had temporarily flown to, "and I'm so indignant I could . . . could burst!"

"Indignant?" This he obviously couldn't understand. "Why should you be indignant? Just now in the compound you practically accosted me and made it quite clear I was disappointing you in the role of gallant. You complained of being bored and threatened to go off with Matt."

"Oh!" She held her head between her hands now, hardly able to bear the indignity of the situation further. "What have I done that you can think of me as a cheap little trollop who would spite you for your lack of interest through your own brother? I wouldn't accept Matt's lovemaking ever, simply because I know I don't love him and could never make him as happy as he deserves to be. I could go out with him and be his crew, miles from anybody, and neither of us would venture to cross that line we drew between us from the start. You don't give me credit for honorable intentions, do you, Mark? I can't think why you assume I can be picked up and dropped in what you call a 'romantic interlude,' either. I would never embark deliberately on an affair of a temporary nature. I'm not mentally constructed for frivolities that involve my own heart.'' Her voice suddenly cracked. ''Why did you think otherwise?'' she demanded almost fiercely.

''I'm sorry, Ruth,'' he said simply and fished in the pocket of his shorts. ''Some perverted creature sent this. I got it before you arrived.''

Ruth smoothed out the folds of the anonymous letter, which had been recovered from the wastepaper basket a long time ago. She paled as she read the letter that was not anonymous to her. She could imagine Glen's bitter diatribe leveled against his wife after the occasion when they had all met together, and she could sense Madge's malice, knowing she was losing her grip over her handsome and successful husband and anxious to blame anyone but herself. But she couldn't understand why Madge would do a thing like this: send a shot out into the dark without even a hope of seeing the mischief she was so ready to make.

''It's rotten, isn't it?'' Mark asked.

Ruth merely nodded.

''I think all anonymous letter writers should be shot. Actually I threw the letter away at once. Then I thought maybe if some action could be taken it would serve as evidence.''

''And meanwhile you thought about it, didn't you? You nursed this horrible cancerous thing!''

''Ruth, I am sorry. I should have known it was lies. You weren't having an affair with this woman's husband, were you?''

''Are you asking me or telling me?'' Ruth grimly inquired. ''According to you I'm capable of anything.''

''All right, so my eye was jaundiced,'' he admitted patiently. ''I find the reference to your having been married absolutely lunatic . . . .''

''Indeed?'' asked Ruth. ''Why should it be so absurd for someone to want to marry me? Am I not a very lovely and attractive person, even according to you?''

"Oh, come," he forced a laugh, "you're not trying to tell me you are . . . have been married?"

"I'm not trying to tell you anything," she quivered, rising to her feet. "If you wait long enough and are still interested, you may get another anonymous letter bringing your information up to date. In the meantime, don't worry about Matt. He's quite safe from this particular social menace!"

She turned away blindly, her chair crashing over.

"Ruth!" He put himself in her path and reached out a hand to detain her. "We can't leave things like this. I feel awful. Talk things out sensibly."

"Men always plead like that when anything gets a little beyond their comprehension. I had no anonymous correspondent informing me about you and I was prepared to stand by my own instinct. You have now reminded me that I am—as you put it—only passing through. I will forget Kanjihan as it will forget me once my usefulness is spent. You asked me to help with the accounts this afternoon. As far as I'm concerned the account is closed. Let me pass, please!"

He stood back obediently. As she swept from view a great heaviness descended on his spirit, and he realized that instinct is not, after all, such a bad prompter. His instinct had been to seize her and hold her closely until she wept in his arms, as he was sure she was now weeping in her room.

But the moment was lost, and it was as though a gulf now divided these two unhappy people from the pair who had found sweet communion in a palace garden.

CHAPTER FIFTEEN

DURING THE WEEKS that followed Ruth was glad of the friendship that had sprung up between herself and Rosala, Rani of Kanjihan. It became a regular practice for an officer of the royal household to appear at the hospital and inquire if it was convenient for the Dr. Memsahib to take tea with Her Serene Highness. And as the monsoon was spending itself, the rain fell less heavily—when it did fall—and it was possible to get a car right up to the hospital, a road having been laid across the quagmire of the swamp itself. Once the guest had been collected the car would drive onto the waiting ferry, and when back on the mainland engage bottom gear for the stiff climb up the road to the palace. The whole journey was accomplished in about ten minutes, as compared with the thirty-five minutes by dandy, launch, and shanks' pony during the wet season.

The main topic of conversation between the two women was, of course, the Princess Kiran, who had by now come safely through three operations intended to build up the imperfect palate and missing gum. None of this showed, of course, but Kiran's speech was much improved and she had never once complained or been anything less than royal throughout the long ordeal she had already undergone. Now it remained for Ruth to open up the drawn-back scar of the lip and perhaps perform a small graft of skin from some other part of the child's body before the operation could be said to be either completed or a success. Ruth wanted the child to be very fit before she attempted this last, and most vital, part of the operation. On its complete success so much depended.

Another of the rani's pet subjects was her school days, for it had been discovered that a favorite mistress from Rosala's school had been transferred to the school where Ruth and Cassie had both been educated, and also where, incidentally, their parents had met for the first time at a fateful Founder's Day celebration.

"I think the fact that we both knew dear Miss Cane makes us—affinities?" Rosala asked on one occasion. "Tell me, did you call her sugar lump?"

"Not quite," smiled Ruth, "but we had the same idea. Actually, we called her sweetie pie!"

The rani sighed with satisfaction over her embroidery. Ruth had just demonstrated a new looping stitch that she was anxious to try out on the next cluster of flowers in the pattern.

"Soon Kiran will be able to go to school in England without fear of being pointed at. Children can be so cruel to one another. I remember how a dreadful girl called me a 'nigger' once! I could have *killed* her!"

The raja entered at this moment, as was his wont at some time during Ruth's visit. She rose, bowed, and sat down again. No more was now expected of her.

"And whom are we gossiping about today?" His Highness asked indulgently as a manservant poured tea for him. "It surprises me how you females find so much to say!"

Ruth smiled. This was obviously the attitude of any husband toward his wife and her friends.

"You to talk, Ajil!" Rosala scoffed. "The last time Dr. Mark was here could I get one word in edgeways for you and cricket?" She turned animatedly to Ruth. "There are test matches—or something—in Pakistan, and those two! . . . Ho! Ho! 'I would have bowled him this . . .' or 'I would have batted thus . . .' so they went on and on! Both of them out for ducks the last time we had a cricket match here!"

Ajil was now smiling more broadly.

"You surprise me, my dear, by knowing what is a duck, and it is not the disgrace you make it appear to Miss Stafford. Dr. Mark and I both bowl rather better than we bat. Did your husband not perform a hat trick and take six wickets for twenty-eight runs, madam?"

"Pooh!" Rosala taunted. "I think it is more spectacular to get runs. But *we* will not talk cricket, eh, Miss Stafford? Another biscuit?"

Ruth took one of the dainties and also had her teacup replenished. Ajil sat in one of the window embrasures, determined not to be dismissed from this little world of women.

"Tell me, Miss Stafford, do you think of marriage perhaps?"

Ruth realized the question was not meant as an impertinence, it was simply an honest regard for her welfare as an accepted member of the palace community. In a country where most females were married by the time they were twenty, she must rank as a somewhat elderly spinster by now.

"I do sometimes, Your Highness," she answered simply. "I am not confirmed in my career to the exclusion of belief in marriage as a woman's rightful estate."

"I think perhaps we have a husband for you here in Kanjihan?"

Ruth flushed uncertainly.

"I don't quite understand Your Highness," she stammered.

"Then I will put things more plainly, dear lady. Why not marry Dr. Mark and settle with us here in Kanjihan? Then I do not have to pay you. I have it here, you note?" His Highness touched his forehead significantly. "It is so, that a husband must support his wife, I gather?" He began to laugh shrilly at Ruth's expression of utter consternation. "Perhaps I am too humorous and you do not admire Dr. Mark at all, Miss Stafford?"

"Your Highness is joking," Ruth decided in some relief. "I can admire Dr. Travers professionally without having to marry him, I hope! Anyway, he is not in the marriage market. He is wedded to his hospital . . . ."

"*My* hospital," the raja said emphatically.

"As Your Highness pleases," Ruth quickly admitted. "I should have said Dr. Travers has no time for anything outside his work."

"Then you have not been trying, Miss Stafford," the raja said gently. "A pretty woman like you should see to it that the heart is involved. Mark is very normal. I have known him all my life."

"But, Your Highness . . . ."

"Away with you, embarrassing my friends, Ajil!" the rani scolded. "There are other men in the world, you know, besides Mark Travers and his brother. I am sure Miss Stafford will find a husband without your help eventually."

"So I will go," the raja decided, yawning behind a hand upon which rings flashed prominently. "Actually, I came to tell you some news, my dear. An archaeological society in London has asked for permission to send a party out to investigate the ruins on the other side of the island." He turned to Ruth once more. "Has Mark shown you his private dig yet, Miss Stafford?"

"No," she admitted, flushing as she remembered that first shattering expedition she had shared with him. "Are there ruins on Kanjihan? I didn't know."

"An ancient cult of sun worshippers once occupied the island, probably driven there by the Mongol hordes many centuries before Christianity was inaugurated. In those far-off days Mount Kanji was an active volcano, and obviously these people were trapped by an eruption that killed all life on the island. Now the trees and flowers grow again on Kanjihan, and beneath the lava is maybe a story the world is waiting to hear. Another Pompeii?"

"And you will give permission for this expedition to come?" asked Rosala.

"Perhaps. I don't believe even Dr. Mark can dig out a whole civilization by himself. But he will mind the intrusion on his privacy, I think. Perhaps you will mention this matter to him, Miss Stafford, and say I am waiting to hear his objections, if any, before I give my permission for this expedition to descend upon us?"

Ruth nodded and the raja wandered off about his business.

There was more talk with the rani after he had gone, this time about movies and the possibility of a travelogue being made about Kanjihan, including a tiger shoot with all the magnificent accoutrements of howdah'd elephants and their splendidly turbaned *mahawats*.

"I think it is wonderful idea, Miss Stafford," the rani said enthusiastically. "There will be a few shots of the children, of course, and Kiran will be shown in close-up . . . ."

They looked at each other suddenly, their feet down to earth with a vengeance.

"I think it will be a good idea to finish that job and then plan such things perhaps?" Her Highness decided and clapped her hands sharply to ask the servant to have the car called for her visitor's return to the hospital.

Rather surprisingly Ruth came face to face with Mark Travers on the veranda of the new house, where she was now in residence with two male domestics—a bearer, who was her personal servant and guard, and an *ayah*, whose duties were confined chiefly to the bedroom and her mistress's toilet.

"You wanted me, Dr. Travers?" Ruth asked formally, wishing she could meet and speak with this man without feeling the color steal warmly into her cheeks.

"Not really, Miss Stafford," he told her. "Gundhalal surprised a prowler near your house and is out after him. It suddenly occurred to me the fellow might have taken refuge inside and I was having a look-see. I came out because—" he smiled ruefully "—obviously I am nothing but a prowler here myself in your eyes."

She didn't mind and watched him go with the same sense of loss she always experienced at such times. Since he had told her about the anonymous letter he had once attempted an apology. The occasion had proved almost as uncomfortable as its predecessor, however, and Ruth begged that they work together professionally without further reference to matters outside this orbit.

"You are banning any possibility of a personal relationship developing between us, Ruth?" he had asked.

"I am simply here to work, shall we say?" Ruth had countered. "I think we will both find it better to forget we tried to warm up what was a perfectly satisfactory frigid relationship."

But Ruth sighed as she ran upstairs to her bedroom calling for Jamsi, the *ayah*. Jamsi did not reply, however, and Ruth shrugged as she flung open the bedroom door. Then she stopped, aghast, for the room looked as though a dozen monkeys had been busy for an hour. Drawers were opened and their contents spilled over the floor. Her jewel case, which had contained such small items as earrings, a pearl choker, and her mother's engagement ring, was lying on the dressingtable, empty. Then Ruth was aware of a spine-chilling sensation which told her she was not alone in the room. She turned stiffly in time to see the curtain across the alcove stir slightly.

"Come out, whoever you are!" she commanded. "Come out or I'll shoot!"

She had picked up her ivory-backed hairbrush and held it like a pistol toward the alcove.

An almost naked figure emerged, carrying an evil-looking *kukri*, the curved knife of the district.

"What are you doing here?" Ruth demanded, trying not to believe that a hairbrush had never looked less convincingly like armament against that wickedly shining blade.

"I want work, memsahib," the man said impudently, deciding to call her bluff and approaching with something akin to a swagger.

"Stop!" Ruth commanded.

Behind the man she now caught a glimpse of Jamsi in the doorway. The woman raised her voice in a scream and fled. The intruder looked uncertain about whether to follow the screamer or go for Ruth, and while he was still hesitating she brought him a sharp blow with the back of the brush and scrambled through the doorway herself, pulling the door shut after her. Her heart pounded as the door was tugged almost from her grasp, then she realized with something like relief that the felon had decided on escape through the window.

There was a commotion now in the compound, and as she reached the veranda, her limbs feeling like jelly, she heard sounds of argument and violence coming from the bamboo grove behind the house. Mark Travers eventually emerged, holding his left arm stiffly in in a blood-soaked handkerchief.

"What happened?" Ruth demanded, finding herself beside him as though concern had lent her wings. "You're hurt!"

"I am a bit," he admitted. "I hear you had company in your house after all. I would have found the blighter if your return hadn't put me off. I don't know how to apologize."

"Apologize?" she demanded. "What have *you* to apologize for? Better let me look at that arm."

He was leaning on her quite heavily by the time they reached the casualty office, and Nurse Angelina exclaimed as she saw the blood dripping to the floor.

"Get him off his feet, nurse," Ruth instructed, "he's just about unconscious."

She examined the deep wound in the forearm and applied a tournique, then decided on an antitetanus injection and stitching.

The nurse set the required tray and then stood and watched the slim fingers stitch first a torn tendon and muscle, then the artery, and finally the skin over the whole.

"It is good, very good," the old nun said when it was over. "Dr. Travers might well have lost his arm but for you, Miss Stafford. Dr. Singh and the young doctor away on Katra.... What would we have done without you?"

"The whole thing might not have happened without me," Ruth smiled. "After all, the offender was robbing *my* house when I startled him. I only hope all goes well from this moment, for all our sakes."

The patient, who had been lightly anaesthetized, now began to mutter incoherently and rebelliously.

"Am I to ready him for bed here?" asked the nurse.

"No. I would call his bearer and have him put into his own bed. Will you see to it, please nurse?"

"Certainly, Miss Stafford."

"Come along now," Ruth encouraged, patting Mark Travers's face as he turned his head from side to side. "Wake up!"

He opened his eyes suddenly, still half in a dream world, and reaching up his good hand touched her cheek, smiled, and sank back into unconsciousness with a sigh that could have been one of utter contentment.

CHAPTER SIXTEEN

IT WAS THREE DAYS after this incident before Gundhalal arrived in the compound, beetle-browed, dragging his prisoner, whining and fearful, after him, looking like a miserable cur about to be whipped.

The old bearer, who had served Travers sahib before his sons, had sworn terrible vengeance on the one who had dared strike at his master and wound him. He had armed himself with his *kukri* and an ancient Mauser and gone off without a by-your-leave to hunt down the offender as one would hunt down an animal. The island was not so big, and having served for many years with the Gurkha regiment, Gundhalal could sniff out the enemy within a mile of him.

He presented his prize to the hospital superintendent, asking permission to take the fellow away and quietly torture him to death for his sins.

At this the prisoner flung himself into the dust and almost licked Mark's shoe.

"Mercy, sahib!" he pleaded, before Gunghalal's bare foot kicked him sharply in the ear.

The man had no possessions and was wearing only a loincloth, and as Mark knew Ruth had missed several things he naturally inquired as to their whereabouts.

"Sahib, I take nothing from memsahib!" the man insisted, far too glibly. "I am an honest man and I wish to work. I am excellent dhobi-wallah. For sixty rupees a month I do all hospital dhobi."

"You had better take him," Mark dismissed him sharply. "Make slow torture, Gundhalal!"

"You can't do that!" Ruth said hastily as the servant dragged his screaming captive off. "This is the twentieth century and nobody condones torture!"

"Hold your tongue, miss," he told her brusquely. "Didn't he nearly kill me? Didn't he rob you?"

"Forget what he took from me . . . ."

Mark called out, ignoring her, "Of course if he should remember what he did with memsahib's things!"

"Mark knows how to handle those thieves," Matt assured her as she turned away biting her lip. "He'll get results if you leave him alone."

"I intend to—leave your brother alone," she said slowly and went about her business trying to forget the scene in the compound and all that might be happening at this very moment.

An attack of chicken pox had delayed Kiran's final operation for another week or two, but she was doing most of the hospital's surgery while the medical director was partially incapacitated, and Matt was kept busy traveling to and from the leper asylum.

"The boss wants you in the office." Matt sought her out to tell her about an hour later. He added almost admiringly, "You really do hate each other's guts, don't you? I can't imagine anybody not liking old Mark, and I certainly can't credit his—or anybody's—not liking *you*."

Ruth didn't answer, for it wouldn't have rung true to say she really disliked Mark Travers. He had angered, offended, and rebuffed her from the outset, yet when he had softened toward her on some rare occasions, she had been more than ready to take whatever he offered in the way of crumbs from what she felt sure was a natural store of abounding warmth and deep affection. It was the only time in her life she had taken the initiative in her unspoken encouragement of Mark Travers, and he had merely humbled and humiliated her, returned her offer with thanks on the grounds that it would hurt his beloved brother much as he would have refused a car trip in a two-seater because Matt would have to be left out of things.

Sometimes nowadays she felt she almost hated Dr. Mark Travers. She knew now they could never be friends. They were created of elements that, when fused together, caused lightnings of desire and thunders of fulfillment. Dispassionate encounters were impossible between them. The sooner she had finished her work here and could return home to simpler relationships, the better.

She looked cool and aloof as she presented herself in the office, though as the gray granite eyes swept over her briefly she had to clutch at her white coat to hide the trembling of her hands.

"Sit down, Miss Stafford," he invited, pointing to a rattan

chair under the window. He indicated a heap of articles on the desk. "I finally got your burglar to talk, and he dug these up. . . . No," he answered the startled question in her eyes, "he was neither tortured nor hanged, drawn and quartered, you will be relieved to hear. In fact, at this moment he's off under escort to jail where he'll stand trial and be allowed a fair hearing. As we've got the loot back it'll be better for him. You must have noticed we're a law-abiding lot on the whole here in Kanjihan. We can usually sleep in our beds with doors and windows wide open, knowing we'll be neither robbed nor murdered. The only way to keep our Utopian ideal is to come down hard on the swine who let us down. That fellow was an outcast Pakistani who had escaped from over the border. It'll be good riddance to the blighter when Ajil hoofs him back again. Now which of these pretty things happens to be yours? One engagement ring with a ruby . . . ?"

"My mother's," Ruth said simply, "and . . . and yes, that's mine, too." This was a small plain band of gold, a wedding ring on a silk cord. She didn't raise her eyes as she put both rings deep into her pocket along with her pearl choker and earrings.

"Your mother's also?" asked Mark Travers significantly.

"No, it wasn't," she told him, her eyes bright and her cheeks suffused. "I think that's all. May I go now?"

"Not unless you're in a hurry. I wondered if—if you would dress my arm for me?" Her eyes widened. "I know it's the nurse's job, but, well, your dressing was so much more comfortable. I can feel every stitch at the moment, like a lot of inverted darning needles, and it's making me as disagreeable as a bear with a sore head. Will you?"

"Certainly," Ruth said, trying not to acknowledge a sensation of warmth in her heart. "I'd better prepare a tray myself and do it here, otherwise the nurse might be offended."

She couldn't find anything wrong with Nurse Angelina's dressing as she took it off, removed the protective cotton wadding and exposed the long weal in the forearm, neatly criss-crossed with her own surgical stitching. Mark was obviously enjoying her professional ministrations, however, and closed his eyes blissfully as she dabbed the itch out of his skin with surgical spirit.

"Lovely!" he sighed. "Do that again, would you, please?"

"You just like hogging attention, I'm beginning to suspect," she told him. "I'm going to do you up and get back to work."

"Actually, I wanted to talk to you," he said suddenly, "and it's confoundedly difficult. May I be frank with you, Ruth?"

They did not readily use Christian names with each other these days, and she looked at him sharply.

"Go ahead," she invited.

"Well, I . . . Matt tells me he's got a job in London. He is to start work on December first. I naturally wondered if he . . . was doing it to . . . to be with you?"

"I didn't even know he'd got a job," she said quickly. "He told me he intended to try his luck in Britain. . . ."

"I had no such warning," Mark said in a tight hurt voice. "Why was Matt so careful not to tell me of his plans earlier?"

"I think perhaps he realized the break would be painful and so best not anticipated. As to your other question, I don't think he's doing it to be with me. I have never encouraged him."

"I know that. But while there's life there's hope, you know. Possibly he thinks you can be won . . . eventually . . . ?"

"I'm not for winning,", she said curtly.

"I thought not. You could give him the most obvious discouragement, you know, if you only would."

"How?"

"Tell him you're married."

"Oh!" Ruth's cheeks flamed afresh. "But I'm not!"

"Really?" He regarded her pocket significantly where the rings jingled together. "You mean you're divorced?"

"No. I'm not married and I'm not divorced. Any more questions?"

"A hell of a lot, if you must know, but you're too prickly to answer them." Now he had risen, and threading his damaged arm through its sling, he regarded her with familiar arrogance. "All right, Miss Stafford, surgeon," he mocked at her, "you win this round. You've got me wondering why the heck I should care whether you're married or not! All I know is that I do care and I despise myself for my vulgar curiosity. I should know better than to invite a second dose of emotional disaster upon myself, but I'm a glutton for punishment. But this can't go on, this having you in my sight yet never in my arms. When I find myself almost throttling a man because I fear he has harmed you, it's time to take stock, lose a little pride if necessary, but at least try to repair lost ground. Will you allow me to open the account between us again, Ruth? Tell me what I must do?"

"Do?" she echoed, and her heart thundered so it almost

drowned the whisper of her voice. She ran trembling fingers over her moist brow. ''What are you trying to say, Mark? I don't really understand you.''

''Would you understand one good arm longing to enfold you?''

She stumbled into that embrace and closed her eyes as his lips descended, seeking her own.

''Oh, Ruth, my dear, I've been so blind! I knew from the start, seeing you at that hotel in Delhi, that you were one woman in a thousand. I can't think of Matt any more, only my own need. There are times when a red-blooded man must stop being a brother to a . . . a . . . .''

She raised her lips once more and took the precious word from his in a more clearly defined way.

This is it! Her thoughts ran in that moment of ecstasy. *This is the only man in the world for me!*

''I'll take you to the bazaar tomorrow and buy you a present,'' his voice crooned into her ear. ''I have always wanted to buy a pretty girl some of those gewgaws the goldsmith makes, and I'll buy you some Indian silk and have a sari made for the white memsahib.''

''Lovely!'' she acknowledged in delight.

''And one day I'll take you out to my dig and you shall eat figs from a dish two thousand years old.''

''Your dig?'' she asked blankly, remembering something about an expedition and the message she had been asked to deliver.

''Yes. I think I've just dug out two lovers, and one—funnily enough— has an incomplete arm.''

She laughed in delight, deciding against spoiling the moment with talk of prosaic archaeological expeditions.

''I'd like to do all these things with you, Mark,'' she told him, ''but I do think I ought to go now. Nurse Indi saw me come in here.''

'' 'Parting is such sweet sorrow,' '' he quoted. ''Kiss me once more, my own, my darling Ruth.''

She complied readily, feeling the firm muscular lips so gentle in their demand upon her own. She opened her eyes mistily to behold a scowling countenance regarding the scene through the unshuttered window. Matt Travers lowered his gaze and strolled on, and with him he took the magic out of the moment.

''What's wrong?'' Mark asked suddenly.

''Nothing, silly. I'm going now.''

''You *do* love me a little?''

''I'll think about it.''

''No, you don't, my girl! Well?'' He barred her way. ''Don't blow hot and cold for God's sake. Simply tell me.''

''I love you more than a little, Mark.''

Their eyes met and somehow merged in the intensity of their gaze.

''You may go now, Ruth.''

He opened the door for her and she went out carrying her tray, her heart singing blithely like a songbird let out of its cage, that feels only the good in the sun and air and has no thought for the hovering and everwatchful bird of prey waiting to still forever the innocent cascade of abounding, naturally expressed happiness.

''OH, NO!'' WAS TORN from Ruth two days later as she read her latest batch of mail. ''This just can't be true!'' Benedict Sharn had written:

My Dearest Girl,

I said I would follow you to the ends of the earth and am about to do so. On Saturday next I am leaving as doctor to an archaeological expedition bound for Kanjihan—where you appear to have taken root, young lady!

I don't think I could have got this appointment off my own bat, but lately I have been seeing a lot of Cassie and it was she who pulled all the strings.

I can hardly bear to read on, Ruth decided, but felt her gaze impelled back to the missive in her hand.

Your stepsister knows just about everybody who is anybody in London, I find, and of course there was a member of her set who has an uncle who was seriously planning this expedition. The seriousness has now gone out of the venture, I'm afraid, for Cassie and a few of her friends have decided they want to come along. All at once they're ardent little archaeologists, and as your raja has given his permission, we will be descending upon you—en masse—very soon.

As far as I am concerned, I simply want to dig you out, my beloved, my wife. . . .

The letter fell from Ruth's nerveless fingers as a shadow loomed on the veranda where she was sitting. Mark Travers retrieved it and handed it back to her, and she could not tell from his expression whether he had glimpsed Benedict's extravagant phrases or not.

"Did you forget to deliver a message from Ajil to me?" he asked calmly.

"Yes. I . . . I'm sorry, Mark," she apologized, feeling utterly flustered. "It was about an archaeological expedition wanting to come and investigate your dig. He wondered if you would mind."

"I would—if I'd known," he said tonelessly. "There are about thirty people coming, including some women. One claims to be your sister."

"Yes, I know. Cassie Belampton is my stepsister, actually."

"Is she an archaeologist?"

"No. I'm afraid not. Mark, are you very angry?"

"Angry? Why should I be angry? Your sister has every right to come and see you. Do you know anybody else in the party?"

"Yes." She knew that now was the time for telling him about Benedict, of their past relationship, but he looked like the Mark of old, who wasn't really interested in her affairs, past, present or future. "I know the doctor in the party quite well," she finished lamely.

"Good! I'll put him up and you can have the women in your house. The rest can bivouac at the dig. All right?"

"Mark, I . . . ."

"Your friends are welcome," he insisted, "and a bit of life will be good for Matt. If you're worried lest I behave like the possessive male animal, forget it. I wouldn't put on a public performance."

She watched him go down the veranda steps and felt as though Mount Kanji had again erupted and blanketed all life and color from the scene.

CHAPTER SEVENTEEN

THERE HAD BEEN no argument, no quarrel as previously, and yet Ruth knew a chasm once more separated her from Mark Travers. She wondered if Matt's behavior had anything to do with it, for he now stalked around the hospital beetle-browed, being merely polite to her and either avoiding or totally ignoring his brother unless the occasion was too public to permit him to do so and get away with it.

What happens in places like this, Ruth asked herself. *Is it merely the climate that makes us prefer personal to impersonal relationships? We're three Europeans, yet we're getting so emotionally tangled it's becoming impossible to coexist!*

For such a little while it had all seemed so wonderful. That expedition into the small town where the dhuka-wallahs squatted in the shade behind their open-fronted shops would remain in her memory for all time.

Mark had casually put his arm around her shoulders as they finished morning surgery and said, ''Come on! I've told Singh we'll be gone for the afternoon.''

How pleasant it had seemed to bath and dress in her favorite golden yellow, knowing Mark also was changing his clothes, maybe wondering how to look his best in *her* company! He had appeared in the compound eventually wearing light tan flannels and a biscuit-colored silk shirt, his bad arm still bandaged but released from its sling.

''Bad business for the medical director to be seen as a casualty.'' He smiled as she joined him, her eyes dwelling on the well-brushed dark hair and neatly clipped mustache. ''I've got my car here out of storage. Ali's been tinkering with it all morning. Where is the blighter now?''

Ali, the Muslim mechanic-cum-electrician to the hospital, now drove the Rolls-Royce up to the compound gates with a white-toothed grin.

''He's fine, sahib,'' he announced.

"Right. We won't need you, my lad." Ali took his disappointment off with him, with many a backward glance at the elderly shining automobile. Ruth permitted herself to be handed into the passenger seat feeling like a queen, and with an exchange of smiles—almost as though the promise of the delight which lay ahead of them bubbled and spilled over their countenances—they sped through the bamboo forest and across the lily-studded swamp to the waiting ferry which bore them to the mainland and the town.

It was difficult to single out one event as significant over all the rest. Mark had bought her a chased gold bracelet; she had liked that. He had spanned her wrist with thumb and finger, exclaiming, "You're slim, Miss Stafford. Small wrists, small ankles, and a ridiculous waist . . . ."

"But all of you is nice," his eyes had said.

After years of Cassie's innuendoes, which had made her sometimes believe a tall woman must also be of elephantine proportions, his words had made her feel comfortably feminine and rather special as a type.

Later they had watched the fakirs in the bazaar and been promised a performance of the Indian rope trick. The magician, however, made excuse after excuse not to get on with the latter. By the time he had found his rope—which had to be a very special piece of rope—he had lost the small boy whose job it was to climb up the rope and disappear. Just any small boy wouldn't do. The magician's assistant was eventually discovered eating *kabi* (figs dried in sugar batter) but by that time the *bhagwan* (spirit) had gone about other business. The magician indicated this "other business" lay somewhere behind his left shoulder, but no one was prepared to go and look for a *bhagwan*, so the entertainment fizzled out.

"In any case," the old magician muttered to the dust on his feet in his native Bengali, "what use a boy with a bellyful of *kabi*!" and he spat mournfully and went back to sleep again.

"It does happen, you know," Mark observed as they stood and watched the raja's plane circling to land after some private "flip of His Highness."

"What does?" Ruth asked, thinking of Indian rope tricks and dancing cobras and other wonders of the native scene.

"People fall in love quite unexpectedly."

"I know," Ruth agreed, and no more was said on that

subject, though he held out his hand and gripped hers as they swung along through the narrow streets together.

It was as though they were assessing rather than demanding of each other at this stage; love was uncertain, like a young girl tripping her way suffused and self-conscious through a crowd of gallants. There were no confidences exchanged, no leading questions asked. It seemed sufficient to nibble at the outer edges of a loveliness too vast to contemplate, and best of all there was no hurry, no urge to snatch at the lowest apple with so many rosier ones higher up the tree.

"Enjoyed it?" he asked as they drove back in the brief twilight.

"Every moment," she assured him and wondered—with sweet panic—if he would kiss her before they parted.

"My arm's been giving me hell for the last hour," he told her as he willingly handed the great car over to Ali. "When can I have these blessed stitches out?"

"Tomorrow," she promised, wondering if she knew him any better for their outing. When would he tell her about Marcia and expect the full account of herself and Benedict? Somehow she didn't relish raking Benedict up, for lately that young man had written as though she was still his wife, as though their marriage had simply been interrupted under duress imposed by others, leaving them in their hearts and in the eyes of God joined irrevocably.

Next day there had been some emergency that kept all staff noses to the grindstone, but Ruth had kept her promise to remove the stitches from the superintendent's knife wound.

"It looks pretty good," she announced as the nurse cleaned up the skin. "How does it feel? Can you clench your fingers?"

"Not fully, yet, but I have every confidence in you to believe I will eventually, Miss Stafford."

That "Miss Stafford" caught her unawares, like a cold shower, then she saw him wink and the warmth in his eyes. The nurse was present, of course, and formality was the order of the day. She must remember. It was not easy for a woman to separate her professional from her emotional self. She wanted Mark to be a little more in love with her with every moment that passed. The difference between them was that he—as medical director of Kanjihan—wouldn't always be prepared to show it.

She knew the brothers had had a row, for she had heard Matt's raised outraged voice after dinner that evening and sensed the coolness in the atmosphere during breakfast next morning. The arrival of the mail, which occurred roughly once weekly, was almost a relief after the strain of the meal, but the news was hardly conducive to happier relationships.

It simply couldn't be true that not only was Benedict coming here in person, and quite legitimately as a working member of an archaeological team; but Cassie—and others like her—intended to descend like so many serpents upon Eden. The bamboo groves, the lily-covered swamp, and the orchid forest would echo to the frivolous and affected voices of Mayfair moppets and their young-men-about-town escorts. They would soon become bored with life on Kanjihan, and then they would look around for mischief.

The person who seemed cheered by the news of the expected invasion was Matt, of all people. He was quite gay during dinner that evening, and when Mark excused himself and went off to the hospital he leaned toward Ruth as confidingly as of old.

"I must hand it to you, you played old Mark rather well," he said admiringly. "You even had me fooled the other day."

"I don't know what you're talking about," Ruth said shortly, for she had been unable to reach Mark all day. It was as though he had donned invisible armour, proof against her approaches.

"No, you *shall* have the credit!" Matt insisted, pouring himself a brandy with his coffee. "You led my brother on a bit—now don't deny it, miss, because I saw you—and you must have known how he has always felt about expeditions visiting the island. But as your own friends and relations were involved you weren't going to have them shooed away, so you occupied Mark's mind pleasantly, conveniently 'forgot' to give him Ajil's message, and the whole blooming party's on the doorstep before he knows a thing about it! Superb, I call it!"

Ruth had listened in dawning horror, thinking Matt must be drunk.

"How dare you!" she challenged him, rising to her feet. "Are you suggesting that I deliberately avoided giving the raja's message?"

"Yes, I do, frankly, Ruth, so spare me your protestations. Mark told me the facts and even I could see the whole blatant pattern of your contriving . . . ."

"You mean Mark thinks I . . . I did it all deliberately?" she asked in a shocked hopeless little voice.

Matt's hands closed around the stem of his brandy glass.

"Didn't you?" he mocked.

"No, I did not. You can believe me or not, Matt, but I'm not quite as despicable as you imply. I would not, for one thing—" she choked and cleared her throat "—sell my kisses for *any* material benefit. I kiss where I love. I didn't love you, but I could probably have wheedled a lot out of you if I'd been prepared to play kissing games."

Matt bit his lower lip and drained his glass.

"I would like to speak to Mark," she went on, her voice trembling. "Will you excuse me, please?"

"Certainly." He stood up stiffly. "He may have left. He's intending doing a spot of night duty on Katra. Dr. Ranjital is down with malaria."

"Oh." She didn't hesitate. "Will he have gone down to the jetty?"

"Probably. Tell Ali to run you down in my jeep."

"Thanks."

She sped away through the darkness, perched beside Ali, feeling tense and miserable.

How could Mark think her capable of such despicable behavior? Yet, she thought bitterly, he hadn't previously held her in such high esteem, either. As far as he was concerned she had merely reverted to type; the "social menace" tag fitted her perfectly.

At the jetty she recognized one of the hospital stewards.

"Anand, is the Dr. Sahib here?"

"Yes, memsahib. He is down there in the launch. He goes to Katra."

"Help me down."

"But, memsahib—!"

Ruth scrambled down into the dark well of the launch without more ado.

She questioned the cabin ahead, "Mark . . .?"

Her voice was drowned in a roar as the motor started up and the propeller thrashed wildly.

"Anand!" yelled the medical director. "Jump in!"

"Sahib!"

Ruth hesitated to declare herself at this stage as she knew there were navigational hazards hereabout.

When Mark Travers had set the course and left the wheel in his steward's hands, he entered the small cabin and lit the paraffin lamp, then allowed the match to burn down to his fingers as he saw his visitor.

"Ruth! What are *you* doing here?" he asked aghast.

"Going to Katra, I think," she smiled almost blithely, then she sobered rapidly. "You and I have to talk, Mark Travers, and if I have to go with you to the leper asylum to do it, then I'm prepared to go—as you see!"

CHAPTER EIGHTEEN

OPENING HER EYES, Ruth regarded the fine mesh of the mosquito and sandfly netting draped around her like an immaculate cobweb, then her vision lengthened into the room beyond. It was an unfamiliar room, and, sitting up with a jerk, she remembered everything.

Back came the wriggle of discomfort with which she had retired last evening following the medical director's most unromantic peroration after he had overcome the shock of finding her stowed away aboard the launch.

"You utterly impossible little fool, Ruth!" he had declared sharply. "What are they going to think up at the hospital when Ali tells them you jumped the boat to find me? What does it look like? Some shady little rendezvous between us, doesn't it?"

"You seem quite capable of answering your own questions," Ruth had replied curtly. "I simply wanted to talk to you. I didn't know you were going to start the motor at that moment and then I couldn't make you hear. It's as simple as that."

"But what was so urgent that you had to follow me at all? We'd just had dinner together."

Somehow Ruth was beginning to wonder about things herself. Had she dreamed a time when she and this man had appeared to be on the edge of falling in love? Now this cold-eyed arrogant stranger was making her feel rather ridiculous about an impulsive gesture she had made in all good faith to right things between them.

"I don't think it was really anything important," she said quietly, wishing she could regain her dignity also. "I'm sorry if this is going to make things difficult for you. I'll explain when I get back."

"Well," he said grudgingly, "that'll have to be that, I suppose. I can explain your presence on Katra. They've often asked about you."

"They?" she queried.

"Ranjital and Hamar and the nurses."

"Oh."

"They'll be glad to see a new face. They don't enjoy many distractions."

"I hope I at least come up to expectations there then."

He looked at her sharply, then shouted some directions to the steward at the wheel.

"Hard to port now, Anand! Steady as she goes; good!" He lit a cigarette after Ruth had refused one, before regarding her mockingly once more. "What if your friends arrive and you're missing? Won't they think it . . . strange?"

"I honestly couldn't care less," Ruth decided, "and since when did you start caring what other people think, Dr. Travers?"

This he digested slowly, drawing on his cigarette until his cheeks were quite hollow, allowing the smoke to escape in curling wisps as he spoke again.

"I think I know what you wanted to see me about," he pondered, "and I have also wondered how to say something to you. Would you mind telling me if you've ever been terribly in love before in your life?"

She tossed her fair hair defiantly.

"Yes, I have. But what . . . ?"

He held up his hand in the old commanding gesture.

"So have I. Heaven on earth, arrow through the heart, the lot. I got over it. Did you?"

"Yes," she said again.

"One doesn't think it possible at the time," he mused, recollecting the wonder of it all. "It doesn't seem decent to have been so deeply involved and live through it to sometimes doubt its very existence."

"We are told time heals all wounds," Ruth said tritely.

"Maybe. But love behaves like a tortoise after an experience like that. Popping its head in and out, scared to be hurt a second time, not even daring to enjoy itself for long. You're rather like a tortoise, Ruth."

"Oh?" she smiled bleakly. "I thought we were talking about you, actually."

"You wanted to tell me you'd like to pop your head in for a while. Your friends coming no doubt reminded you of a life left in a state of suspension back home. Well, I do understand, and I shall help your friends to have a good time while they're here."

"My 'friends' number one," Ruth said dryly. "I can't lay claim to a whole archaeological expedition."

"Then shall we say you can count on my discretion?" he asked. "If you think I presumed during the more charming moments of our acquaintance to lay claim to your heart, I assure you such is not the case. As I have tried to make clear, one is wise not to take these things too seriously after the proved transience of one's initiation into love."

"Let's conclude the tortoise is safer with his head in," Ruth almost snapped.

"Exactly. Unless he knows where he's going."

Their eyes met like two arrows, point to point, each trying to pierce the other.

"Unless he knows where he's going," she echoed breathlessly.

"And our tortoise *is* a little uncertain, isn't he?"

"Katra, sahib!" shouted Anand from the wheel, granting them both a profound relief from the tension of that conversation.

Word for word Ruth remembered it as she folded back the mosquito netting and tucked it up on the beam protruding over the bed. It had been dark when they had arrived at the leper colony the previous evening, so she hadn't seen much of her surroundings.

"You'll be all right here," Mark had said, putting a storm lantern into her hand and ushering her into the room she now occupied. "You'll understand we don't run to servants on Katra. We do for ourselves. You'll find a bath."

Looking out of the window, she now saw that she was in one of a row of separate chalet-type buildings painted black and white and with deep overhanging roofs. Each chalet had a minute veranda, and conspicuous on the other verandas were large zinc baths. Rather nervously Ruth investigated her own, and sighed in relief to find some thoughtful person had erected a rattan screen, which more or less enclosed the veranda and enabled her to bathe in private.

She had just emerged from the water, wondering how one emptied the bath, and had fastened a robe around her, which she found hanging behind her door, when a voice called cheerily, "Are you there, Miss Stafford?"

Ruth appeared, toweling her head, to see a young woman setting down a tray of tea, toast, and marmalade.

"For me? I really don't want to impose on you . . . " she said doubtfully.

The young woman, who was undoubtedly beautiful even in a country famed for its beautiful women, wore a nursing dress in the usual navy blue calico so familiar to Ruth's eyes. Her crisp white cap sparkled like a tiara on the silk-dark, neatly parted hair.

"Miss Stafford, how are you?" They shook hands warmly. "I am Nurse Indiri. You have heard of me?"

"Of course." Ruth was too ashamed to admit that she hadn't taken much interest in Katra's staff. It always seemed a world apart.

"We have heard a lot about you," said Nurse Indiri, pouring Ruth's tea and settling down for a brief gossip. "Personally, I have never met a woman surgeon before. We had a woman pathologist at St. Christopher's . . . ."

"In Bayswater?" Ruth asked promptly.

"Oh, no. I trained in Bagshaw. The north riding of Yorkshire."

"So you trained in England, nurse." Ruth sipped the tea, which was piping hot and very refreshing. "What are you doing here, of all places?"

Still perfectly at ease, Nurse Indiri looked toward the window. There was a view of sandy beach and the inevitable palm and casuarina trees leaning away from the wind.

"I can only work in a leper colony now," she explained simply, "though I have shown no signs of activity for more than five years."

"I'm sorry," Ruth said quickly, hating herself for her thoughtlessness.

"Oh, I am not sorry!" the other assured her. "I am very happy here now. I am allowed to go home on leave to visit my family periodically, but since Bhil and I became engaged to be married, I am not so keen to leave him."

"Who is Bhil?" asked Ruth gently.

"Bhil Hamar. He is second-in-command here."

"I see. Congratulations, nurse, belated though they might be. I really am in a fog about Katra. It's time I came to see for myself. I had visions of an absolute shambles of a place with the sick and dying creeping about like a flock of lost sheep."

"You're joking, surely, Miss Stafford?" laughed Nurse

Indiri, and for the first time Ruth saw the cleverly dressed hair was pulled down to hide what was merely a stump of the left ear. "A shambles under Dr. Mark? You must know him better than that. Anyway, I am to be your guide, and you'll see our 'lost sheep' for yourself. What size shoes do you wear?"

"Six and a half," Ruth said blankly. "Why?"

"You will take simple precautions, Miss Stafford," Nurse Indiri said simply. "I will send you a pair of gumboots, size sevens will have to do, and a coat to wear over your own clothes. You'll find these things on your veranda directly. Meanwhile, enjoy your breakfast. I'll be watching out for you."

When she was attired in the gumboots and wearing the doctor's coat—much too big for her—Ruth strolled along the beach, curious to see what was on the huge boarding near the jetty where three motor launches were tied up. A mechanic was busily occupied with a greasy rag, looking like any mechanic busy on any boat, apart from the fact that his face looked masklike from the disease from which he had suffered for years and which was now—it was hoped—cured.

Province of Kanjihan (Ruth read)
Katra leper asylum
Unauthorized persons keep out!

This was repeated in both Bengali and Hindustani. Ruth was sure there weren't many trespassers troubling Katra.

She took the rather good silver-sandy road that led between flowering palms and bottle-brush trees. She saw a gardener busily planting artichokes in a clearing and behind him rose the feathery green fronds of asparagus. She bypassed a village with neat little houses built around a compound where children played. Beyond she saw the welcoming figure of Nurse Indiri waiting at a gate.

"Found your shambles yet, Miss Stafford?"

"No," Ruth smiled ruefully. "You're not going to hold that against me, are you, nurse?"

"Of course not. Most people, if they think about leper colonies at all, picture places of absolute human despair. The village you just passed houses our paroled patients. They have shown no signs of activity for six months or more, but while being encouraged to lead normal lives, they're not quite out of the woods and must still have treatment. Sometimes they settle down in the village so happily we have difficulty discharging them when they're due. Over there is the clinic where Dr. Mark and Bhil are supervising the treatments of walking patients now. I will take you through the hospital if you like, or will it distress you, do you think?"

"If I were not distressed I wouldn't be human, nurse," Ruth said quietly, "but I am a doctor and hope I can control my feelings. I've come to Katra and I'll see everything, if you don't mind."

RUTH WAS VERY QUIET when Mark Travers joined her for lunch.

"Well?" he asked. "What do you think of it all?"

"I don't know," she shrugged. "I wouldn't know what to say if God asked me what I thought of heaven, either."

"A strange parallel," he decided.

"Not really. I would feel similarly impressed, overawed, and dreadfully humble, I think." She looked at him suddenly. "I wonder if anyone really knows you, Mark?"

"Why do you ask that?"

"Because you aren't just Dr. Mark Travers, an uncompli- cated general physician. You are so many people. One man sees you as a brother, one woman remembers you as a sweetheart; the raja tends to forget your functional capacity and tries to keep you his friend. But thousands of souls see you only as Dr. Mark, and here on Katra you're almost a . . . a deity."

"Don't say things like that, Ruth," he said sharply. "I'm no Schweitzer."

"No, and you have no public sympathy, either. Mark, I could help Nurse Indiri with surgery."

"But . . . ."

"She's getting married in about three months' time, and I'd like to do it as soon as possible. She's such a lovely girl otherwise."

"Leave out the 'otherwise,' Ruth, and no, don't suggest surgery to Fany."

"But why? . . ."

"NO!" Mark forbade. "That girl has learned to live with her disability, is loved despite it. If you interfere you don't know where it might end."

"What do you mean? Surely it's my job to restore everyone I can?"

"Maybe. 'Everyone' is the operative word. If you restore

Fany's ear, can you restore Bhil's fingers on his left hand? Then can you restore all their patients who take their hope from these visible signs that once these two were afflicted as they are? It's too big a chain reaction, Ruth. You see Fany Indiri as a beautiful girl with a blemish. I see her as an intelligent nurse-in-charge who will settle here on Katra as a happily married woman doing the job she loves and being the inspiration she has always been.''

"Sorry I intruded," Ruth said in a low voice.

"That's all right, you meant well. You didn't have any luggage, did you? Because I'm sending you back now."

She knew better than to argue.

"Does that mean you're not returning to Kanjihan with me?''

"It does. Anand will take you. He knows the navigation in daylight. I want you to ask Matt to come over this evening, and you take over there, will you?''

"Very well. When . . . when will you be back?''

The moment had grown suddenly personal despite their recent offhandedness with each other.

"Oh, soon," he promised and flicked his finger under her chin. "Now don't tell me you're going to miss me, Ruth?''

"I might," she told him. "I've sort of grown used to . . . being mauled lately.''

CHAPTER NINETEEN

CASSANDRA BELAMPTON RAISED her smooth head from the soft pillow on the chaise lounge and called softly, "Coo-hoo!"

Matt Travers paused in his tracks, smiled indulgently, and came toward the otherwise deserted veranda with a backward glance at the hospital.

"Hello, Cassie! Why aren't you at the dig with the rest?"

"Because I'm not the great big horsey type like the others, dahling. That's why. Little Cassie's got no energy today. I think I need a doctor."

Her green-flecked eyes flashed up a sensuous invitation, and Matt straddled a chair and regarded her, wondering if this curled-up, diminutive kitten was in reality the mature woman he was assured she was—by Ruth. Cassie Belampton was the first female he had met who made him feel big, strong, elderly, and important all at the same time. Most of the other people in his life seemed to emphasize his youth and inexperience. He was Mark's "kid brother"; he was the "young" doctor, and he was the emotionally callow fellow who had fallen in love—and rather hard—with the first pretty woman he had met.

Now that Ruth was in his past he felt much more worldly for the experience. He had loved and been rejected, but he had grown a thicker skin for the rebuff; his heart was now lightly calloused. No longer could he be termed naive. He could even regard Cassie's dark lashes flickering at him, see her hair spread over a cushion, and imagine its silky softness running through his fingers, without visible reaction. He was comfortably aware that he was receiving flirtatious encouragement from the occupant of the chaise lounge, and he reveled in the utter physical enjoyment of such a situation without turning a hair.

"Don't you think little Cassie looks ill, Matt?" she asked, unwinding her legs and brushing a toe against his well-developed calf in its thick white hose, which showed off the brown of his skin so sharply. "Feel my poor head."

Matt obligingly did so. The forehead was cool, slightly moist, and agreeable to the touch.

"My pulse?" invited Cassie, holding out her hand.

Everything about her was so tiny, Matt realized. She was like a miniature, or a Dresden figurine, but beneath the spotted silk of her sundress he saw the sharp pout of her breasts and realized he must not underestimate the powers of the adult female—pint-size though she might be.

He released her hand sharply as the fingers were beginning to entwine his own.

"Oh, Matt!" she exclaimed sharply. "Don't you like me a little?"

This, he decided, standing up, was a moment rare in his experience. Someone else had taken the initiative and left him with a choice: to answer yes or no, and so steer the course of future events.

"Of course I *like* you, Cassie," he said with careful emphasis. As her eyes begged a little more from him, he added, "You're a sweet little thing. But you're not ill at all, you scamp!"

He now felt at least thirty-five, and it was a wonderful feeling. She was regarding him with open admiration and looked up at his six-foot-two as though he was Hercules.

"No, I'm not ill, Matt, darling, but I am a teeny bit sick of the crowd I'm with. That's why I sneaked a day off. So I could be e with *real* people, wonderful people like you. I . . . I think you're awfully courageous and clever, Matt. Have you ever shot a tiger?"

"Oh, yes," he chuckled, sitting down again. "Dozens. Well," he added modestly, "I was born in India."

"You make me . . . breathless," Cassie told him. "I never saw anybody like you, honestly. All the young men I know are namby-pambies. I really thought you were a film star when I first came here. Well—" as he laughed "—I've been frank with you, at least. Now, what do you think of me?"

They played a game of dare with their eyes before he replied.

"I think I would rather tell you that away from—" he looked toward the hospital again "—distractions." How easy the game of love became with experience, he decided.

Cassie rose suddenly, and he was surprised to feel her mouth firmly pressing against his own. A sharp pleasure exuded from the contact, quite separated from the fountain of his loves and hates. He parted his lips slowly and—putting his hand to the back of her head—condescended to play his masculine part in the exchange of kisses.

"Excuse me," came Ruth's voice, soft and embarrassed, "But Dr. Travers is asking for the new syringes. Could I have the storeroom keys, please, and I'll get them."

"No! no!" Matt said, jumping up and plucking Cassie off him like a burr. He felt twenty-six again very quickly as he realized his brother would probably be blazing. "I'll get them, Ruth."

He bounded away, leaving the stepsisters regarding each other watchfully.

"Well, come on!" Cassie invited at last, sinking back on the chaise lounge and regarding her orange-colored fingernails. "Transcribe your oozing disapproval into words, big sister!"

"You do give me an unenviable role, Cassie," Ruth shrugged, looking helpless. "Why must you dally with Matt Travers, of all people, and in the middle of the afternoon during an outpatients' clinic?"

Cassie smiled maddeningly.

"I'm afraid one is inclined to forget the mundanities of times," she chirruped. "I can just imagine dahling Matt saying, 'I can spare you two seconds, Cassie, and then I must go back to my outpatients' clinic like a good little doctor!' Oh, come off it, Ruthie! He forgot you all for a lamentably short while and became human."

"Doctors can't afford to forget," Ruth persisted, and looking sharply at the other added, "or be distracted into a state of forgetfulness by anyone else. Don't you forget that if the functioning of the hospital is disrupted in any way you'll have to go, Cassie."

"Just me, I suppose?" the other asked tonelessly.

"Unfortunately, no. The genuine members of the expedition would suffer with you. If you want it put any plainer, Cassie, you came as a member of that team and you'll stick with them in future. I personally object to seeing you lying around on this veranda making sheep's eyes at every passing male. You are in full view of the hospital staff room."

Cassie had begun to quiver until she was atomized rage.

"Oh, how I hate you, Ruth!" she blazed at the other. "You holy hypocrite! I suppose you and Bendy weren't distracted when you were supposed to be studying medicine in Edinburgh? You were human enough to sneak off and make love somewhere, weren't you?''

"Be quiet, Cassie!" Ruth commanded sharply. "Let's leave Benedict out of this.''

"Yes. Let's leave everybody out of it except me. That's always been your way. I am the original sinner and you are the lily-white maiden. Pooh! Some maiden!''

"Cassie!" pleaded Ruth in horror, for she recognized the fragrance of the pipe smoke now percolating the ruthlessly hot air of the late afternoon. The smoker could not be far distant. "Do control yourself. These tantrums are childish.''

"I'm going to get this off my chest if it kills me," Cassie almost screamed. "I never did believe in that non-consummation nonsense. Bendy confided in me that you were his real wife. Only the fact that you didn't have a baby gave you a loophole of escape. You're nothing but a horrible big fraud!''

Two sharp slaps finally succeeded in silencing Cassie for a moment, a moment pregnant with naked malice.

"I'll remember that along with all the rest," she said, fingering her stinging cheeks almost lovingly. "You're calling a tune you won't like Mrs. ex-Sharn!''

As Cassie disappeared into the house Ruth heard a cough behind her. She did not turn her head, however.

"Did you get around to ordering coffee, Ruth?" asked Mark Travers casually.

"No. I . . . I'll do it now.''

She was almost sorry to meet the cook rounding the veranda with a tray, for this gave her no respite.

Mark solemnly pored three cups and instructed the boy to take the third cup upstairs to Missie Sahib.

"Miss Belampton is your stepsister, I think you said?" he asked casually. "That means you are actually unrelated outside of the marriage of your parents?''

"That's right," Ruth admitted, feeling rather faint now from the reaction to that row with Cassie, and beginning to realize just what that young lady had said—or implied—which could clearly have been overheard by anybody within yards of the house.

"But you think of her as your sister, don't you?''

"No! No!" Ruth said sharply, trembling and almost weeping

with humiliation. "I never have thought of her as anything but a physical thorn in the flesh. And that's not purely one-sided. Cassie doesn't care much for me, either. We just happen to be chalk and cheese. It's unfortunate."

"It must be. Especially when the cheese is thrust into intimate communion with the chalk. I suppose one can't help absorbing some of the other's background and affairs?"

"If you're trying to tell me you heard our conversation," Ruth said bluntly, "if such a commotion can be called a conversation, that's all right. I realize Cassie isn't exactly a cooing dove when she's angry."

"I did hear," Mark admitted. "I heard enough to make me curious about one thing, but you might think it an impertinence if I ask it outright."

"Oh, do ask whatever you like," Ruth invited magnanimously.

"Very well, I will. Sir Benedict and I chat sometimes during the evening, you know, as you girls must chatter here. He told me—in a moment of alcoholically induced confidence—when you had given him a partiuclarly discouraging time, that he was once married to you. I can't say this was any surprise or shock. That letter I got told me as much. But Cassie's rantings did jar a little, I must confess. Now marriage, to me, means many things outside of a signed contract. No woman is a wife until she . . . ." Now the gray eyes were boring almost down into her very soul. He leaned forward so that his next question was scarcely more than a whisper. "Were you ever his wife as I mean it, Ruth?"

It was a simple straightforward question and she understood it perfectly. All she had to do was frame one small monosyllable in reply. Instead she racked her brains for the reasoning behind his admitted curiosity.

"I really don't see that . . . ." she countered at length in utter confusion.

"Ruth?" he insisted, kindly but very firmly, and held her chin so that she couldn't turn her head away again. "You gave me permission to ask. Now you must answer."

Some devil made her resist him as long as she could. When the trembling denial finally left her lips it was accompanied by the scalding of her tears, and as she turned away blindly to find a quiet corner and the blessedness of privacy, she heard him bound away from the veranda and go off, whistling blithely, across the compound.

BENEDICT SHARN SAID SHARPLY for the sixth time that evening, "I never knew anybody could change as you have changed, Ruth. Have you forgotten how we used to walk near the Forth Bridge and swear we would last as long as all that iron and steel did?"

"You keep reminding me, Bendy," Ruth sighed. "You must have quoted everything we ever said to each other."

"I remember because *my* love was sincere," Benedict said reprovingly. "Have you forgotten what we actually *did*, Ruth, in all the freshness of our young love?"

"No," Ruth told him candidly. "I even remember how—in the midst of all our young love—your father appeared and managed to make me look like a cheap little schemer. And I remember you didn't meet my eyes when you followed him out of the room to talk in terms of resigning me."

"You don't know what a hell I was in!" Benedict groaned.

"I was too busy suffering in my own," Ruth told him promptly. "Oh, and Bendy, did you actually tell Cassie that the terms of the annulment were really false? That we were—in physical fact—man and wife?"

Even in the darkness she felt his embarrassment cloak him . . . .

"I . . . I may have hinted as much. Has the little devil squawked back to you? It's not as horrible as it sounds, Ruth. You must believe me. After my father died and you left, I saw Cassie, and she made some suggestions as to how I might regain your interest and your love. Actually, she made a dead set at me herself. Wherever we dined or wined, or whenever we went to a theater, there were photographers and newshounds, and I grew tired of seeing myself in various rags described as 'Miss Cassandra Belampton's latest escort.' One night at her apartment I told her about it and she threatened to 'frame' me."

"You've been seeing too many movies, Bendy!" smiled Ruth.

"I never go. But I still know what 'framing' is. She locked us both in her bedroom, after inveigling me in there somehow, and said, 'Bendy, all my friends think we're practically engaged, you and I. You're not going to let little Cassie down with a bump, are you? Because if you are, little Cassie is going to scream and scream and then Aimée will come running and it'll all look very queer. And if little Cassie turns the gas on after you're gone. . . .' Honestly Ruth, that pocket-sized witch went on like that at me, and I had to think for my very life. I told her that it was on my conscience that our 'annulment' was secured on a false statement. That actually we had been man and wife together and also that at one time you feared you were pregnant.''

''Oh, Bendy!'' Ruth cried out. ''All this . . . ? To a girl like Cassie?''

''I tell you I was desperate. I told her I was approaching the authorities to have our annulment waived, and then it would mean divorce if we still wanted to end things.''

''And Cassie believed you?''

''I was pretty convincing. Actually, it was all wishful thinking on my part. I half believed myself. Anyhow, it worked. Cassie went quiet and let me go. A week or two later she told me about this Kanjihan trip, saying I might like to see my 'wife.' I jumped at the chance, I can tell you. But now that I am here, you're a . . . a stranger. I can't even put my arms around you without feeling you shudder. Is it . . . too late for us, Ruth?''

''I'm afraid it is, Bendy. Six years too late. You see, time moves on so relentlessly. You can't lose touch with your partner for six long weary years and expect to carry on the dance exactly as you were.''

''I suppose not.''

In the background, a record player blared out an ancient foxtrot and a few couples were dancing desultorily in the compound.

Mark Travers, looking around for one person in the throng, suddenly found her. Bending down, he asked, ''May I?'' and Ruth rose readily and felt his arms enfold her as they swayed into the dance. Happiness, she was discovering, was moments such as these, unquestioned and seized ere they fled as other happiness had fled before. Her cheek was cool against his, and all the scents of the night were minimized by the carbolic and tobacco scents of *him*.

Benedict Sharn watched the two glide past and, swallowing his chagrin, mentally phrased a cablegram addressed to the Velades Clinic in New York.

CHAPTER TWENTY

GLEN WROTE:

My Dear Ruth,
For heaven's sake, when are you coming back? I know I said stay as long as you wish, but even dear Cassie has written to say old Ajil is looking as good as ever and that she doesn't know what you're doing of a specialized nature nowadays. Ajil pays a comfortable check into your account (and mine) each month, but I don't think we should push him too far, do you? After all, you're not general surgeon to do odd jobs about a "wog" hospital after all my work on you—and with you—darling.

You can tell me to mind my own so and so business if you like but this prolonged absence of yours has me worried. I feel that either Sharn is pestering you sick or you have rebounded into some impossible romantic interlude with one of Ajil's European staff.

Believe me, Ruth, these types only look good in the jungle habitats. Put Tarzan into your grandma's drawing room and he would only be an embarrassment.

In reverse, I will not coolly submit to my finished product, my very attractive and efficient female assistant, wasting her sweetness, and her talents, in an attack of jungle fever.

Report immediately that you are winding up your business and coming back, Ruth, or even I will pack a toothbrush and fly out to see what's up.

Yours, Glen

Panic seized her momentarily, and she actually believed—for as brief a moment—that Glen had hit on the truth. That she was using his time and the raja's monthly check to help pursue her own selfish ends.

Of course it wasn't true, she realized in relief. The real purpose of her stay here was Kiran, and even Glen didn't know about her. His Highness had preferred that the princess's disfigurement should not be the subject of a written report. Reports got into others' hands sometimes, he had argued, and the rani was particularly sensitive on the subject of their daughter.

"When your work is completed to the satisfaction of all, Miss Stafford, you can tell Meriton about it in person, can't you? Meanwhile, I must congratulate you on my new scar—or should I say the lack of it?" And they had both laughed as he affectionately fingered the almost imperceptible white line that was all that remained of the tuck with which he had been discharged from the hospital in Calcutta a year ago.

"Perhaps I should not feel so ashamed, Miss Stafford," the raja had proceeded, "but for the fact that my face was torn by a *dead* tiger. He was a mangy brute and one in my shooting party brought him down. As it was the fellow's first kill he was naturally very excited, and he was holding up the animal's pad while I examined the head when cadaveric spasm set in. The chap dropped the pad and ran for his life, and I got the dead claw embedded in my cheek. There was much blood and fuss and I was flown to Calcutta to have a few stitches and some antibiotics."

"Why not Dr. Travers, your Highness?" Ruth asked. "Have you no faith in your own hospital?"

"Implicit faith, Miss Stafford. But could I have shared this confidence with Mark, do you think? We were schoolboy friends together. Now I am the raja. He would have laughed and made a schoolboy out of me again. A *dead* tiger, I ask you!"

Ruth could imagine Mark Travers slapping his thighs and laughing indeed over such an incident. Though Ajil took the dignity afforded by his royal rank very seriously, Mark probably remembered only too well the pranks of their common youth together and thought of his friend still as "old Ajil" rather than as Rajah of Kanjihan.

"I will keep your secret, Your Highness," Ruth promised. "Dead or alive, I don't think I would care to come to grips with a tiger."

"But you must attend a shoot before you leave us, Miss Stafford," Ajil insisted. "What do you think I keep those brutes of elephants for? I will arrange great excitement for you when your work is finished.''

"As Your Highness pleases," Ruth bowed obediently, knowing better than to argue her preferences in the face of what was intended as a supreme compliment,

On this morning Ruth had been up at first light, having been awakened by the arrival of the man who delivered the mail. Now she sat digesting Glen's letter, sentence by sentence, and answering each question he asked to her own satisfaction.

No, they must not push the raja's generosity too far. As soon as Kiran could safely be passed as fit from her attack of chicken pox she must have her final operation. After a few days she—Ruth—would know if the lip was going to knit satisfactorily, and then she could leave instruction with Mark Travers and make preparations for her departure.

Was Benedict pestering her sick?

That, also, merited a negative. Bendy had seen only too clearly from the moment of meeting that her erstwhile feeling for him was as dead as the dodo. There is a point in our human relationships beyond which we dare not trust our luck. Knowing when to bow out is as important as making an entrance. Benedict Sharn had watched his old sweetheart viewing him first cordially, then with lessening regard, until downright revulsion was written on the cards should he continue to press his suit with her. Even now he couldn't think where he had failed her, and though he couldn't bring himself to wish her ill, he rather hoped she would realize her mistake when it was too late and so take a large dose of her own medicine for a change. As for him, there was the unknown quantity of Olga Velades ahead, and the promised appointment at the clinic. Old Regis wrote regularly hoping he was having a good leave. Well, it was a damned rotten leave and now he wouldn't be sorry to see the end of it.

Ruth didn't like Glen's reference to a ''wog'' hospital. Mr. Meriton would think of Nurse Indiri and her Bhil, Ranjital, Singh and the rest as ''wogs,'' and she was appalled by the thoughtless mental cruelty of most white people. Here in Kanjihan she had met intelligent, devoted, and dedicated Indians, who had better manners than to sneer at Europeans for the lack of pigment in their skin. Also, she was angry to think of the Travers brothers coupled with a fictitious character who was noted for hurtling his physical perfections gymnastically from tree to tree, and little else.

Didn't Glen realize that there was a society and a code of behavior outside of grandma's drawing room? Mark Travers hadn't looked so bad that evening at the palace. He had represented Europe fairly enough without forgetting for one moment that he was a guest not only in his host's house, but also in his country.

How true was Glen's suggestion that she might be in love with such a character?

This Ruth hardly dared investigate herself recently. She had always been as sharply conscious of Mark Travers as she had been indifferent to his brother. He couldn't enter a room or stroll across the compound without a physical awareness causing her very spine to tingle. Sometimes he reared like Fate in her consciousness and seemed as unavoidable. When he had fought the felon barehanded for her and declared his fearful concern in such unmistakable and memorable terms, she had surrendered as to the inevitable. It was as though it was right she should be in Mark Travers's arms and hearing the halting phrases of his adoration.

Love should be all action, she had since decided. When love starts to think and question, romance may fly right out of the window.

This seemed to have happened to them.

Mark hadn't had a particularly high opinion of her to start with. He had been injected with the poison of the anonymous letter, and though his better self tried not to let it influence him, she had only to make the merest slip for him to view her with deadly suspicion. He had suspected her intentions regarding his brother, and he had suspected that her motives in coming to Kanjihan were all of an ulterior nature. Slowly—oh, so slowly—he had reestimated her and allowed his heart to speak. He seemed at times to want to love her despite her obvious human frailty, but when Benedict had arrived, open armed and possessive, he had withdrawn into the bland role of host and almost offered his blessings as he threw them together and created opportunities for their reacquaintance.

Well, it didn't work, Ruth reflected and trembled a little as she remembered his insistence on her answering the question that apparently was important to him, after that row with Cassie.

Why did he want to know, she asked herself fretfully. *He*

*hasn't made any advance since. I can't hang on in Kanjihan
waiting for him to speak, and anyhow, there's my career to think
of. As Glen says, I wasn't trained as a specialist to spend the rest
of my working life on a small island in the sea off nowhere.*

But at least give me the chance, cried her heart, involuntarily
leaping as she recognized the bush-shirted figure striding to join
her.

"Good morning, Ruth!" he greeted quite jovially.
"Couldn't you sleep?"

"I slept," she answered him, "but I think these first two
hours of the day are too good to miss. I'd rather go to bed early
than sleep through them."

"Let's have chow," he suggested and clapped his hands
sharply. "Come along, Gundhalal!" he called to the old
servant. "Where's breakfast?"

"He be right here, sahib, memsahib," the old fellow
promised in a fluster. "All missie sahibs—" he indicated the
upstairs region "—make much work."

"You're not taking breakfast upstairs, are you, Gundhalal?"
Ruth demanded suspiciously.

The old man grinned apologetically.

"Only for Missie Baba," he explained with a shrug. "No
trouble for that. But so many baths! . . ." and he rolled his eyes
heavenward and disappeared.

"Missie Baba's going to get up for breakfast in future," Ruth
decided harshly. "Cassie must be made to realize this isn't the
Ritz."

"Don't interfere, Ruth," Mark Travers said quickly, and, as
she questioned him, "I don't like anyone hating you. Cassie's
hate, that day, was tangible. You don't know how far to play a
cobra."

"Thanks for your concern," she said as the cook appeared
with fried Patna rice and succulent sweetbreads on a dish,
followed by the *ayah* carrying coffee. "Cassie can't hurt me,
Mark, and her bark's always worse than her bite."

"Hm," he pondered. "Matt seems to like the minx."

"Oh."

With deliberate casualness he observed, "Sharn tells me he
has been recalled to New York. He's asking the expedition to
release him as soon as possible. He says he'll be sleeping out at
the dig from now on."

"Oh!" Ruth said again.

"Won't you . . . miss him?" came rather less casually.

Ruth pondered. These heart-to-heart investigations of her innermost feelings didn't seem to lead anywhere. He looked a little confounded when she said, "Of course I'll miss him. I've grown used to seeing him around."

Work that out, her eyes flung at him.

"By the way," she said as he didn't appear to have lost his appetite, "I'll have to be getting away from here myself very soon. My boss—" she tapped her pocket where Glen's letter lay "—is getting impatient."

"Oh," he said with real interest, "has the mail arrived then?"

She suddenly felt like weeping and storming at him. She has told him she was leaving and he just couldn't care less, it seemed.

"I don't suppose I'll be missed, either," she murmured with a suspicion of self-pity as he found his own mail and rooted through it.

"Oh, I dunno," he shrugged. "The staff, everybody likes you, Ruth, but that won't affect any decisions you have to make. That's life."

"Yes, that's life," she sighed.

Mark Travers read his mail with apparent satisfaction. Ruth wondered if he was normal enough to have relatives; even a maiden aunt perhaps, who wrote to him regularly, called him "dear boy," and warned him against taking chills.

"Good!" he nodded, putting all the envelopes into his pocket and regarding her again. "Now what were we talking about? Ah, yes. You have to get back to London soon, you say. Well, when do you want to do Kiran?"

"How about next Thursday?"

"So be it. I'll go and get her myself Wednesday evening. We'll put her in hospital for the night and prep her, then you can have first theater before this lot stirs." He cocked his thumb aloft where female voices were chattering animatedly. "Thank heaven you're not the academic type, Ruth!"

"I'm not so sure how to take that," she decided. "Surely by the nature of my profession I *must* be an academic type?"

"No," he denied. "Even with your head in an isotope you'd still be wholly a woman."

"Well!" She didn't know quite why, but she liked to hear

this, then as feet clattered down the stairs her pleasure was disrupted by her companion's sudden attempt at escape.

"Good morning, Dr. Travers!" said the leader of the female contingent of archaeologists brightly. "Just off, are you? I always think we drive you away, you know."

"Not at all, Miss Bray," Mark said gallantly, "but our hours are rather keen. We like to start early and break in the heat of the day. I hope you're all comfortable? . . . Have everything you want? . . ."

He's simpering, Ruth thought in amusement as he stood behind chairs and saw the four women seated. Only Cassie was being borne along on the expedition's back as a nonprofessional; she had secured her place in the team simply by the expedient of putting money at their disposal. After the first few days she had tired of the work and, despite Ruth's injunctions, spent her time roaming around at will.

Ruth finished her coffee, well aware of her own lack of interest in the wonderful finds out at the dig. Had she been a true academic type she would have been agog, but Mark had said she was all woman. All woman perhaps, but not a whole woman. To reach completion a woman needed a man; nature supplied the elements but individuals were more selective.

I know how I feel, Ruth pondered as she crossed the compound, *but I can't throw myself at him. He pays me small attentions and I'm in heaven, then he looks through me as though I wasn't there. Very soon I won't be there, and I don't think he'll really notice. I sometimes wish I were a nice quiet unemotional fossil. Inanimate objects really have the best of it!*

CHAPTER TWENTY-ONE

MATT TRAVERS TURNED from the sink where he had been scrubbing up and saw an unexpected figure draped in the operating room doorway.

"Cassie!" he exclaimed. "What are *you* doing here?"

"You weren't at dinner," she observed with what appeared to him to be a nervous flutter of the hands. "I missed you, Matt."

"Did you now?" That sensation of elderly and superior pleasure once again permeated his being. "Whom do you think you're kidding, my dear girl?"

"Really, it's not the same without you about," Cassie insisted, rocking on her high heels like a child playing at dressing up. "I think the others put on your good nature and make you do more than your share of work."

"You may have something there," Matt smiled indulgently. "But one of my patients had a hemorrhage, you see, so it was up to me to give him a transfusion. We usually do our own patients, even though it means a bit of overtime. Now I'm going to have a last look around and knock off."

"Can I come with you?" the girl asked eagerly.

"What? You mean around the wards at this time of evening?"

"I won't excite the patients, will I?"

"I hope not. But it's not usual for visitors to appear at this hour. Especially one wearing such a pretty and—I may add—rather revealing dress!"

"I'll pretend to be a doctor," Cassie said, reaching up and taking Ruth's white coat from behind the door. "Now, how do I look, Matt?"

"I hope I don't meet up with anybody like you who really *is* a doctor, Cassie! I'd never be able to keep my mind on my work. Now come on, and no, we *do not* hold hands on the wards!"

Cassie walked a short pace behind the tall figure of Matt

through the dim wards, thoroughly enjoying herself—at first. So this was what it was like to be Ruth; the loose white coat, though rather long on her, gave out an aura of dignity and authority that was typical of her stepsister. Cassie had never forgiven Ruth for her natural capacity for experience and her aptitude for acquiring it. Ruth had always gone headlong into everything with a sense of dedication: her work, her love affair, her life. Cassie, who had so much more of the world's goods, was terrified of giving herself to anything or anyone. Her friends would desert her if she economized on their expected "treats," and she knew it. In her heart of hearts she admired Ruth and all she stood for, but rather than acknowledge this she mischievously sought to bring about her stepsister's downfall, there being a perverted satisfaction in destroying that which shows up the flaws in oneself.

Matt felt a head here, took a pulse there, spoke soothing words into wakeful ears, and Cassie nodded kindly and distantly, resembling a small goddess distributing her approval like largess.

In the surgical wards, however, her magnanimity failed her somewhat. There was a strong odor of ether mixed with iodoform for one thing, and two patients were having blood transfusions supervised by the night nurse, a very pale, almost corpselike nun of the Portuguese order. Cassie watched the blood slowly dripping from the upended vacolitres and felt herself grow pale. She had once visited a friend in hospital and become faint, she remembered. The friend had laughed and declared, "They'll be popping you into bed if you don't watch out, Cassie! You look awful. Go on home before you fall down!"

Yet she was as healthy as a young tree, and always had been. It was this atmosphere, this suggestion of sickness and death and blood and bandages . . . .

"Where did Cassie go?" Matt wondered as he suddenly missed her at his heels, then the nurse called him over to see a wound that had suddenly started to discharge, and he was all professional again.

Cassie was looking blindly for a way out when she staggered into a small room, startling its occupant into wakefulness. She sat down on a chair and put her head down on her knees. Even in that moment she had to remember Ruth thrusting her neck down and saying on one occasion, "Any fool knows you simply need blood in your head when you feel faint. Really, Cassie, all that panic over a cut finger!''

After a moment or two she felt better and looked around her. This must be a private ward. Was the occupant—she almost panicked again—in isolation for something horrible?

''Hello!'' Kiran greeted kindly from the bed. ''Are you a doctor, too?''

''No, I . . .'' Cassie now saw the twisted lip and shrank a little, so that Kiran noticed and slid down self-consciously between the sheets.

''I'm here for my operation,'' she said somewhat defiantly, ''then I'm going to be all right.''

''Good!'' Cassie decided, smoothing her hair. She suddenly realized a small brown child was addressing her in very good English and asked, ''Who are you?''

''I'm Kiran. I'm Miss Stafford's patient.''

''Oh?'' Cassie decided to join the game of making oneself a person of importance. ''I'm Miss Stafford's sister,'' she said in a singsong voice.

''Are you?'' Kiran was truly impressed now. ''I've had two operations already, and when I'm better I'm going to school in England.''

''Your parents must be rich,'' Cassie decided.

''Oh, they *are!*'' Kiran assured her. ''My father is the Rajah, you know.''

''I didn't know,'' said Cassie, her eyes very round, wondering why Ruth had never mentioned this little princess in her conversation.

''Miss Stafford came especially to attend to me,'' Kiran enlarged solemnly, ''and I'm a secret. I hope I haven't been chattering?''

''Not at all,'' Cassie assured her, and at that moment the door flew open and Matt stood revealed, looking sharply from one to the other of them.

''So here you are!'' he gasped, and pushing Kiran down onto the pillows with stern instructions to sleep, he hauled Cassie outside the room with him.

''You shouldn't have gone in there, you know!'' he scolded, and his brow was suddenly damp with perspiration.

''Why?'' Cassie asked blandly. ''Is the child infectious or something?''

''No. Oh—'' he shrugged fatalistically ''—just don't go shouting it around that you were turned loose, that's all.''

''She must be a princess at least,'' Cassie said demurely. ''A pity she's . . . like that.''

''She won't be like that much longer,'' Matt snapped, then bit his lip as he saw tears well up into the eyes regarding him.

''Don't cry, Cassie,'' he said more gently. ''I couldn't bear to see a pretty girl cry!''

She decided to initiate him forthwith and stand the consequences.

Outside the night was warm and starlit and the bamboo grove smelled sweet and earthy.

It was very late before either Cassie or Matt Travers retired. Cassie lay on her bed like a cat, pleasantly satiated with masculine attention, her mind still clear and designing.

Matt sat on the edge of his bed and smoked heavily. It couldn't be love, he pondered, not this time, but it was something equally necessary to existence, and who was going to look such a pretty little gift horse in the mouth? Somewhat wryly he decided a poor doctor's life wouldn't suit a girl like Cassie, so she obviously wasn't intending that he should take her seriously. He wondered about her life in London, if he would ever see her again after this brief interlude that had succeeded in making them imagine they were two of a kind.

RUTH FELT THE STAB of light on her eyes as she opened them and sank back onto her pillows.

''Dr. Memsahib?'' Gundhalal questioned her again. ''To get up now, please?''

Ruth felt as though she was looking through a curtain, and saw the face under the cleverly wound pink turban anxiously regarding her. She knew this was the day decided upon for Kiran's final operation, that she had asked to be called early. Her mind was crystal clear about all these things, yet she had difficulty in framing words with her dry lips.

''Bring . . . Dr. . . . Mark . . . .'' she said with difficulty.

Then Cassie's face appeared and retreated, and Cassie's voice announced cheerfully; ''You're off-color, aren't you, old girl? You look ghastly . . . ''

By closing her eyes and grimacing Ruth indicated she didn't care a hoot about her looks at that moment.

"Bring Dr. . . . Mark . . . ." she said again.

"All right. All right." Cassie paused on the threshold thoughtfully. "Won't Matt do? Or the Indian doctor?"

Ruth levered herself up on one elbow trying to focus her eyes and failing. She felt herself engulfed by a wave of nausea.

"I want Mark!" she pleaded weakly, and Cassie's lip curled as she pondered her discovery. So this was why Bendy had huffed off down to the dig, was it? Ruthie was in love with the elder of the Travers brothers!

The rigorous one, she decided, remembering that nest of heat in the bamboo brake last evening. *He strikes me as being the sort who would cough and apologize before submitting to his natural instincts!*

Rigorous enough to hide any personal feelings he had about the news of Ruth's sickness, certainly. Cassie gained no satisfaction from watching Mark Travers finish shaving, collect his stethoscope, and pocket a thermometer, while handing her a dish containing a hypodermic syringe and a small vial.

"I'm not happy in sickrooms," Cassie explained as they reached Ruth's bedroom together, "so I'll leave you to it if you don't mind."

She then went to her own room next door, put her ear to a thin partition, and eavesdropped quite blatantly.

Ruth, who had decided to sail away on the cloud hovering to accommodate her, felt the jab of the needle in her thigh and came back to earth with a bump.

"Mark!" she exclaimed, wanting to cry suddenly. "I feel awful."

"I know you do, but I don't think you're so bad. Our genus of mosquito is very considerate on the whole. He usually only lays us low for about forty-eight hours. In fact, this is the first time he's popped his head up since you and I made our assault in Ajil's plane when you first arrived. Remember?"

Ruth managed a weak smile and sought a handhold. As he obliged and squeezed her fingers gently she sighed and closed her eyes again.

"I wanted you, Mark," she whispered. "Do you understand?"

Fever, he pondered, *usually makes us speak truth. But she'll get better, bless her, and the tortoise will pop his head in again, no doubt.*

"I'll be available whenever you need me, Ruth," he told her, and for a moment touched her fingers with his lips. "Now sleep. I'll tell the *ayah* to sit with you."

Suddenly, however, she sat up and said quite rationally, "I've got to do Kiran. You know this is the day, Mark!"

"Yes, I know." He pushed her down gently. "We'll do her on Monday."

"Someone might see her," she persisted fretfully.

"But no one knows about her except us, Ruth, so no one's interested. Why should they be? *You* haven't told anyone, have you?"

"No, of course not." She became suddenly fretful again. "You don't think *I* would betray a trust like that, do you, Mark?"

"No, Ruth. I don't."

"I wouldn't lie to *you*, of all people."

"Go to sleep, Ruth, and stop worrying. I'll look after Kiran personally. You must get fit for Monday."

Gradually she relaxed and then began to breathe quickly and heavily as the fever mounted and the drugs he had injected took over.

There was nothing more he could do for the moment, so he called the *ayah* and instructed her clearly in her native Bengali. Then he strolled out into the compound feeling strangely lost and lonely. This would be how it would feel when Ruth had gone away for good, as though one could expect never to see the sun again, or something equally drastic.

"So what are you going to do about it?" he asked aloud of a startled grandmother langur in the branches of a wild pomegranate tree. "Ask her to share your lot here in Kanjihan?"

The langur began to chatter angrily. She didn't like humans apparently sneering at her, and she was glad when this one— who had always behaved quite well in the past—shrugged his broad shoulders and strode away, leaving her to suck the sweet pips of the fruit she held in her paw and to spit to her heart's content.

"PLEASE . . . HOW'S RUTH TODAY?" Cassie asked prettily, finding Mark Travers having coffee alone on his veranda.

"She's much better," Mark told her. "Cassie, I wish you wouldn't roam around so openly unescorted. If you want to go off somewhere take Gundhalal or Ali. I must look after you until Ruth's fit again, you know." He smiled gallantly.

"But I can take care of myself." Cassie laughingly accepted the coffee he poured for her. "I may look like a schoolgirl, Dr. Travers, but I'm twenty-two and quite a woman of the world."

"You don't say!" He tried to look impressed. "You've only been out in the world for a year, young lady. Before that Chancery kept a firm hold on you."

"Did Ruth tell you that?" she pouted prettily. "Ruth tells everything. She promised to keep secrets and then tells—always." She lowered her long lashes conspiratorially. "Of course it cuts both ways. Sometimes she tells me things other people have told her. I like it best when she tells me about her romances. Poor old Bendy little knows I could tell him all about those presumably sacred moments of tenderest passion. I even know how they cheated to secure their annulment. You know about that, of course?" Mark's expression told her nothing, but his complexion was now a dull purple instead of its usual dark tan. "It should really have been a divorce. Bendy told me himself. I wouldn't be surprised if legally they weren't still married, you know."

"Should you be telling me this?" Mark asked sharply.

"No." She looked up innocently. "You're right. I shouldn't. Actually, I came to ask you if it's all right to include some pictures of the little girl with my magazine article?"

"Little girl . . . ? Article . . . ?"

"You're rather dull this morning, Dr. Travers," she said with exaggerated patience. "I'm writing some articles for a magazine back home on this trip. After all, not everyone has the chance of visiting places like Kanjihan, and they'll lap it up. Of course there isn't a lot of human interest, but I've squeezed out what I could. I think mention of the little princess and her . . . her trouble and all that's being done to help her will make a wonderful human interest story, don't you?"

"Give the child a name, please!" Mark said curtly.

"But you know her name, don't you? The Princess Kiran . . . ."

"Who told you of the existence of . . . of Kiran?"

"Oh!" Cassie's hand flew to her mouth in horror. "Don't be angry with Ruth! It's me. I shouldn't have told . . . !"

"You should, and I'm glad you did, young lady. You'll write *nothing* about Princess Kiran or the royal family of Kanjihan for your wretched magazine. What can your sister have been thinking of?"

"Well, I told you," Cassie said unhappily, "Ruth does

chatter, but I'm sure she means no harm. She . . . she'll kill me for this!''

She looked really scared, he thought.

''Cancel the articles and I'll keep our secret,'' Mark said firmly. ''If the raja finds he can't trust people, Cassie, just anything might happen. You must wipe Princess Kiran right out of your recollection. Promise?''

''I promise,'' Cassie said, biting her lip. ''I'm sorry, Dr. Travers. You won't tell Ruth I . . . I let the family down, will you?''

''I won't tell.''

As she turned away, her head downcast, she had all her work cut out not to let her bottled-up mirth escape in cascading trills of triumphant delight.

So much for the humiliation of Benedict Sharn's rejection! So much for Ruth, who had dared to strike her! A very satisfactory settling of accounts all around.

CHAPTER TWENTY-TWO

THOUGH RUTH, in her feverish delirium, fancied eons of time were washing over her burning head, she was actually kept in bed for only three days. She was hauled to her feet, feeling tottery, on the evening of the third day by Nurse Angelina, who had come over to the house especially to escort her to and from the bathroom and keep vigil over every confused moment. After a bath, however, she merely felt rather weak and very, very hungry. With a sensation of shock she looked down at her ochre-colored hands and saw her face in the mirror was also somewhat oriental in appearance, especially as her cheekbones were naturally high and wide.

"Thank goodness I don't feel as bad as I look!" she told the nun.

"Oh, that is the drugs, Miss Stafford," the woman said blithely. "Dr. Mark is a great believer in injecting meperidine at such times. He doesn't realize a pretty girl may prefer being ill to losing her complexion!" And the nun laughed merrily, stopping in midair, as was her habit, and frowning sternly to say, "Now back to bed with you and no more nonsense!"

"But I feel quite well now. Can't I have dinner with everybody else?"

This argument was the "nonsense" the nurse had forecast, however, and Ruth was hustled back to bed, tucked in as for midwinter in northern Scotland, and then given a very small piece of breast of chicken and a few green beans.

She settled off into the last of her night sweats, however, feeling happy and looking forward to the morning when she had been told she could rise as usual. She was rather disappointed to be visited by Matt just before she slept, for throughout her fever she had always known when Mark was near her. His touch on her wrist or brow was like a lifeline upon which she subconsciously drew herself nearer to the bank of full recovery. There was nothing of a personal nature between her and Matt these days. He was kind, professional, and faintly on the defensive. Also he smelled vaguely of the perfume Cassie favored, which came from some exclusive salon in Paris, cost the earth, and was called La Femme Fatale.

Maybe Matt had only sat next to Cassie at dinner, but it was as though in Ruth's sight, fresh and cleared by her fever, he carried Cassie's brand on him and now cared rather less who knew it.

Mark did not come in that evening at all, but next morning she awoke very early, feeling quite herself, though conscious of having lost weight, and decided on a quick dip in the eternally tepid water of a bath and a stroll across the compound in the hope that she would find him breakfasting on his own veranda. He was an inveterate early riser and read various textbooks on medical subjects while even the hospital was still asleep.

She dressed in her—and his—favorite shade of blue, finding she had to draw the belt in two more inches, then, grinning at her yellow complexion in the mirror, she went out into the cool sharp air of first light. Even the birds were only stirring with an occasional protesting squawk from the branches of fig and eucalyptus trees, as though some precocious member of the family was being told to shut up and go back to sleep again.

Ruth's appearance in the compound was the signal for a giant crane to rise from his inverted umbrella in a nest in a dragon's blood tree and flap off toward the swamp. She could imagine the great fuss of his settling in the now stagnant water, and his goose-stepping yellow legs in the shallows, at once so elegant and so absurd.

It was a lovely day, she decided, and seeing Mark on the veranda she wanted to run and present herself, saying, "Look! I'm here!" and skip and twirl for his approval.

Instead she walked demurely and saw him half rise as though to go indoors, then deciding at least to await her arrival.

"I hoped you hadn't had breakfast yet," she greeted, her own delight spilling over into dimples. "I'm famished."

"Good!" he commented. "You've been a little behind schedule, this being a first attack, but we'll be able to tackle theater on Tuesday, all being well. As to breakfast, I've had mine. Gundhalal has instructions to allow you anything you fancy within reason. You have only to let him know."

Until that moment Ruth had been conscious only of the width of the table between them. Now she felt the slap of a barrier falling into position. It was as tangible against her chest as though it was a solid oak five-barred gate, and he was—yes, he was—excusing himself to go inside, fully expecting her to behave like a sensible ex-patient and run off and order breakfast on her own veranda.

She turned away sharply, the blood staining her jaundiced cheeks as she stewed in the embarrassment of realizing that her appearance had apparently been an intrusion.

Why, why, she asked herself, losing all interest in the thought of food and desiring only the privacy of her room again.

She knew that at the beginning of her illness her feelings had escaped from her control, that she had in fact made it quite clear to Mark Travers that he meant more to her than she had previously allowed him to realize. She had been glad to lay her emotions naked before him, ridding her mind of their weight, and he had apparently as gladly gathered them up in acceptance of a situation as mutually desirable as it was inevitable. They had tried to dislike each other from the start. That is always a bad beginning between a man and woman who are emotionally unoccupied, for once the emotions are involved just anything can happen, and usually does. It is sexual indifference that permits of platonic relationships between the sexes.

Mark had tried to sheer off when a warning note was sounded, but the magnetism between them had apparently pulled too strongly to be dissuaded for long by such items as anonymous letters and an exhusband appearing masterfully on the scene in the role of present sweetheart. Mark had watched and noted the leisurely resolving of all these things. She had proved herself an able specialist surgeon. She had handled the situation with Matt, and his blatant worship of her, patiently and with the gentlest of discouragements so that he remained unscarred from the experience. She had welcomed Benedict to Kanjiahn as a member of the expeditionary party, and when they were tactfully thrown together by Mark Travers, she had patiently borne all Bendy's protestations and declarations and merely repeated her decision to allow the sleeping dog of the past to lie content and advocate that they go their separate ways.

All this she knew Mark had observed, though he had observed it from the no-woman's-land into which he had withdrawn since the invasion of his island province. He had merely stooped to clarify some point or other in his mind before retreating again, as though afraid of being trapped into some situation for which he wasn't quite ready. She couldn't openly pursue him, but time was suddenly not on their side any more. Months had sped by almost unnoticed, and now she was being pressed to wind up her affairs and return to England.

Why didn't Mark speak, knowing all this? Was he going to allow her to leave—even help to speed her away—without one single invitation into the realms of mutual sensory madness that punctuate, and make worthwhile, the most sedate and otherwise rigorous lives?

Her illness had seemed to toss the gauntlet between them, and he had appeared to accept the challenge, as hungry for the admission of a deep-seated need as was she.

But here she was with her face hot in her pillow, obviously the victim of a delirious presumption. She had been Dr. Mark Travers's stricken colleague and nothing more. With all her eagerness and love shining in her eyes he had practically told her she was intruding, and if such a blow needed softening she could order what she liked for breakfast from Gundhalal.

Oh, humiliation indeed!

Cassie tapped on the door and entered quietly, looking somewhat doubtfully at the still prone figure of her stepsister.

"Are you better, Ruthie?" she asked gently. "I thought I heard you get up ages ago. Don't overdo things, will you?"

Ruth quickly gathered her features into the mask she reserved for Cassie and rolled over.

"I'm the original little yellow goddess," she announced brightly. "Watch you don't get malaria, Cassie! Yes, thank you, I'm better. What day is it? Ah, Sunday. Nurse Catarina usually holds a hymn and prayer service in their chapel for us Anglicans. Are you coming?"

"To sing hymns?" Cassie made a face. "No. Actually, I might go yachting. It's quite safe, isn't it?"

"You'll be safe with Matt," Ruth said, trying to feel an interest in the other's welfare. "Just do as he says and watch the boom doesn't decapitate you."

"I had imagined lying around and looking elegantly idle," Cassie countered, fingering a copy of the *Indian Medical Journal* that lay on the bedside table. "I hope sailing isn't going to be *work*."

Ruth said even more brightly, "Well, what about breakfast, eh?"

But Cassie pulled Ruth back as she was about to leave the room, and then she reached up—much to Ruth's consternation—and kissed her.

"Even though you're as yellow as a buttercup I *still* love you, big sister," she declared. "You *are* sure that you're better? That everything's all right?"

"Of course everything's all right, juggins," Ruth assured the other. "In fact, I've almost finished my work here and I may be flying back next week. Hadn't you better think of leaving, too?"

"I suppose so." Cassie sighed hard and flounced off to her room.

Ruth descended the stairs, feeling strangely affected by the conversation in the bedroom. Cassie wasn't normally so considerate of her, and her previous demonstrations of affection had been of the "kiss of death" variety. For instance, when their parents had decided to marry both girls had been called upon to act as bridesmaids. Ruth was fourteen at the time and Cassie eleven. Ruth was allowed to wear a full-length dress of blue taffeta and net for her role as chief bridesmaid, and the younger girl was attired in a short frock of the same material, her feet encased in ankle-strapped shoes over white socks. It was not Cassie's way to complain that she, too, wanted a long frock and cuban-heeled silver slippers; this was somehow too straightforward for Miss Cassandra Belampton's complex nature. Instead she was dressed in her own regalia, apparently quite content, and when stepping out of the car outside the church, with scores of people milling around to watch, she had firmly planted her black patent shoe on Ruth's trailing net overskirt and delightedly listened to the prolonged r-r-ip of the other's finery. Somebody rushed forward to hustle the bridesmaids into the shelter of the church porch, and somebody else offered a safety pin. Cassie had simply reached up on her patent-leather toes and kissed hard while investigating Ruth's shocked misery with interested green eyes.

Could Cassie have helped it?

Only Miss Belampton knew that, but obviously one couldn't bawl her out after being kissed so vigorously.

There were other occasions when Cassie had destroyed and kissed. Ruth's broken sewing machine had earned such a salute, and so had the surrender of her first boyfriend—to Cassie. Ruth never knew that young Peter broke their swimming date because

Cassie told him she had gone off with someone else. Ruth saw Peter, who was just eighteen, driving off in one of the Belampton cars—with Cassie, of course. A car was a great attraction, and apparently Peter preferred it to her, even though it meant having the kid along, too.

Why had Cassie kissed her just now?

What was there to break—or take—here in Kanjihan? She couldn't know how Ruth felt about Mark Travers, unless it was written all over her countenance, and in any case, her own preference was for Matt, who seemed capable of handling the minx quite well.

I'm unjust to Cassie at times, Ruth decided. *There's good in her—must be. I'll remember to look for it in future.*

Now the whole household was up and about. The women of the expedition greeted her cheerfully.

"So glad you're on your feet again, Miss Stafford, and I hope we didn't disturb you with our comings and goings!" greeted the elderly Miss Bray.

"I never heard you at all," Ruth admitted. "How's work progressing?"

"Oh, so-so. Volcanic rock's a bit of a stinker to get through, you know, but we *have* found a cave, and there's a skeleton, pots, writing, everything. You must see it, my dear. Actually, the professor wants to hold a picnic out at the dig, as a small return for all the hospital staff has done to help us. I'm going to see Dr. Travers after brekker, and I shall insist he bring you. It'll buck you up after your illness. What do you say?"

Ruth smiled and decided it depended on Dr. Travers, didn't it?

CHAPTER TWENTY-THREE

YOU CAN BE WITH SOMEONE in the flesh and a thousand miles removed from him in spirit, Ruth concluded with a bitterness alien to her; and yet where there is true love and understanding, distance makes no obstacle.

Here they all were at the dig, Mark, Matt, herself and Cassie, and a horde of merry-faced, low-caste natives, who served in any capacity as casual laborers to the expedition, offering curry puffs and rice patties and sandwiches containing every known filling for the heathen unfasting English.

There was plenty of laughter, too, though it washed over Ruth's head, leaving her like Queen Victoria, not amused. She was not without a sense of humor, but laughter wells from the emotions, and she had battened down the fountainhead that gives rise to joy, lest it sour into tears that sought to relieve her in moments when her self-control was suspect.

She knew she was taut and unnatural in her reactions, but hoped her recent illness was excuse enough for this. She saw uncovered before her remnants of the ancient civilization of Kanjihan and heard a commentary, sounding equally dead and uninspiring, from the lips of her self-appointed guide, a London professor in ancient history and a well-known archaeologist.

". . . so what we thought was a skeleton was really two," his voice droned on, "a male and female so closely entwined they must have been lovers. Obviously the eruption caught them unaware and the young man, naturally enough, threw himself on the girl to protect her. *C'est l'amour magnifique,* eh, Miss Stafford?"

Looking down at the tangle of dry bones Ruth decided, "I suppose there is love like that."

"So my dear wife assures me when I forget our wedding anniversary and such occasions. You know, I personally think occasions should be enjoyed for themselves and then decently forgotten, like these two. Had they lived to remember, could they ever really have recaptured the pain and horror, the blinding revelations of love faced with decision, in a yearly anniversary?'' The elderly face was now living and animated. ''Can one feel again as one did the day one married and saw at the altar a girl who had changed overnight from a very dear and close companion into a beautiful remote stranger?'' The professor shuddered. ''It's a small wonder all bridegrooms don't bolt from the church!''

''They obviously don't because it's just another form of love faced with decision,'' Ruth said brightly. ''And I'll bet the dear and close companion was there all the time, thinking how *you* had changed overnight into an impersonal tailor's dummy!''

''You're too young to be so cynical, Miss Stafford,'' Professor Harburn chided. ''How dare you outmaneuver an old hand like me! I'll be saying it with flowers on our next anniversary if I'm in your company much longer. We're discussing love, fidelity, and practicalities, Dr. Travers. Are you for or against anniversaries?''

Ruth was well aware of Mark behind her; her scalp had pricked in the old familiar warning.

''Some anniversaries,'' he said thoughtfully. ''On the whole we're a lot of ridiculous sentimentalists at heart, and I don't suppose you are any exception, sir. When a day has nothing to commend it we'll shut ourselves away with the remembrance of a day that had. Memory is really anniversary, isn't it? We select special occasions for our own delectation.''

''We're going to be on to Freud any minute,'' Professor Harburn said darkly. ''I must go and keep an eye on those people in the other department. I can trust you, of course, Dr. Travers, as a fellow—if only amateur—digger?''

''Too right!'' smiled Mark in a pseudo-Australian voice. ''Bolting off, too?'' he asked Ruth as she turned to leave the dimness of the large cave whither the professor had escorted her.

''Not particularly. But I've had all this explained to me.''

''And reached what conclusion, may I ask?''

Ruth looked again at the skeletons and a pain stabbed her heart.

''That there's always been tragedy in the world,'' she said as though to herself.

''But tragedy is not necessarily an end,'' he pointed out. ''Earthquakes, the violence of nature, the belligerence of men . . . all these bring about individual ends, but they will not stop love or inspiration from functioning, which would be the greater tragedy. I think we are given the necessary fillip to override our disasters, and yet we find ourselves confused and disarmed when faced by smaller hurdles.''

''I would have thought you were the complete hurdler at all times, Dr. Travers,'' she said acidly, confronting him. ''You've always struck me as being complete master of all your situations.''

''Then you must be quite unaware of my most provocative situation, Miss Stafford. It's a very good maxim that advises us, 'He who does not know which way to turn, let him stand still and ponder.'''

''But not retreat,'' Ruth flung at him, knowing full well he understood her. ''You're much too preoccupied with the behavior of tortoises and other creatures of retractive habits. I have never seen *your* head out of your shell long enough to recognize it!''

''Well! well!'' He took refuge in a long draw on his pipe. ''When you retail your memoirs of this day into other ears, Miss Stafford, they will not include the fulfilling of my natural desires at this moment. *My* scalp will not provide material for one of your girlish chats!''

He went off leaving her alone with the storm lantern, her heart beating like a sledgehammer in her chest.

What did he mean?

What *could* he mean by that?

How could one love a person who made one so angry? In reverse, how could one be so angry with a person unless one loved him so much?

We were within a fraction of an inch of hurling ourselves into physical combat there, Ruth pondered ruefully, taking a long quivering breath and deciding that with Kiran's operation facing her in the morning she couldn't take any more of Mark Travers that day.

She returned to the picnic group and deliberately sat beside Benedict, who was coolly concerned with his anticipated return to the States.

''You must come over and see the clinic one day, Ruth,'' he invited. ''Maybe I'll even give you a job—if you want one.''

''I'll bear that in mind, Bendy,'' she told him, feeling suddenly friendly toward one who nowadays could be relied upon to stir no emotion whatsoever in her breast. "I'll certainly bear that in mind."

"SWAB!" RUTH CALLED CLEARLY and then clipped the severed flaps of the upper lip apart. "Would you remove a tooth for me, Dr. Travers? Your grip is harder than mine. It's only a milk tooth, but it may rub and interfere with internal healing."

"Certainly," Mark agreed, taking a pair of dental forceps the nurse was holding out. "Is this the one?"

"Thank you." Ruth put a plug in the dental cavity and sprayed the unconscious child's mouth with a saline solution. "I think we can carry on now. The palate has built up so well I think a graft from the forearm will be quite unnecessary. I shall stitch fairly loosely, leaving a slight gap, carefully dressed, which I hope will granulate naturally. The child will have artificial feeding for two days so as not to disturb the dressing."

"Very good, doctor," said Nurse Angelina in acknowledgement.

Ruth drew the silk thread through the severed lip, carefully stitching the side that had hitherto been imperfectly separated from the palate.

"She looks normal already," the nurse declared. "It is wonderful what can be done. God be praised!"

"Amen," said Mark Travers humbly. "I must say you've done wonders—" he hesitated "—Miss Stafford."

Later, as they washed up together, he observed, "I thought you were nervous of this final op? You tackled it almost eagerly at the finish."

"My mind was somehow settled," she spoke into the towel. "It was completely on my work. One has to be confident about some things." She glanced at him as she removed her turban and shook her hair free. "Who'll be using this theater when your brother has gone?"

"No one is irreplaceable," he said expressionlessly. "There's a fellow called Ram Dan taking over. Calcutta's turning them out by the score these days. No shortage of recruits."

"I thought I had noticed strange faces around lately. Well—" she looked at him boldly now "—I'll go and write some letters, if you'll excuse me . . . ? Tell various people I'll be coming home soon."

He allowed her to leave without comment, though his

countenance was dark with his thoughts as he watched her out of sight.

"Women collectively are a bit of a bore," he murmured, "but one woman can be hell! Unadulterated hell!"

THE ISLAND GARDEN of Inj with its intermingling fragrances of fruits, flowers and spices, its silver-sanded horseshoe bay with its breakwater of pink coral and colorful plant and fish life too numerous to mention, was an ideal retreat for a romantic interlude.

Matt Travers lay prone on the sand, his sharply white yachting shorts stark against the bronze of his skin, his brown eyes lazily and indulgently regarding his companion, tiny and yet extremely feminine in her brief red-spotted bikini.

"Don't you dare!" Cassie warned as she opened her eyes, heavy with sun and heat, and anticipated the descent of his lips. "Stop it, Matt!" She wriggled away from him, frowning, and sat up. "The way we're going on I'll be having a baby or . . . or something," she said fretfully and energetically put her hair to rights.

His laughter was spontaneous, and while he laughed she watched him, uncertain whether to join in or cry.

"Cassie," he said at length, "you funny little thing! Kissing won't give you a baby!"

She drew herself up and looked out to sea, so incredibly turquoise, a sea deepening in shade until it was almost a black line against the royal blue arch of the sky.

"I know my biology, Matt," she said darkly, her amber eyes unwinking. *Like those of the tigress,* he decided. "I learned it in a girl's school, both classroom and shrubbery varieties. I know that when a girl really wants a baby—" she looked at him squarely "—she gets one somehow."

Matt visibly swallowed and a sweat broke out on his forehead.

"D'you know what you're saying, Cassie?" he asked hoarsely.

"Yes, I do, worse luck. I'm liking, too much, our being together like this. Hell, Matt, I'm selfish and . . . and cruel by nature. I can't bear to love anybody so much. Please, please don't make me."

His answer was to pinion her to the sand while he digested slowly the emotions welling inside him.

"I don't think you're selfish and cruel, Cassie. There's not enough of you to . . ." He kissed her again, battening down the fever her small stirring hands roused in him. Rolling onto his back he said, "You're right, Cassie. Let's be still for a while and just think. You're rich, aren't you? So marrying you is quite out of the question."

"Why?" she asked sharply.

"Rich wives aren't decent things to have, my dear kid," he jeered. "No woman's going to make me look like a study in still life. My wife will live on my pittance as a doctor, in a house of my providing, and not be afraid of cooking my supper on occasion."

"Yes, sahib," she said cheekily with a mock humility. "That sort of existence sounds absolutely stinking, but I suppose it's only what I deserve. But how do I get rid of my money? Daddy tied it all up in neat little securities so that I would never want during my lifetime. Unfortunately, I can't consult him now that I'm falling in love—I think—with a poor proud humbug!"

His eyes warmed again.

"Really, Cassie? Do you think we could make a go of it?"

"Oh, I don't know," she suddenly panicked. "Maybe it's this place . . . this climate. . . ."

"Then we'll stay in it," he suggested. "How about that?"

Her eyes flickered over him again.

"Matt, I . . . we don't know each other very well, do we?"

"All that's important, surely? Anyway, my life's an open book. I have no shady hidden corners that I know of."

"I believe you. But I'll bet you're a brute when you're angry. I haven't seen you angry, Matt, and I think I would be afraid of you."

"But why should I be angry with you?" He smiled indulgently. "You're a funny little thing, Cassie. I feel awfully protective toward you, as a matter of fact. Tell me why I should be angry with you." He nuzzled her golden shoulder suddenly. "Have you been playing doctor again without my knowledge and poisoned all my patients?"

"Idiot!" she laughed. "I had enough of doctors and hospitals that one evening. I'm not a ministering angel. No, it's a question of standards of behavior. I think you're so steeped in the pukka sahib school, Matt, that you wouldn't condone half the things little unprincipled me does. For instance, if somebody annoys or offends me, or is even outstandingly better or sweeter than I am,

I never rest until I've got my own back. I . . . I just stoop to *anything*. You don't know.''

"Do go on," he said as though intrigued. "Give me an example of this horrific side to your nature."

"Certainly," she said obligingly. "Better to tell you now than have you discovering after we're married and *murdering* me or something. With a doctor disposal is so easy. I . . . I'll tell you a bad thing I've done recently, and then you'll know me at my worst. It concerns Ruth. Most of my sins do," she shrugged.

"Go on," Matt encouraged.

"You told me you used to, well, admire Ruth at first. I don't hold that against her really," Cassie said hastily, "because I've grown up seeing everybody admire and love Ruth. At school, in sports. . . . She even confided in love—the fool—when she was running away to marry Benedict Sharn, and I, of course, wired Sir Esmond, his father, and he caught them just after the ceremony and succeeded in bringing it all to nought. Shall I go on?"

"You must have been a horrible schoolkid," Matt pondered, "but so many girls are cats. What about the Cassie of today?"

"When our parents were killed Ruth left me, took an apartment, and more or less washed her hands of me. All at once our mutual friends—as I considered them to be—stopped coming to the house. Ruth had been the attraction, you see? All my life," Cassie proceeded vehemently, "I seem to have been living in Ruth's shadow. Even you had to fall in love with her first!"

"But she didn't fall in love with me," he pointed out. "You'll be one up on her if you follow through with this business, Cassie."

"I haven't really shocked you yet. Ruth criticized my behavior, especially with you. She's a dog in the manger sometimes, you know! She made me very angry and when I let her know it she . . . she slapped me! I nursed that for a day or two; then your precious—and equally perfect—brother questioned me about the possibility of my shoving off in the very near future. I could see he didn't think I was very good medicine for 'ickle bruvver.''

"Really?" smiled Matt. "I never knew."

"So while I was in a fine old state of animosity toward these two I discovered they were, well, that way about each other.''

"*I* knew," Matt said. "I minded a bit at first, but after you made your presence felt I . . . ."

"I made my presence felt there, too," Cassie proceeded. "I really enjoyed myself for half an hour or so. I had discovered about Princess Kiran, as you know, and I heard Mark impressing upon Ruth the need for secrecy until the operations were safely over; so while Ruth was ill I pretended to Mark I was writing some articles for a magazine and I mentioned Kiran and her affliction quite casually. I even asked if he would mind me taking some pictures of her as she was."

"You *what?*" Matt gasped.

"Don't be tiresome, darling, you heard every word I said. I explained to Mark that Ruth had told me about Kiran, as she told me everything else, including her romantic interludes. I looked at him in a way that—without naming names—let him think I could tell him how passionately he kissed according to Ruthie. Just in case he wasn't sick enough by that time, I threw in for good measure the fact that Ruth ought to consider herself still married to Benedict as the union had actually been consummated."

"And had it?" Matt asked faintly.

"Not on your life! My shining light wouldn't step out of line, and they were followed from the church. I actually bulldozed poor old Benedict into taking that line when I had him in my corner for a bit, but I never really believed him. All he made very clear was the fact that he was still Ruth's captive. What are you doing, Matt? Where are you going?"

The younger Dr. Travers was stalking down the beach in the direction of the wooden jetty, where the yacht was tied up.

"Matt?" questioned Cassie, now fearful, having to run to keep up with him. "Aren't you going to . . . to speak to me again? You—" her voice grew shrill "—you're not going to leave me here, are you?"

He indicated that she should take her place in the well of the boat.

"No! You might drown me!" she wailed afresh.

His answer was to lift her up bodily and, with one almighty slap, throw her like a parcel toward the stern.

She watched him, very respectfully, as he untied the yacht and shoved off from the jetty.

CHAPTER TWENTY-FOUR

FOUR DAYS AND then she would start on her journey back to England and—what? Ruth had never before found the prospect of her future so empty and uninviting.

It's a ridiculous and morbid state of mind induced by the climate, she told herself firmly as she wandered in the palace gardens, for Rosala had insisted on her staying at the palace for at least a week before her departure. *When I recapture my lost energy I'll take a new interest in my work, and*—a veil of pain blotted out her sight for a moment, for she could not conceive of anything life had to offer other than her work these days—*and I mustn't be so emotional in future about people.*

She paused to watch an orange and white butterfly as big as a fan weaving like an exotic ballerina among the bauhinia blooms. Rosala had a plot pecularly her own that she called "little Brighton," and here a gardener worked among unfamiliar flowers like delphiniums and giant hollyhocks, canterbury bells and phlox. On a lawn of savannah grass the young princess Kiran played openly without a veil with her young brother. They had a guest, a ten-year-old boy who was directing the course of their games and at times pausing to be the budding raja he was. As Ruth stopped to regard the three indulgently she heard the young Vikramji say, "I'm going to marry you some day, Kiran. I like you."

The princess looked up brightly and decided, "That's nice. I like you, too."

"What's the matter with your lip?"

"It has been cut," Kiran said gravely, "but it's getting better now."

"I shall come to marry you on a white elephant," Vikramji proceeded, and then the smaller prince broke up the romantic interlude with the challenge that there weren't any *white* elephants, for if there were, his father would have one.

Ruth strolled on, feeling comforted that at least she had done what she had come out to do and given Kiran the chance of a normal life. Only the new weal of the scar showed on her perfectly balanced bowed lip. In a year or two even that would have to be searched for under a magnifying glass.

Behind the palace great preparations were underway for the tiger shoot that His Highness was arranging for tomorrow. The party, including the doctor brothers and interested members of the archaeological expedition, were traveling by elephant alongside the course of the Goonch river into the jungle haunts, where sher (tiger) were to be found. Even now a party was out planting kills to tempt Mr. or Mrs. Sher to come out and play with the hunters when they arrived.

Ruth personally dreaded the whole business, but a shoot was Prince Ajil's supreme offering to the VIPs of his acquaintance. One had only to see his eyes on Kiran these days to realize that Miss Stafford qualified as a particularly VIP in the raja's estimation.

Also it gave His Highness an excuse for parading his elephants and their splendidly attired *mahawats*, much as an English peer might parade his new limousine for his friends' envy and approval.

But most of all, Ruth dreaded seeing Mark Travers at close quarters again. She had carefully removed all her personal equipment and luggage from the island, so that as far as she was concerned the final break had been made. Benedict had been replaced and released a week ago and had gone off by train as far as Calcutta. Ruth understood the raja was sending his personal pilot with her as far as Delhi, to save her the strain of a train journey during the hot weather. She expected to catch a connecting plane without holdups this time as the rains were almost over and had been too light this year, as they had been too heavy, causing serious flooding, the previous year.

"All your arrangements are in excellent hands, Miss Stafford," Prince Ajil had assured her, "so do not worry."

He was in extremely good spirits himself and inclined to tease, with mysterious references to a secret that he could not share with "chattering women."

"So he has a secret," Rosala scoffed, "and now we know about it! Is this the way you keep a secret, Ajili, to tell us and make us curious? This way we will surely worm it out of you!"

But His Highness had merely laughed and made his escape.

"Do you understand men, Miss Stafford?" the rani asked blankly.

"I refuse to try, your Highness," Ruth had said on that occasion.

"Surely they are beyond comprehension at times!" Rosala sighed. "Playing secrets . . . like children!"

Wandering to the stable-yard entrance, Ruth watched the exciting scene of the royal elephants being scrubbed and manicured in readiness for tomorrow. One great gray tusker rumba'd gently from foot to foot, rattling his tethering chains like accompanying castanets. This beast had taken a fancy to her, much to Ajil's amusement, and now he waved his trunk and trumpeted a greeting, his horrid little eyes rolling pinkly in their sockets. The boy-mahawat beamed ingratiatingly, pleading that she approach the beast and give it a tidbit.

"I have nothing," Ruth said rather nervously, but an old man appeared from the stable and put two stale pieces of rice bread into her hands.

"*Tek hai memsahib,*" he smiled toothlessly and encouragingly.

Ruth swallowed and walked up to her elephantine "friend," wondering how the creature would show its gratitude. She offered the bread and the trunk hovered delicately over her outstretched hand; she could feel the creature's breath damping her skin. Then the bread was removed and hooked into the pink cavern of the mouth beneath. The other piece followed and Ruth turned away, feeling pleased with herself at not having succumbed to her natural feminine fears. There was a moment of horror, however, for the elephant's trunk descended again and wound itself around her arm.

"What do I do now?" Ruth asked the old man faintly.

The ancient one only understood Hindustani however, and it was the boy who ran up and exclaimed, "Subha, he wishes you should pet him a little, memsahib."

Ruth reached up and stroked the snakelike trunk with her free hand, determining to keep her distance from the affectionate Subha in future.

"There's a good boy then," she crooned, and slowly the trunk unwound and released her. "Good boy! Good boy! Make him let me go now!" she instructed and kept up the patting to show there was no ill feeling while the *mahawat* commanded the creature to kneel down in readiness for his scrub.

It had all been rather nerve-racking, and she felt no better for turning away and almost bumping into Mark Travers.

"Oh!" she exclaimed in genuine surprise. "I didn't know . . . !"

His gray eyes had never left her face. She wasn't again going to be taken in by that lean and hungry look of his, which told her she was someone in particular one minute and denied her very existence the next.

"Thinking of working in a circus, Ruth?" he asked in a voice as uncertain as her own had been.

"I sometimes think I do," she said and made her escape for the second time in a few minutes from a source of possible danger. She was breathing hard, only too conscious of *that man's* presence in the palace precincts, when she reached her room, and there another surprise presented itself, for Cassie was draped in the window embrasure looking somehow distraught.

"Ruth!" she greeted wildly. "I've been waiting for you. You've got to help me, do you hear? You've *got* to help me!"

"Why, what's wrong?" Ruth asked sharply. "Don't look as though the world has come to an end, Cassie!"

"I think it has." The younger girl began to weep wildly. "It's Matt. I'm in love with him, Ruthie, and he won't even speak to me!"

Thinking she hadn't heard right, Ruth echoed, "*You* in love, Cassie? Does Matt know it?"

"He must," the other declared unhappily. "I've told him, and written him, and he still takes no notice of me. *Do* help me, Ruthie!"

"But what can I do?" Ruth asked gently. "Do you think it's wise to throw yourself at Matt with such declarations, Cassie? After all, it's the man who should take the initiative and keep it."

And I should know, she thought wryly.

"Well, there's one thing I ought to tell you, Ruthie," Cassie said in the old wheedling way. "You see, Matt's rather mad at me for one thing. I . . . I did something rather awful to . . . to get back at you for bullying me, and he behaves as though I'd damned you for life."

There was an uncomfortable silence.

"Hadn't you better tell me what you've done?" Ruth asked.

"Yes, I suppose I'd better, then you must tell Matt it's all right and he's got to stop it. Do you hear?" Cassie wept a few wild tears and then snuffled into her handkerchief. "I was willing to give up everything for him," she moaned softly, "for the first time in my life."

"Well?" Ruth insisted, trying not to sound impatient. "How do I come into it?"

"I don't consider you do, but evidently Matt thinks his precious big brother's being hurt through you, so it's a sort of ricochet action."

"Tell me!" Ruth commanded, tiring fast of the situation and Cassie's absorption in her own private misery.

"Yes, well—" now Cassie realized she could evade no longer "—if you promise not to be wild with me. I merely found out about Princess Kiran—quite by accident—and told Mark you had discussed her with me. Then I . . . I told him about you and Benedict."

"*What* about me and Benedict?"

Cassie drew a pattern on the tessellated floor with her sandal toe.

"That your annulment was a . . . a lie." Cassie raised a hand as though to ward off an expected blow. "Benedict told me himself," she added defiantly.

"You know it isn't true, Cassie," Ruth said, her chest rising and falling agitatedly. "Anyway, I'm glad I know what's been going on lately. Thanks for owning up."

"You're not mad?" the younger girl asked. "I told Mark first. It was he who brought me up here to talk to you before the others come. Now you can make it up with him and let Matt know I've done the right thing, can't you? Then we can all be happy again!"

Ruth walked to the window and looked out.

"It's not as easy as that, Cassie," she said fretfully. "You can't undermine relationships and then wave your little wand and put them right again. I didn't know why Mark turned frigid on me so suddenly, but you haven't brought a great love affair toppling, so don't fret about that."

"I . . . I haven't?" Cassie questioned hopefully.

"No." Ruth looked out and saw the object of her thoughts walking along the terrace with the raja. "If Mark Travers had really loved me he would have been temporarily shattered by such revelations, I suppose, and then have risen above them simply because he *loved me*. After all, you don't love someone for the things they've done, but because of what they are, which makes them occasionally do things to upset you. That may not sound very clear to you, Cassie, but it's clear to me. I would rather have had Mark forgive me for my apparent lapses than simply have them wiped off the slate by your admission."

"But if you and Mark don't get back together, Matt won't . . . won't . . . ." Cassie's eyes brimmed again and she threw herself on her stepsister, sliding down until she was hugging her calves in the humblest of pleadings. "Oh, Ruthie, please! Please!"

Ruth unwound her almost fastidiously.

"Now look here, Cassie, when Matt comes I shall certainly tell him you did all you could do to undo your mischief, and that I hold nothing against you. I shall also tell him that you never held the power to do me real harm. Maybe I have old-fashioned ideas about love, but all this merely goes to show I was perhaps in danger of making a very real mistake."

"Then I'll leave you," Cassie ventured ruefully, trailing toward the door. "I can't think what you expect a man to do, Ruth, to show he's in love with you. Must he go through fire and water?"

"If I'm prepared to do the same—yes," said Ruth firmly, her thoughts going back to that now revealing conversation in the cave at the site of the excavations. "If someone can't even jump the hurdles, what about the apparently insurmountable obstacles that love is reputed to take in its stride?"

MATT WAS VERY MUCH a man these days, Ruth realized afresh, marveling at this discovery. Cassie's very juvenility seemed to have matured him, impressed a permanent crease in his erstwhile smooth brow.

"All right, Ruth, I love the monkey," he admitted in some desperation, "and I think in her cockeyed way she's more than fond of me. But there's responsibility in loving a girl like Cassie, and I've concluded the only way to handle her is in assuming absolute mastery over her from the start. I have to find out where it hurts and then periodically hit hard. Do you understand?"

Looking very respectful, Ruth murmured, "Cassie should have had a father like you."

"She'll probably expect some sign as an outcome of this conversation," Matt said grimly, "but she isn't getting one immediately. I don't think she's quite ready to heel yet."

"But don't be too harsh for long, will you?" Ruth asked anxiously.

Matt narrowed his brown eyes.

"All her life people have been too soft with Miss Belampton," he decided. "If I'm taking her on for the duration I'll have her as a wife, not a vicious schoolkid. She'll think twice before she upsets me again. Okay?"

"Okay," smiled Ruth. "I won't interfere further, Matt."

CHAPTER TWENTY-FIVE

THEY BIVOUACKED IN THE FOREST as darkness fell, and here under the giant cedars was darkness indeed, for only an occasional star flashed like a fairy light through the interlacing greenery above.

It seemed rather absurd to Ruth that they should be camping, with all it entailed of fire lighting, cooking, the putting up of several tents, and tethering and feeding the elephants, with the palace and all its amenities only about seven miles distant. It took a horde of servants in a hundred capacities to look after the party, and they had trailed along, poor souls, on foot all day, burdened with all the equipment for a night in camp.

This was great shikar (sport) and it took a shikari to appreciate it.

The tiger they were trailing had successfully eluded them all day, but as he had the reputation of having turned man-eater, as a beast too old to hunt the fleet-footed deer, there was an added incentive to catch him. A tiger prefers to prowl at night, and at this very moment the raja, Matt, and the youngest male archaeologist (who, it was hoped, would keep his mind on the present long enough to appreciate the dangers of the situation) were perched up in machans (seats built in the trees) at points along the outer perimeter of the camp, waiting for the tiger to evince enough curiosity to come and at least look at what was going on.

They had enjoyed a kind of venison for supper; the raja's bodyguard had dropped a fine buck. As Matt was otherwise engaged, Cassie had retired to her sleeping bag, along with two other females in the party, and only Ruth seemed to be unable to settle or quite believe the fantastic day was over.

So as not to disturb the others, she wandered outside and leaned against a tree in the glow of the camp fire. It was cool here in the forest, for not much direct sunlight ever penetrated.

She actually shivered in her thin blouse over jodhpurs, and immediately a loose coat was slid around her shoulders, a coat pleasantly redolent of tobacco smoke.

"Thanks." She tried not to show her nervousness. "Have you a cigarette, please?"

"I have. In this very jacket."

Mark Travers offered her his case and lit the cigarette for her. "I didn't know you smoked," he observed.

"But then—" her voice was even slightly coquettish "—you don't really know very much about me, do you?"

He pondered this and decided, "I didn't think our acquaintance called for a history sheet. I know as much as I need to know. Would you rather be alone?"

"Not particularly," Ruth said, feeling all the old dangerous symptoms his nearness stirred in her. "I hope I'm not intruding on *you*."

He laid down the rifle he was carrying and indicated a nearby log.

"I'll be glad of your company," he said sincerely. "Sit down and let's have a natter." She obeyed and he began to stuff his pipe with the patient deliberation peculiar to men at such times. "How are you enjoying the shikar?" he asked.

"Well, actually it's not quite registering. I suppose when I'm back at my apartment I'll suddenly realize that I was on a tiger shoot with an Indian prince and party, and the glamor of everything will suddenly dawn on me—too late."

"I think you could enjoy it all now if you only would, Ruth."

The change in his tone had the desired effect on her. She was disarmed temporarily and trembled against him.

"If only you would, Ruth?" he insisted, and now his arm crept around her waist and she knew that to turn her head would mean to be kissed.

"I'm enjoying everything well enough as it is, thank you," she heard her voice say and she held herself rigidly away from that seeking arm. "In many ways I'll be glad to return to England."

"You had a socially gay life?" he inquired, as though that moment of intimacy had never been.

"No. I got out to dinner occasionally and I like the theater, plays, mostly. I read a lot and listen to the radio. I may get a television set this coming winter."

"It *is* winter in the U.K.," he told her. "I got *The Times* by airmail just before I left the island, and they're having snow; diggin 'em out in Yorkshire and Scotland."

"Brrr!" she shivered. "I'm going back at a bad time then."

"You're still intending to leave on Thursday?"

"Of course. I've cabled Glen Meriton and the woman who has been caring for my flat."

"Supposing I came to see you one day. Would you give me dinner at your flat?"

"I'd be delighted to, Mark. Honestly. I'd even make you a curry!"

"You mean you can cook?"

Now her laughter tinkled genuinely.

"I like to think I cook rather well," she told him. "You must have gained the impression I'm not domesticated because here one's servants do absolutely everything. I find cooking is both relaxing to the mind and stimulating to the appetite."

He puffed in silence for a few moments.

"I think you know, Ruth, that I won't be coming to dinner, don't you?" he asked at length.

Her heart missed a beat and then raced a little.

"I suppose I do," she said in a low voice.

"In fact, if you and I say goodbye in two days' time, it'll be goodbye forever?"

"That, also," she whispered.

"Why did you send Sharn away?"

"I didn't send . . . ."

"You were responsible for his coming and his going, if only as an objective, weren't you?"

"I . . . I suppose I was."

"So he didn't gain his objective?"

"If it *was* me, no, he didn't."

The log rolled a little and she had to clutch at him to prevent herself falling off. He merely steadied her and then allowed her hand to go.

"I felt sorry for Sharn in a way," he mused. "I suppose after Thursday I can start feeling sorry for myself."

"Really, Mark!" She rose and walked a few paces away from him. "What's the point of this conversation? If only you were consistent I might understand you. If I changed my mind about leaving on Thursday you would probably stow my baggage yourself and command me to go as planned. Some demon in you only desires the unobtainable. I've been in Kanjihan for almost six months, and most of that time your behavior toward me has been unbearable!''

"And when it wasn't unbearable?'' he queried.

"Oh!'' She clicked her tongue irritably.

Now he was behind her. She could feel him looming over her. "And when I wasn't unbearable,'' he insisted, "was I merely, well, bearable, or rather more in your estimation?''

"I refuse to pander to your wretched ego,'' she said crossly.

He whirled her around to face him and his eyes were light and clear in the reflected firelight, almost luminous.

"Ruth, there are moments when only truth will satisfy us. Punishing as it may well be, we must know where we stand with each other. You are too ready to put yourself on the defensive. This can only mean you're uncertain. I was once before prepared to spend love on someone, but I would not exchange love for lovemaking. With me the one is an offshoot of the other, but is not nearly sufficient in itself to maintain two people for life. Women are overinclined to emphasize the demonstrative side of any relationship. Ruth, I'm telling you now, I love you.''

Because of her confusion and a vague awareness that the sky was falling in around her ears, she almost groaned, "You, Mark, to speak of love!''

"Yes, me!'' he insisted almost angrily. "Do you think it's been easy admitting such a thing even to myself, with so little to suggest the possibility of a happy ending? I had sniffed the smoke of your past affairs wafting in ahead of you; my own brother laid his heart at your feet so obviously and embarrassingly I simply had to hold aloof, and pity and yet hate him for his courage in taking you at face value—''

"Which isn't always a bad idea,'' she interjected.

" . . . when you walked your feet raw on that occasion I took you up the mountain, I had to admit qualities in you I didn't want—wasn't then prepared—to accept. Physical love I shrank from, for obvious reasons, but I wanted you at times, Ruth—'' he closed his eyes as though even mouthing her name was a caress "—more than you'll ever know! When we kissed in Ajil's garden . . . when you appeared to be responsive to my advances . . . .'' He sighed and then shuddered. "I was afraid, I admit it. There was Matt confiding in me, trusting me, and there

was the memory of Marcia, so ready with her kisses to take the
sting out of her lies. I actually thought of women as soft
seductive creatures devoid of integrity. But you confounded
me, Ruth. You were prepared to fight back whenever I
challenged you, as though your kisses were like compulsions
against your greater wisdom, as though you surrendered only
this very little to nature while withholding so much you
considered more important. Sometimes I even hoped you were
beginning to love me, and then you would suddenly shoot my
hopes down in flames, as when you invited Sharn out here.''

"I didn't invite him, Mark," she said weakly.

"I believe you, Ruth," he accepted this. "Funnily enough I
always believe *you*. That's why I have—perhaps imperti-
nently—given you the third degree on occasions. Other people
have slandered and abused you, but it was *your* word I believed,
sometimes against all my reasoning. I was, of course, utterly
confounded when you brought Sharn out here—"

"I *didn't bring him!*" she insisted.

"No." He passed a hand over his brow as though to wipe out
the erroneous impression once and for all. "Forgive me, Ruth,
but I'm telling it as I thought it. We were getting rather close, in
the most pleasant of companionships, when you sprang Sharn
on me—expedition and all—and apparently deliberately failed
to pass on a message entrusted to you regarding this invasion of
my privacy. What could I think? Because I was falling more and
more in love with you I hoped—naturally enough—that you
cared a little and had brought the other half of your emotional
life here to be able to decide clearly where your real preference
lay. If you remember, I gave you every opportunity of renewing
your acquaintance—if that covers it—with Sharn.''

"You did," Ruth said grimly.

"You apparently presume *I* didn't go through hell during
those first few days!" he almost blazed. "Sharn was discussing
you with me as though he had your ticket back to London and a
remarriage in his pocket. He hinted more. As you were not
behaving like a maiden in love, but were rather brisker,
snappier, less endurable than usual, I asked what I wanted to
know of you, and in your answers I was satisfied. Sharn—
though he didn't admit it—was on his way out of your life.
When he left my house and went off to the dig altogether, I was
convinced and dared to be a little happy again. Then you became
ill. Oh, Ruth . . . !''

She wanted to put her arms around him, but desisted. Instead she took up the story from him.

"Cassie got hold of you, I know," she told him, "and then there were two words against mine. My intrinsic honesty didn't shine so brightly, did it? And I had, apparently, gossiped with a particularly silly female about a highly confidential matter. A sacred trust, in fact. Isn't that how it goes, Mark?"

He saw the pain in her eyes, and his own stared in surprise.

"No, Ruth," he said, completely disarming her, so that she was unable to bear his gaze longer and turned away. "After what I had already been through, Cassie's tale didn't count for much with me. She was a little too eager to impress me with your failings before she particularized. I happened to have gained the impression for myself that you not only didn't gossip—or 'chatter' as she put it—but that you were at times too introspective for your own good. I did wonder how she could know about Kiran, but I presumed you'd talked in your delirium or something. Actually, it was all cleared up to my satisfaction when Kiran told me herself the 'lady with the leopard's eyes' had paid her a visit one evening, saying she was your sister."

"Then you never really held what she told you against me?"

"Heavens, no!"

"But, Mark—" she looked up at him helplessly "—after I got better you were so cold. You . . . you sent me away from you."

"I know," he muttered moodily. "I'd been doing some thinking. The whole business seemed suddenly utterly preposterous."

"We're speaking of you and me, of course?" she asked acidly.

"Yes, I—"

"I knew it!" she told the jungle darkness almost triumphantly. "We were bound to hit the buffers somewhere along this now familiar route. The tortoise has gone shy on me again! Well, let me tell you, Mark Travers, you've done it with me for the last time!"

"But, Ruth . . . ." He was almost smiling, she perceived, her anger rising.

"You needn't go on!" she said passionately. "I've heard it all before!"

"Hadn't you better let me finish?" he asked whimsically.

"No!" she denied him. "At the moment I feel hard and bright and in perfect control of my emotions. We could go on reminiscing until I felt like weeping, but it isn't happening again. Now, good night!"

Distraught, as she was, she wheeled off into the trees instead of back to the women's tent.

"Ruth!" she heard him call as he stooped to pick up his rifle and plunge after her.

She had realized her blunder and had turned immediately, well able to see the glow of the camp fire as a guide to her whereabouts. Cruelly she did not answer him, however. Why should he concern himself about her when the very idea of their being in love had been denounced as "preposterous"?

She heard him calling her name at first coaxingly, then with very real concern.

"Answer me, you little fool!" he at last commanded.

Just then there was a crashing in the undergrowth and the raja's voice shrilly shouted.

"'Ware, camp! Tiger!"

A rifle bullet sang, and then another.

"For heaven's sake, have you got him, Ajil?" Mark yelled, half demented.

"No. My flashlight startled him, and before I could get my sights on him he made off in your direction. Take care, Mark. He's nervous now, and knows we're after him. Is everybody back there who isn't armed safely under cover?"

"No." Mark's voice seemed to break. "Ruth's wandering around somewhere. I haven't a flashlight with me, but I can't go back without her!"

Though conscious of the danger of the occasion, Ruth thought she had never heard a sweeter phrase in her whole life. "I can't go back without her."

She plunged in the direction of the voice almost blindly.

"I'm here, Mark!" she called for all to hear. "I'm all right!"

Then she froze, for from the bush immediately ahead of her gleamed twin amber lamps. It was some seconds before she realized she was looking at the man-eater.

"Mark!" Her voice wasn't so confident now, but she realized she must keep her head. "Where . . . where are you?"

"Here, Ruth."

"You sound to be on my right," she decided. "He . . . he's here, Mark, looking at me. What must I do?"

"Keep talking, Ruth, for God's sake! I won't speak again."

The tiger decided to snarl, unable to decide between attack and retreat.

It seemed an eternity to Ruth before anything else happened. She continued to stare the tiger out, and recited "Twinkle Twinkle Little Star" at the same time for Mark's benefit.

"Urrr!" grumbled the tiger uneasily, probably wondering what was happening also, and prepared to live and let live with his stomach full of the stinking meat of the bait.

Then Ruth felt the draught of a bullet pass within a yard of her own head and saw a blue white flash light up the area. There were two more shots in quick succession, then her legs crumped beneath her as she felt herself gathered up and crushed and she was scolded and kissed all at the same time.

"You little fool! Darling, are you all right? Never do that again! If the brute had decided to . . . ."

"But he didn't," she murmured contentedly, hearing the raja approaching through the undergrowth and not caring who saw her in Mark's arms. "You're sure he's dead?"

"Yes. I got him with my first. The other two were for good measure and to relieve my nervous tension over you. You're sure you're all right, Ruth?"

"Yes. Just a bit of reaction, of course."

"I'm going to fasten you up in your sleeping bag myself with my own hands and put a padlock on you. I couldn't go through an ordeal like that again!"

She dutifully peeped at the tiger, which was now displayed in the light of the attendants' flashlights, but she was glad to leave the scene of violence and go to sleep with the memory of Mark's voice crying—and sounding so stricken—"I can't go back without her!"

"Preposterous" their love affair might well be, but at such times it would not be denied.

CHAPTER TWENTY-SIX

ROSALA RANI PAINTED her caste mark between her straight black eyebrows and wrapped her yellow silver-edged sari over her smooth shining hair.

"Amineh!" she called to her woman-servant. "Please see if Miss Stafford is ready for the drive."

Amineh bowed and backed out of the royal dressing room into the cool marbled corridor. She hastened along to the room that had been allotted for Ruth's use and, after tapping on the door entered and bowed again.

"Are you ready yet, Dr. Memsahib?"

"Yes, Amineh. I'm ready. I'll go out into the courtyard now."

She had fast learned the local protocol and knew that no matter how friendly one might be with princes, it must not be they who are required to wait while one hitches a stocking or finds a handkerchief.

Therefore she was on the front terrace, admiring four magnificent horses harnessed to the shining phaeton, when Rosala finally appeared with her children. Though the township of Kanjihan was familiar with the sight of the rani and her small son, the daughter was an almost legendary figure who was rumored to be in purdah, away at school, sickly, and other things. Now Kiran was dressed as a small replica of her mother in the palest of pink and silver saris over white punjabi breeches. She wore new silver sandals and was pleasantly conscious of all her finery.

"To see this day!" Rosala murmured devoutly and clapped her small hands noisily, so that a cloud of doves rose from the cotes all along the terrace and weaved, rustling, among the palace domes. "Go tell our Lord the thanks of my heart!" the rani bade them. "Oh, Lord of the Herds, what avail us our Kingships if there is sorrow dwelling with us!"

Ruth heard, duly impressed by the outburst, and yet knowing full well that Her Highness was sufficiently mercurial to be discussing the palace's new washing machine the very next moment. She would often pause to indulge a small personal religious outpouring of her own, called *puja*, and then continue scolding one of the children, or a servant, or anything she had been doing previously. Now she solemnly stepped into the phaeton, a remnant of Kanjihan's less motor-conscious past, sat a child on either side of her and indicated that Ruth should sit opposite.

"Always my tummy feels queer when I ride behind horses," she confessed excitedly. "I do it because your queen looks so good in a coach. I ride through the bazaars and I wave my hand so," Rosala demonstrated, also bowing graciously from side to side. "I play at being a queen."

She's a married woman, the mother of two children and exactly as old as I am, Ruth pondered, *and she plays at being a queen!*

For a moment the eyes of the women met, and as though there had been an impact in the glance, Rosala frowned slightly as the bodyguard, a Subhadar-major, climbed up next to the coachman and two postilions jumped up behind.

"I tell you *everything* about me, Miss Stafford," Her Highness went on reproachfully, "and you smile in your cool English way and confide nothing."

"But what do you want to know, Your Highness?" Ruth asked. "Believe me, my life isn't as glamorous as yours."

"Nor has it known such tragedy, I think," Rosala sighed. "My father was murdered in the Calcutta riots, and my mother was stoned and frightened until she lost her reason. I think there is no virtue in suffering. You agree we are meant to be happy?"

"I do, yes."

"Then how will you be happy eventually? Always work, work, work?"

"Most of the time, I expect, but it's happy work on the whole."

"It has brought happiness to your friends in Kanjihan." Rosala stopped speaking to bow and wave toward a group of laborers in a field. She indicated that Kiran should do likewise, then she leaned back again and said mischievously, "I discovered my husband's precious secret. Shall I share it with you?"

"I don't think you should, Your Highness. A secret is—after all—a secret."

"But it concerns you, and I think how foolish to keep secret that which it will make you happy to know."

As Ruth still looked dubious Her Highness said gaily, "I can tell it to my children. If you care to eavesdrop that is your affair. Narhad, Kiran," she said ringingly, "your Uncle Mark is leaving Kanjihan. He is going to London with Miss Stafford."

"Oh, mama!" said Kiran, solemneyed and ready to cry. Ruth's heart had turned quite over.

Was the Rani teasing and testing her reaction to Mark's name being introduced into the conversation?

"Everybody going away," Narhad said gloomily. "Why, mama?"

"Because I think they love each other. Like papa and mama," she answered brightly, her eyes on the waxlike figure opposite. "Tell me, Kiran, does Miss Stafford look angry or otherwise?"

"She is blushing," the princess decided, captivated by this habit peculiar to white-skinned people.

"I'm sure I'm not!" Ruth said and took out her handbag mirror to look. "I simply haven't turned a hair because I don't believe your secret. Of course Dr. Mark isn't leaving Kanjihan, or he would have told me!"

Mark had said nothing that morning after the shoot other than, "I'll see you before you go, Ruth," because everything had been public and he was in a hurry to return to the island. She had felt, however, that there was much more to say and next time they met he would be sure to say it.

Rosala's "secret" had disturbed her profoundly, because she did not associate Mark Travers with acts of madness, and to fly off out of Kanjihan with her would be an act of delicious madness.

"I have made you happy, Miss Stafford?" Rosala queried gently, seizing the prince by the seat of his pants as he hung over the carriage door to watch some children playing in the dust.

"It can't be true, Your Highness. Dr. Matt is leaving by train next week. They couldn't both go."

"Why not? Ajil has replaced them quite successfully. You must have seen Dr. Heeralal and the new surgical officer at the hospital?"

Can this fantastic thing be true, Ruth asked herself, and all at once her heart soared and sang like a bird in her chest. She wanted to do a devout little *puja* there and then, but instead she closed her eyes and battened down the joy welling within her.

"I am so happy for you, and you are not angry with me?" Rosala asked, unable to quite understand the other's immobility when she herself was so volatile in emotional stress.

"I am very happy, and thank you, Your Highness," Ruth assured her. "But I just can't believe it's true, somehow."

"Then you'll see," Rosala promised, nodding her head. "Tomorrow morning on the landing strip. Remember to be surprised!"

THE LAST EVENING at the palace Ruth felt extremely lonely, with an unaccountable brooding heaviness of spirit that she couldn't fathom. Maybe it would have been better had Rosala not let her into the "secret"; then the morning's surprise would have seemed heavenly.

As it was she found herself thinking of reasons for Mark Travers visiting London, and there were plenty that didn't include her, except the role of traveling companion. Maybe Mark was simply taking well-earned leave, for she couldn't imagine him saying goodbye to Kanjihan forever. Or perhaps he wanted to assure himself that Matt was making a move in the right direction, or wanted to bring himself up to date with new drugs and treatment. He could be doing anything.

There had been a certain amount of "atmosphere" during dinner, and Ruth had the uncomfortable feeling that their Highnesses had quarreled very recently over something. Rosala went off with her women when the meal was over, and after a desultory walk in the garden Ruth also retired early.

She awoke to the screeching of the parrot outside her window. The bird was reputedly more than eighty years old and spoke Hindustani and Bengali along with one English phrase he had learned from the old rani's governess-companion, who—according to the raja—had been a character akin to the Anna who occasionally put the King of Siam in his place.

"Take your bath, my gel!" the parrot shrieked now for Ruth's benefit. "Take your bath! *Tora chini, tora char . . . pukka sahib! Maro Polly! Maro!*"

Now Ruth recaptured all the thrill of anticipation as she remembered Rosala's forecast regarding Mark. She could imagine them all (Mark, Matt, and Cassie, accompanied by

Gundhalal), coming to see her off, and at the very last moment
Mark would step into the plane with her, apparently to say
goodbye privately, and there he would stay while she registered
consternation and eventually confessed that she had known all
the while.

Their Highnesses joined her for breakfast on the terrace,
though normally neither of them stirred until noon.

"You'll be leaving us in half an hour, Miss Stafford," the
raja announced somewhat curtly, as though he was still angry
with his wife from the previous evening. "I do not need to say
again I am deeply grateful to you, do I?"

"Of course not," smiled Ruth. "I did my job and everything
happened according to plan. I am indeed happy to have enjoyed
a success with Kiran."

"And Miss Stafford must come and see us again," Rosala
invited, glancing up at Ajil and away again.

"Of course," Ajil endorsed this. "Come to my daughter's
marriage, if not earlier, dear lady."

Ruth made suitable little exclamations of pleasure and
anticipation, her ears straining for the sounds of arrival from the
island.

The raja suddenly dropped a bombshell, however.

"I am instructed to tell you, Miss Stafford, that Dr. Mark is
too busy to come and see you off," he announced, his eyes on
his cup. "He added that you'll be hearing from him."

Ruth felt the coffee turn bitter in her mouth.

"*Not* see me off?" she questioned, noticing that Rosala was
deliberately looking away. "Has a messenger been here then,
Your Highness?"

"Late last night a message arrived. But I will escort you to the
plane, Miss Stafford, and see you safely airborne. You must
understand that things keep cropping up with doctors."

"Yes, I do understand," Ruth said brightly, her heart taking
its now familiar dip down into her shoes. "Is Dr. Matt busy,
too, and my stepsister?"

"They, also, will not be coming here," Ajil confirmed,
looking suddenly very royal as he stood up and brought the
conversation to a close. "In ten minutes, Miss Stafford," he
warned her and frowned at his wife on his way into the palace.

Rosala rose also and investigated a hanging basket of her
favorite orchirds.

"I do not know what is wrong, Miss Stafford," she said, as

though anticipating the other's question. "What I told you was true, but when I told Ajil I had blabbed he was angry with me. Now he won't tell me anything more. But I'll show him. Last night I shut him away from me, when he would have tried to patch up our quarrel, and I can keep my door locked tonight also, if he is not kind to me."

"Don't quarrel on my account, Your Highness," Ruth said tiredly.

"But I feel I have let you down in some way, dear Miss Stafford. We can't allow these men to kick us around, as they say on the films."

"Cassie at least could have come," Ruth frowned. "I'm only traveling six thousand miles!" she added cynically.

"Mark had planned to accompany you," Rosala insisted. "I will not have you doubting that. Something is the matter on the island."

"But what *could* be the matter?" Ruth asked blankly.

"I heard Ajil instructing the *chuprassie* to see that all water is boiled before use," Rosala mused. "I also saw the aide-de-camp dashing off to the town in the Land Rover, and he hasn't returned yet. I remember all this happening once before when cholera broke out in a house on Benares Street."

"Cholera?" Ruth echoed soundlessly.

"There is no Benares Street now," Rosala went on conversationally. "Ajil burned it down and built new houses for the survivors. We lost twelve of our people in that particular outbreak."

"But why couldn't I be told about a thing like that?" Ruth inquired. "I'm a doctor, like the others."

"It is my considered opinion," Rosala said sententiously, "that Dr. Mark asked Ajil to get you safely out of the way. He would not wish his beloved to be in danger. Here comes my husband now, so I'll leave you with all my heart, dear, dear friend."

The rani kissed her lightly on both cheeks and slipped away into the shadows without a backward glance.

"Are we ready, Miss Stafford?" asked the raja mock jovially.

Ruth decided to toss down the gauntlet.

"Would Your Highness be trying to get rid of me?" she asked.

"Trying to . . . ?" Ajil laughed in confusion. "Really, Miss Stafford, your English sense of humor!"

"I haven't any at this moment, sir," she said firmly. "I simply think I'm being bundled out of the way because of an epidemic maybe . . . ? Cholera?"

"Who has told you?" the Rajah demanded, then bit his lip as he realized his mistake. "An odd case or two," he admitted, "but no epidemic yet. It will be all right for you to go. You cannot possibly have been a contact."

"I'm not leaving," Ruth rebelled, "and I'm going back to the hospital at once. In the event of an epidemic developing I naturally want to be on hand. Also I happen to be very fond of Mark Travers."

"He will *kill* me for this!" Ajil put his hand extravagantly to his brow. "All right, the car will take you down to my barge," he suddenly decided. "Once on the island you will not be able to leave until it is cleared by the authorities. You understand?"

"As Your Highness pleases," Ruth said obediently, her heart rising with every step she took across the paved yard to the waiting car.

The raja turned as a small inviting sound came from the alcove behind him.

"You may embrace me if you like, Ajil," smiled Her Serene Highness, the rani, holding out her arms.

CHAPTER TWENTY-SEVEN

As THE PARTY waited for the ferryman to repair some minor fault in the boat's engine with the usual "piece of string and puja," Mark Travers had the disconcerting sensation of being suspended between two worlds and belonging to neither.

It was true that he was now no longer director of medicine—that purely honorary title!—of Kanjihan province. Dr. Heeralal had taken his degree and worked for six months in Liverpool at a hospital for tropical diseases, so he was obviously a natural for a job like this, though Ajil had been induced to make the yearly salary look a little more inviting.

The surgical officer who was taking Matt's place was a graduate of a Calcutta hospital and was simply glad of a job that provided board and lodging.

There was no doubt that Kanjihan hospital would go on without pause in these capable hands; but how would he fare, a specialist in name only, tossed onto a market where there were, reputedly, so many already unable to get decent jobs?

Still, if he was to ask Ruth to be his wife, as he fully intended to do at the earliest possible moment, he could not, in all conscience, pluck her from her own valuable niche in the world of medicine and surgery to join him and the frustrations he endured daily. He had seen her work, deftly and confidently; he had watched her reform Kiran's incomplete palate, operating in an area so small and awkwardly placed it was almost like working in the dark, and yet she had never once hesitated or stated that whatever the outcome, it would have to do. Meriton had at least passed on to her the fastidiousness of a profession that was content with nothing less than near-perfection. Had there been failure she would simply have tried again—and again.

It might be years before he could support a wife, or at any rate equal her own salary, which pride demanded. Still, when you are in a state that cannot endure the thought of never seeing someone again, it is as well to follow the direction of your heart's indicating, trusting more than usual to your luck to see you through.

Matt was breaking bread at the side of the road to attract an intinerant peacock and his brood. The fowl obligingly spread his "fan" and Cassie gasped in delight.

"The dahlings!" she exclaimed and then was left pouting as Matt casually rejoined the party without acknowledging her.

Finally they embarked and made the crossing. The archaeologists bowled off in their waiting truck, and there was some argument when Miss Belampton refused to ride with them and indulged in a noisy and public weep on the landing stage.

Ali was not waiting with the car, so Matt and Cassie were despatched in the only available *gharri* and instructed to send him back immediately. Meanwhile, Mark strolled into the undergrowth behind the bent casuarina trees and there smelled camp smoke. He did not encourage vagrant life on the island. Even the archæological expedition was an intrusion, in his opinion. Only the sick were welcome here, and there would be no "squatting"—with its accompanying squalor—if he could help it.

He came into a small clearing where the valuable bamboo had been ruthlessly hacked away, and here was erected a long, low, ungainly Arab-style tent. Two camels were tethered nearby, regarding him with the peculiar pitying arrogance with which they inspect all other forms of life, and which gives rise to the belief that only on the humble camel was conferred the seventh and ultimate name of Allah by which He is known in heaven.

Mark was not impressed by the animal's hauteur, however, or their film-star eyelashes, heavy as silken fringes. He was impressed by the flies buzzing around the beasts, and most especially those invading an open festering sore in one camel's neck.

Long ago Mark had banned livestock from the island. Goats were driven in to be milked, and away again. Animals and their droppings attracted flies, and flies in the tropics carry all kinds of diseases. But Mark's particular *bêtes noires* were camels, with their poor resistance to syphilis and such horrors.

"Hi!" he called loudly, for nobody human was in sight.

A small boy and a very old woman crept out of the tent, allowing a waft of foul air to emanate with them. They might have been any nationality, or bits of all of them. There was something of Korea in the flat mongoloid face of the old woman, yet the small boy, if otherwise attired, could have passed for an American Indian. He had straight black hair, a hook of a nose, and was brick-colored. Later Mark discovered the boy covered himself with red clay as decoration, being rather ashamed of his yellow skin in a country where other children were pleasantly brown.

"What are you doing here?" Mark demanded in Bengali. "You can't stay here. Hospital. I am a doctor."

The old woman required the boy to translate all this into some patois of their own, then she smiled toothlessly and instructed the interpreter to tell the gentleman she knew there was a hospital here, and was happy he was a doctor, because her grandson—the boy's father—was inside the tent and very sick.

"Well, you can't stay here with those brutes! . . ." Mark stared malevolently at the camels before the doctor in him came uppermost and he sank to his knees and crawled into the tent.

It was impossible to see anything after the brilliance of the light outside, and the stench was abominable, so he instructed the boy to fasten the tent flap back, and when the lad obeyed, his great-grandmother muttered awe-inspiring imprecations on the probability of her grandson dying of a chill.

This firm belief was probably embedded in the old woman's mind for all time. Whatever ailed the sick man, the free inlet of fresh air to his body would surely kill him.

Mark had no medical kit with him, but two of the three elements of diagnosis were still open to him, to observe and to palpate. He quickly observed that the sufferer was a bad color, that his eyes were glazed with high fever, and that he evinced all the muscular contortions of extreme pain. Palpation told him that the lower abdomen was swollen in the otherwise wasted body, that here was the seat of the pain, and his nose told him the man had been in a state of incontinence for some time.

Outside he shook his head sharply as he remembered past horror.

"No, it can't be!" he tried to convince himself.

It was impossible to tell what was wrong without pathological tests. It could be aggravated dysentery, caused by camel-infected flies settling on the family drinking water.

Ali was looking around for him when he returned to the jetty.

"Don't come near me, boy," he advised sharply. "I'll drive

myself up to the hospital. Meanwhile, see that nobody goes near that lot.'' He indicated the camp behind him and drove off.

Thus it was that the dreaded cholera came to Kanjihan island, making internees out of visitors and inhabitants alike. The palace and town were informed and advised to take their own precautions. Katra was asked to stand siege, allowing no one to land. The asylum would be adequately provisioned from the air, it was promised.

Police blazed the trail—in reverse—of the infected caravan, and Matt Travers was put in charge of civilian inoculation, making his headquarters on the raja's barge, with a gangplank leading to the jetty. Because she refused to leave his side, Cassie was instructed in the use of a hypodermic syringe and, before long, was making the necessary injections, acting as medical clerk and generally being useful.

''I'm half-dead, but I like it, and damn you!'' she said rebelliously that first evening, and Matt's features softened into a grin for the first time in days.

The old woman succumbed to the disease within hours, and by morning the boy—who was a small fifteen—was complaining of pain as he passed copious quantities of blood. He ceased to fret over the prompt slaughter of the family's camels in his own fight for life, and there in the isolation hut, standing a little apart from Kanjihan hospital proper, his future—if any—was irrevocably reshaped by the violent death of his great-grandmother during the night, and of his father an hour later. He was not to know that during his babyhood his mother and the rest of his family had been similarly wiped out. They were itinerant tinkers by trade, never staying anywhere long enough to benefit by the hand of progress and education.

Still holding his breath, Mark realized no other cases had been reported. The staff had feverishly inoculated each other, and when Heeralal went down with an attack of dysentery there was a sudden mild panic. The archaeologists had been warned to keep to their own side of the island.

There was so much to think of, Mark fretted and winced away from the acrid smell of the burning flesh of the two fatalities, the only possible end to it. He realized, as he took a breather in the small room to which he had confined himself in the isolation hut, that he had expected to leave the next day in Ajil's plane with Ruth.

Ruth! Her name lit up like a neon sign in his brain. If she heard about this he knew she wouldn't go, but there was no knowing with cholera. It would strike down the clean living with the filthy, the immaculate with the foul. He himself, despite recent precautions, might well be nurturing the killer in his own bloodstream.

Though it was two o'clock in the morning he radioed the palace and gave Ajil charge of Ruth's safe despatch, asking that she be kept in ignorance of the outbreak.

When he would see her again, he didn't know, but she would be safe somewhere in her pristine surroundings, and it would be his pleasure and comfort to think of her thus occasionally.

In the morning Nurse Angelina, who, the most austere of all the staff, always undertook isolation work with an unnatural feverish sacrificial joy, began to groan, hold her stomach, and run a temperature. She was put to bed by a nursing volunteer, Komala Indi, and an orderly who had recovered from cholera in childhood and was therefore considered to be immune.

"Oh, God!" Mark silently pleaded. "No more of it! Please, no more of it!"

The padre, who attended to the spiritual needs of the nursing sisters, arrived to give the sufferer extreme unction, but she took such a lively interest in proceedings for herself, telling the nurse where to find her shroud when it should be needed, that Mark began to hope the inoculations she had had would withstand the violence of her attack.

Almost unconsciously his ears strained for the sound of Ajil's plane. Ruth probably thought his nonappearance indicated that the tortoise was in him again. Maybe she would wash her hands of him entirely, and he would find himself not only out of work—in England—but also out of favor for all time with the lady he both loved and desired.

Because he had not slept he felt a deep wave of depression engulf him. In the blackness of his mind he saw half the population of Kanjihan clutching their guts and groaning on the streets, unable to gain admittance to the crowded hospital.

A faint moan escaped him in sympathy and he raised his eyes to see an angelic figure actually bending over him. The figure wore white, had short fair hair and blue eyes, and the most tremulous of smiles, like a child who awaits a spanking from a loved one and hopes to soften the blows.

"Well?" asked the voice he knew so well. "Where do we start?"

His depression slipped from him like a cloak, and his vision changed to seeing the streets of Kanjihan clean and wide and shining with public health.

"Ruth!" he gasped, rubbing his eyes as though fearing he would rub her away with the ache in them. "Oh, Ruth! My own Ruth!"

There were no questions and no answers required. She was in his arms and she was telling him she wouldn't have left without seeing him, cholera epidemic or not.

"I just want to be with you, Mark, wherever you are and whatever you're doing. You should have known that all along."

"Oh, Ruth!" he gasped again and added foolishly, as though it could possibly make any difference, "I threw up my job to follow you."

"That doesn't matter." She kissed his cheek and the tired eyes in a persistence of devotion. "I threw mine up this morning. The raja is cabling Glen to that effect. Withersoever thou goest, Mark . . .?"

"Thither go I," he added gently and smoothed her hair and placed his lips, trembling, on hers in a gentle passionless communion.

Passing the door, the padre observed them and wondered if he had remembered to bring his supply of marriage licenses with him.

What the press says about Harlequin romance fiction...

"The most popular reading matter of American women today."
— *The Detroit News*

"Women have come to trust these stories about contemporary people, set in exciting foreign places."
— *Best Sellers*, New York

"Harlequin novels have a vast and loyal readership."
— *Toronto Star*

3 GREAT NOVELS

**Harlequin brings you
a book to cherish …**

three stories of
love and romance
by one of your
favorite
Harlequin authors …

**JOY
ROMANCE
LOVE**

Harlequin Omnibus

**THREE love stories in
ONE beautiful volume**

The joys of being in love...
the wonder of romance...
the happiness that true love brings...

Now yours in the HARLEQUIN OMNIBUS
edition every month wherever
paperbacks are sold.

The **HARLEQUIN CLASSIC LIBRARY**
is offering some of the best in romance
fiction—great old classics from our early
publishing lists.

On the following page is a coupon with which
you may order any or all of these titles. If you
order all nine, you will receive a free book—*Meet
the Warrens*, a heartwarming classic romance by
Lucy Agnes Hancock.

The first nine novels in the

HARLEQUIN CLASSIC LIBRARY

1 **Do Something Dangerous** Elizabeth Hoy
2 **Queen's Counsel** Alex Stuart
3 **On the Air** Mary Burchell
4 **Doctor Memsahib** Juliet Shore
5 **Castle in Corsica** Anne Weale
6 **So Dear to My Heart** Susan Barrie
7 **Cameron of Gare** Jean S. MacLeod
8 **Doctor Sara Comes Home** Elizabeth Houghton
9 **Summer Lightning** Jill Tahourdin

Great old favorites...
Harlequin Classic Library

Complete and mail this coupon today!

Harlequin Reader Service

In U.S.A.
MPO Box 707
Niagara Falls, N.Y. 14302

In Canada
649 Ontario St.
Stratford, Ontario, N5A 6W2

Please send me the following novels from the Harlequin Classic Library.
I am enclosing my check or money order for $1.25 for each novel ordered,
plus 59¢ to cover postage and handling. If I order all nine titles, I will receive
a free book, *Meet the Warrens*, by Lucy Agnes Hancock.

☐ 1   ☐ 4   ☐ 7
☐ 2   ☐ 5   ☐ 8
☐ 3   ☐ 6   ☐ 9

Number of novels checked @ $1.25 each = $ _____

N.Y. State residents add appropriate sales tax $ _____

Postage and handling $ _____.59

TOTAL $ _____

I enclose _____
(Please send check or money order. We cannot be responsible for cash sent
through the mail.)
Prices subject to change without notice.

Name _____
               (Please Print)

Address _____

City _____

State/Prov. _____

Zip/Postal Code _____

Offer expires August 31, 1980   0025633760